"I knew you'd come for me" she whispered

"I'll always con[barcode obscures text]

Their lips met [barcode obscures text] and fog and brine. [barcode obscures text] he could freeze a [barcode obscures text] was pure, untainted by an[barcode obscures text] need.

Casting him a look he would never forget, Liz murmured, "You saved me."

He couldn't think of an answer, so he kissed her again.

Alex stared at her tearstained face and said, "Are you okay? How about the baby?"

"I feel okay. The fall doesn't seem to have affected either one of us."

Knowing the situation could have been much worse, Alex was relieved to hear Liz's words. His love for her was overwhelming in its intensity.

But the questions remained—who had tried to kill his very pregnant wife and what would happen when the culprit discovered she was still alive...?

Dear Harlequin Intrigue Reader,

The holidays are upon us! We have six dazzling stories of intrigue that will make terrific stocking stuffers—not to mention a well-deserved reward for getting all your shopping done early....

Take a breather from the party planning and unwrap Rita Herron's latest offering, *A Warrior's Mission*—the next exciting installment of COLORADO CONFIDENTIAL, featuring a hot-blooded Cheyenne secret agent! Also this month, watch for *The Third Twin*—the conclusion of Dani Sinclair's HEARTSKEEP trilogy that features an identical triplet heiress marked for murder who seeks refuge in the arms of a rugged lawman.

The joyride continues with *Under Surveillance* by highly acclaimed author Gayle Wilson. This second book in the PHOENIX BROTHERHOOD series has an undercover agent discovering that his simple surveillance job of a beautiful woman-in-jeopardy is filled with complications. Be there from the start when B.J. Daniels launches her brand-new miniseries, CASCADES CONCEALED, about a close-knit northwest community that's visited by evil. Don't miss the first unforgettable title, *Mountain Sheriff*.

As a special gift-wrapped treat, three terrific stories in one volume. Look for *Boys in Blue* by reader favorites Rebecca York, Ann Voss Peterson and Patricia Rosemoor about three long-lost New Orleans cop brothers who unite to reel in a killer. And rounding off a month of nonstop thrills and chills, a pregnant woman and her wrongly incarcerated husband must set aside their stormy past to bring the real culprit to justice in *For the Sake of Their Baby* by Alice Sharpe.

Best wishes to all of our loyal readers for a joyous holiday season!

Enjoy,

Denise O'Sullivan
Senior Editor
Harlequin Intrigue

FOR THE SAKE OF THEIR BABY

ALICE SHARPE

HARLEQUIN®

TORONTO • NEW YORK • LONDON
AMSTERDAM • PARIS • SYDNEY • HAMBURG
STOCKHOLM • ATHENS • TOKYO • MILAN • MADRID
PRAGUE • WARSAW • BUDAPEST • AUCKLAND

ISBN 0-373-22746-9

FOR THE SAKE OF THEIR BABY

Visit us at www.eHarlequin.com

Printed in U.S.A.

ABOUT THE AUTHOR

Alice Sharpe met her husband-to-be on a cold, foggy beach in Northern California. One year later they were married. Their union has survived the rearing of two children, a handful of earthquakes registering over 6.5, numerous cats and a few special dogs, the latest of which is a yellow Lab named Annie Rose. Alice and her husband now live in a small rural town in Oregon, where she devotes the majority of her time to pursuing her second love, writing.

Alice loves to hear from readers. You can write her at P.O. Box 755, Brownsville, OR 97327. SASE for reply is appreciated.

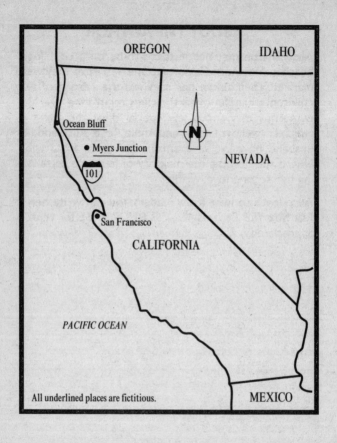

OREGON

IDAHO

Ocean Bluff

● Myers Junction

101

San Francisco

NEVADA

CALIFORNIA

PACIFIC OCEAN

MEXICO

All underlined places are fictitious.

CAST OF CHARACTERS

Liz Chase—The heiress and businesswoman resigns herself to a divorce in order to move into the future and find peace before her baby is born. Then her imprisoned husband walks back into her life....

Alex Chase—The former fireman and confessed killer of Liz's uncle has limited time—before his new trial—to discover the truth, protect his wife and reclaim his freedom.

Devon Hiller—The wealthy, manipulative autocrat had so many enemies it's a toss-up who wanted him dead the most.

Sheriff Roger Kapp—His hatred of Alex Chase leads to a slipshod investigation and a hung jury, but he won't rest until he gets Alex behind bars for good.

Ron Boxer—The leasing agent at the Harbor Lights Mall, he's the big brother Liz never had, as well as a trusted friend and confidant.

Emily Watts—Ron's prickly sister and Liz's friend, she has secrets of her own.

Harry Idle—The former shopkeeper blames the late Devon Hiller for all his problems.

Dave Sullivan—The one man at the fire station who never loses faith in Alex.

Battalion Chief Montgomery—The chief holds a crucial piece of information about Kapp's scheming.

Sinbad—The ever hungry, ever loyal Siamese cat is yet another victim.

This book is dedicated to my newest darling,
Carmen Amelia Sharpe,
with enduring love.

A huge thanks to Tom Hanky and Station 14
of the Albany Fire Department for their generosity
in helping me with this book. Thanks also to
Donna Beamer of the Heritage Mall, and
Jennifer Jones for her spiffy ideas and
incalculable support.

Prologue

Devon Hiller lit a hand-rolled Cuban cigar and leaned back in his chair. Under strict doctor's orders not to smoke, drink or become unduly stressed, he amused himself by blithely indulging in all three. Hell, he wasn't dead yet.

It was good to have the house to himself again. A cleaning crew would come in the morning and pick up after the party, but for now he was just glad to be rid of that crowd of brown-nosers. And that included his niece, Elizabeth, though he had to admit issuing ultimatums to her had been the high point of his evening. Never mind her husband, a ticking bomb if there ever was one. What could *he* do about anything? Nothing, that's what!

As Devon took a generous sip of cognac, he thought he heard a noise in the foyer and straightened in his chair. Parking the cigar in a heavy crystal ashtray, he peered into the gloom as the door to his study silently drifted open.

"Who's there?" he barked.

A figure moved in the shadows.

"That you, Elizabeth?" he chuckled as he set aside

the snifter. "Back again, are you? Changed your mind? Good, good. I knew you'd see it my way."

The figure stepped into the light. Not Elizabeth.

"How did *you* get in here?" Devon demanded. The look on the intruder's face caused an alarm to go off in Devon's brandy soaked brain. His gun was in the wall safe. Palming the antique letter opener he always kept on his desk, he slowly got to his feet.

"I thought I made it clear I wasn't going to do business with you," he growled as he rounded his desk. A show of strength, that's what was called for. Just as he decided to throw in a few words of warning, he finally noticed a long green cord stretched between the two gloved hands.

The intruder's lips curled into a smile that sent Devon stumbling back, groping for the phone. His attacker moved swiftly, pulling Devon away from the desk, slamming him onto the Persian carpet. The impact caused the letter opener to tumble free.

Still Devon struggled, gratified as he felt his fingers wrap around the green fiber, then gasping as a sharp pain drove all other thoughts from his brain. He was conscious just long enough to glimpse the hilt of the letter opener erupting from his chest.

He died knowing that, in the strictest sense, his bad habits had finally caught up with him.

Chapter One

The jarring ring of the doorbell startled Liz Chase awake. She sat very still for a moment, trying to remember what she'd been dreaming, but the images dissolved without ever taking form.

The bell rang again. Setting aside the paperback novel that had lulled her to sleep in the first place, she heaved her very pregnant body from an aging rocker and mumbled, ''I'm coming.'' Curled up by the cold fireplace, Sinbad, her Siamese cat, opened one blue eye and yowled.

Through the parted drapes she saw a light-colored truck pull away from the house and a jolt of uneasiness rocked her. It had to be close to ten o'clock. Who would plan an unannounced visit at this hour? Who would apparently send his or her ride away before making sure Liz was home?

Wishing she'd gotten around to installing a chain on the door, she cautiously pulled it open as she switched on the outside light.

For a moment, she couldn't believe her eyes. Was this one of those dreams within a dream where you thought you were awake but you weren't? She whispered, "Alex?"

He blinked at the sudden influx of light just as she shivered from the gust of cold wind that blew a handful of fallen leaves around her feet. He was dressed in jeans and a heavy jacket and looked far better than he had a right to look.

"Liz," he said at last, running a hand through his thick, dark hair. "My God, if you aren't a sight for sore eyes."

She managed to mumble, "I thought…how…"

"In a minute, sweetheart. Just give me a minute."

Heart racing, she glanced over his shoulder. Across the narrow country road, she caught a glimpse of her only neighbor's lights. She searched her own heavily shadowed yard for—

For what? Sheriff Kapp and a posse of deputies?

She found nothing but the forbidding shapes of denuded fruit trees twisting in the wind, dancing to the mournful sound of ocean breakers hitting the base of the cliff below.

Alex cleared his throat. "May I come in?"

A death grip on the door kept her on her feet while she considered his question. Her instinct was to say no.

"Dave Sullivan gave me a ride," he explained as though giving her time to gather her wits. "I didn't want you running around at night," he continued. "Not with the baby coming."

As her free hand flew to her midsection, her indecision fled. "I think you should leave," she said, pushing on the door.

He blocked it with his hand. "Honey, wait. I need to talk to you. It's important."

Except for a few glimpses of him in the courtroom

when she'd testified at his trial, she hadn't seen him since the night he killed her uncle. She'd thought she'd never see him again. Wasn't that what he'd wanted?

"Liz, please." He had somehow moved across the threshold. Letting go of the door, she pushed against his chest, but he caught her hands and held onto them. "Liz!"

For the first time, she met his gaze straight on. His stormy eyes and gaunt cheeks hinted he wasn't sleeping or eating well. His skin was pale, unnaturally so for a man who had spent most of his life outdoors, whose passion was fighting infernos and saving lives, who camped and hiked year-round. Jail time can do that to a man, she figured, trying to imagine what he'd look like after ten years behind bars, twenty.

"I'm home," he said gently.

She felt a biting pain behind her nose as tears gathered there but went no farther. She fought with herself to discount the way his voice caressed her, the sudden ache his presence created, an ache she'd spent months trying to overcome, to deny. Pulling away, she said, "No—"

"I'm home," he repeated fiercely, his face mere inches from hers, his breath warm against her chilled skin. His gaze bored two holes into her. "Home, Liz."

And feeling the pressure of his hands clasped around hers, sensing the heated power of his body standing so close, she felt every last ounce of self-control and pride slip away. Horrified at her own weakness, she nevertheless burst into tears, slumping against him, relying on his quickness and strength to save her from hitting the floor in a pitiful heap.

He caught her with forceful hands. Supporting her against his side, he shut the door, shielding them both from the wild cold night and prying eyes.

It's all been a terrible mistake, her heart chirped like a demented songbird. *Haven't you somehow known it all along? He's your husband and he's home.*

For the first time in months the planet fell back on its axis.

"You're really here," she whispered as he wiped away her tears with trembling fingers whose touch she'd thought she'd never again feel. Then he lowered his head and kissed her.

How many nights had she dreamed this very thing? Alex's soft, sensuous mouth pressed against hers, his big hands gently cupping her face, his lips everywhere, grazing her forehead, eyelids, mouth, chin. She held onto him as tightly as she could, afraid he might vanish from her arms the way he always vanished from her dreams, but he was flesh and blood and real.

A million questions rattled around in her brain. She shut them out. For the moment, it was enough to go on feelings and her feelings were telling her that everything she'd thought about her husband for the past several months had been unequivocally wrong. Damn the facts, damn his own confession. Damn the way he'd turned away from her, shut her out. All wrong.

Her husband.

Not for long. Not now...

Like the relentless advances of an unwelcome suitor, reason refused to leave her alone. Things weren't so simple. She'd come a long way in the past six months, further than Alex knew. She'd had no choice.

Pulling herself away, she whispered, "What are you doing here?"

"I came because of you." Tugging on her hands, he led her toward the light cast by the floor lamp. "Look at you." His gaze dropped from her face to her distended middle and he put a hand on her belly, lightly cradling his baby. She involuntarily flinched at the intimacy.

"I missed all this," he said. His gaze lifted again and his expression was so carefree he almost looked like the boy she'd fallen in love with over twelve years before. "Do we know the sex?"

"No," she said, her voice shaky. She'd worked hard to eradicate the surreal quality that had suffused her life for the past several months, thanks to him, but now it was back.

His gaze swept over her, leaving her breathless, re-awakening memories of him she'd fought desperately to forget. *Alex after a fire, alive and safe; Alex in bed, reaching for her, loving her…*

"You cut your hair," he added, fingering the tousled blond tresses. "I like it."

She'd cut her hair because he'd loved it long.

"Honey, you look like you've seen a ghost. Come sit down."

Summoning her resolve, holding her breath, she blurted, "I'm not moving from this spot until you explain how a man who should be in prison is suddenly here in my living room."

He looked at her as though the answer were obvious. "I know you're surprised—"

"You could say that," she whispered.

His gaze traveled every square inch of the room as he took off his jacket, revealing a black shirt she'd never seen before. It didn't fit him very well; it was too tight across his broad shoulders, too short in the sleeves. He caught sight of the cat who now sat on his haunches, both almond shaped eyes wide open. "Sinbad, you little devil, how are you, boy?" He picked Sinbad up and as Liz watched, the cat rubbed Alex's chin in a show of affection and trust. Liz found herself thinking that life was easier if you were a cat.

Alex put Sinbad down and draped his jacket over the back of a chair. He stared at the unused fireplace for a moment, then back at her. "You still can't stand an open flame in the house," he said softly.

She shrugged as he strode to the door with the unconscious grace that had first attracted Liz in high school. Back then, she'd been a shy freshman and he'd been the star varsity basketball player, the resident bad boy, four years her senior. It had been love at first sight.

He locked the door then yanked the drapes closer together, blocking out the black, moonless night.

From what—or whom—was he hiding?

Rolling up each sleeve in turn, he faced her again, more in control now, thinner than in the past but still unbelievably fearless and every inch the man she'd pledged to love for eternity.

She said, "Why are you stalling?"

Staring at her as though she might disappear at any second, he whispered, "Because I can't believe I'm really here. I thought I'd never see you again."

She nodded, well acquainted with that particular feeling.

He moved close to her and added, "There's going to be a new trial."

A veritable tidal wave of relief flooded Liz's central nervous system. Her legs felt wobbly again, but all she could think about was that a new trial must mean new evidence and some kind of…well, mistake or misunderstanding.

"Come sit down before you fall down," he insisted, taking her arm.

She obligingly sank down on a chair and stared up at

him. "I'm okay," she insisted, relieved when he let go of her. It was hard to think clearly in his presence, let alone form a coherent thought when he actually touched her.

And then his statement resounded in her head. A new trial? How could that be? She knew his case had gone to jury two days before. The television and radio had been full of little else; the newspaper had all but locked him up and thrown away the key. She'd avoided watching, listening to or reading anything that had to do with his trial. What was the point? He'd confessed. He'd shut her out. He was history.

He pulled the ottoman near her chair and sat down opposite her, so close their knees touched. Propping his hands on his thighs, he leaned closer still. "The jury was unable to reach a unanimous verdict."

"They're hung?"

He nodded.

Liz rubbed her hands together. The old house tended to be cold anyway and having the door open for so long hadn't helped matters, nor did the tension presently building in her chest. "How could that happen when they had your confession?"

His gaze met hers and slid away. "My lawyer was too good."

"And that means?"

"I told him not to mount a defense, but he said he couldn't do that because it would provide grounds for a mistrial. He offered up enough witnesses and enough doubt about the way my confession was obtained and the way the evidence was handled that it planted a seed of doubt in some of the jurors' minds. The D.A. has warned me there'll be a new trial. My being out is only temporary."

As she tried to assimilate all this, she started to shake. Alex retrieved his jacket and draped it around her shoulders. He stared down at her, his face caught in shadows, holding her gaze with glittering intensity.

"Sheriff Kapp is foaming at the mouth," he said. "He told me he's coming after me. That's why I'm here, Liz, to warn you. It's imperative you and I have our stories straight. This time Kapp will build a tighter case. This time his pride is on the line and re-election is right around the corner."

The jacket was still warm from Alex's body heat, and she pulled it close, burying her hands in the heavily piled lining. "You want me to lie for you?"

His brow wrinkled as he sat back down.

She realized with a sinking heart that she'd been foolishly nurturing the hope that a miracle had occurred, that he truly was innocent and that someone on the jury had realized it. That hope now shriveled up and died as had all the other hopes before it. She said, "Nothing's really changed."

"Everything's changed. I thought you were safe, but you're not, that's what I'm trying to tell you, that's why I'm here."

She pointed at the door and said, "I want you to leave. Right now. Go."

He managed to look bewildered for a moment. "*How* can you ask me to leave?"

"You have no right to come back here and try to make me feel…"

"Feel what, Liz?"

"Anything," she mumbled.

He got to his feet in one fluid motion. "I suppose that explains the divorce papers delivered to the jail?"

She narrowed her eyes as months of frustration and

grief fueled her anger and words too long unspoken flowed from her mouth with a life force of their own. "When you killed my uncle, you killed *us*. You killed any feelings I had for you. You killed our future. And you did it for his money. Was his money the only reason you married me in the first place? Was Uncle Devon actually right about you?"

Alex stood over her, eyes blazing again, fists balled, and for the first time in her life, Liz felt afraid of him. She sat frozen in her chair as he dropped to his knees by her side.

"You know why I married you," he said, his voice deep with emotion. "In your heart, you damn well know why and it had nothing to do with money."

Every womanly part of her knew he was right. It was just that his abrupt arrival had jolted her. She'd spent months mourning, she'd made herself sick with grief. It had been a long and difficult journey to escape the yawning abyss that had threatened to swallow her and her baby. She wasn't about to allow herself to stand so close to the edge ever again.

"I don't understand this charade," he added in a hushed whisper, sending new chills down her spine that had nothing to do with the temperature. "We both know what really happened the night your uncle died. Okay, I signed on for the long haul. I was willing—I *am* willing—to protect you and our baby until my dying breath. Nothing's changed when it comes to that."

Liz shook her head. "What are you talking about?"

He pushed himself to his feet and glared down at her. "You know what I'm talking about."

She shook her head. "No, I don't. What do you mean you were willing to sign on for the long haul? What's going on here, Alex? Stop talking in riddles."

When he finally spoke, his voice was low and ominous, as though he sensed a thousand ears pressed against the windows, listening to their every word. Standing over her, his expression grim, he said, "Remember the night your uncle died? We went to his house to tell him about your pregnancy. There was a terrible fight."

"We left the party and you were called to an emergency at the station," she added. "The old church at Taylor's Crossing was on fire." She shuddered as she thought about that fire, mercifully without victims.

Alex stopped dead in his tracks and pinned her with a laser stare. "When I left you, you were still furious with Devon."

Tears puddled in her eyes as old feelings of inadequacy welled up inside her. "Of course I was furious. For years I tried to please that man. I never could. That night was the last straw. The things he said—"

"He didn't want you saddled to someone like me," Alex said. "He wanted better for you than one of the Chase boys."

One of the Chase boys. Sure, Alex had come from a disreputable family but he'd grown into a wonderful, trustworthy man. Her uncle had refused to see that. To him, Alex would always be the boy he'd forced Liz to break up with in high school—the boy with no future.

Did wonderful, trustworthy men commit murder? an inner voice demanded.

Alex a murderer. It didn't sit right, it never had.

But he confessed.

It always came down to his confession.

"Later that night, you went back to his house," Alex said softly.

"How do you know that?" She'd never admitted that bitter, pointless trip to anyone.

Alex said, "I saw you."

Before he killed her uncle? Had she been that close to being able to stop him? A cry of anguish erupted and died in her throat. "I thought Uncle Devon might have had a…I don't know, a change of heart," she mumbled. "Except he didn't have a heart and I should have known it. I guess I was still hoping he might come through."

"But he didn't."

"Of course not. It was foolish of me to think he would. He was more sure than ever that I'd eventually do just as he wanted, like I always did. He said he was going to call his lawyer in the morning and set up the papers giving everything he had to a local nature conservatory. He didn't care about the wetlands, it was just his way of showing me he had control. Because he judged everything by its monetary worth, he thought I did, too."

Alex cleared his throat. "He never understood you."

"It doesn't matter anymore."

He stared at her so hard she felt the back of her skull throb. Finally, he said, "Don't ever tell anyone else you went back there that night. Do you understand? Not a soul."

"Why—"

"Not a soul," he repeated. "Promise me."

She took a deep breath. "Okay."

"You didn't tell Kapp, did you?"

"I was in shock when he came, but I kept thinking the less I said the better it would be for you. After he left, I called your lawyer. I told him I wanted to help you. I couldn't believe you'd ever kill anyone. But he confirmed that you'd confessed. He said you didn't want any help from me, you didn't even want to see me or talk to me. Alex, do you have any idea how much that hurt?''

"I—"

"Because for all intents and purposes, I lost you that night. I thought I was going to lose our baby, too. I'd lost one before and the thought of losing another... The doctor put me in bed for a week."

"I—"

"It doesn't matter if you're out on a technicality. You're still a murderer. I won't have you around me or my baby."

To her astonishment, Alex laughed. He laughed until a single tear rolled down his cheek, then he sat abruptly in one of the wing back chairs that flanked the stone-cold fireplace and buried his face in his hands.

Liz watched him with growing alarm until she found herself standing by his side. She shrugged off his coat and laid it aside. He apparently sensed her closeness for without looking up, he reached for her, caught the hem of her sweatshirt, pulled her onto his lap. He rested his cheek against her breasts, his chin on the curve of her belly.

While one tear did not a crying-jag make, she'd never seen Alex shed even that before. She'd always been the one to weep at the drop of a hat, not him. She wrapped her arms around him and smoothed his hair with an unsteady hand. She tried to dismiss how sitting in his lap made her feel. The way her body came alive. The way the world suddenly seemed to be okay again despite the fact that nothing was okay. It was like finally waking from a long, dreary sleep.

But where would this feeling of renewed life take her? Into heartbreak territory, that's where. Into a new trial, the outcome of which didn't matter because he was guilty and that was enough to destroy them. She concentrated on feeling pity. It was safer.

Eventually, he looked up. She fought the urge to touch his lips with her own. How else does a woman comfort a man she loves, even a man she knows she shouldn't love?

His expression guarded, he said, "I found your long green scarf."

She blinked a few times, totally at sea.

"The one I gave you for your birthday because it matched your eyes."

"I know which scarf you mean," she said. "But I don't understand—"

"You left it behind. I only had a second before I heard the sirens so I did the only thing that came to me. I hid it."

Blood pounded in her ears, making it hard to follow his words.

"Liz," he said gently, "I passed you a few miles from your uncle's estate. It's a narrow road and it doesn't go much of anywhere else. You were driving back into town."

"I didn't see you."

"It was dark and my old black truck looks like half the other black trucks in the county. But you have that white sports car."

"I don't understand, Alex. What's this got to do with my scarf?"

"I found your scarf in your uncle's hands. For an eternity or two, I just stared at it, trying to make sense of it until I heard the sirens. Then I untwisted it somehow and hid it. By then, the sheriff was there. He took me into custody. I tried to call you. I tried for hours. You weren't home.''

Liz had a hard time finding her voice. Her throat felt dry and raspy. She said, ''After I talked to my uncle for the last time, I went to my office at the mall and started packing my things. I wrote a letter of resignation. I was going to give it to him the next day. I was going to quit.''

''When I couldn't reach you, I thought it meant you were hiding,'' Alex said. ''The sheriff started talking about finding you. He started saying that everyone, even him, had heard you threaten your uncle. He said everyone knew you were just waiting for your uncle to die so you'd be rich. He said maybe you'd killed your uncle. I've had time to think about it since then. I think he was goading me. At the time I just wanted to strangle him.''

''Why would he do something like that? He was my uncle's protégé, and while we weren't exactly friends, he's always been pleasant to me.''

''He wanted me to admit I killed your uncle.''

Liz found herself on her feet, trembling. ''What are you saying, Alex?''

He took her hands and held them firmly. ''I think your uncle came at you with that letter opener and you struggled with him. I think your fear gave you enough strength to protect yourself and our baby. I think that during the struggle, the letter opener got turned on him or he fell on it, I'm not sure which. I think it was an accident or self-defense.''

She pulled her hands away and backed up. ''You think *I* killed my uncle?''

Brow furrowing, he nodded. ''Yes. Of course I do.''

''And then allowed you to take the blame for me?''

''Well—''

She felt all the blood drain out of her face.

"Liz—"

"I didn't kill him," she cried, hurt beyond bearing that he could think she would betray him.

He looked as pale and stunned as she felt. He swore under his breath and stared at her.

"I didn't kill him," she repeated.

Chapter Two

Alex swallowed so hard she could see his throat work. His eyes narrowed dangerously. Their stares stretched on and on until Liz finally sat down on the ottoman. "I don't understand. You confessed. Now you're telling me you didn't murder my uncle?"

"I didn't murder your uncle."

"But you thought I did?"

"Yes, I did," he said, and closed his eyes. She could only imagine what he was thinking and feeling.

"I went to tell Devon he could give his blasted money to a flea circus for all I cared," he added, opening his eyes and searching her face. "I wanted him to leave us alone. Don't you think I know how hard it's been for you to keep peace with him, to do things his way, how impossible it's been? But telling you to divorce me, to 'get rid' of our baby if you ever wanted to see a dime of his money—when he said those things, he burned his bridges as far as I was concerned and I wanted him to know it.

"He was in the den, crumpled on the floor in front of his desk, your scarf tangled in his fingers. He was warm. My EMT training kicked in and I felt for a pulse, I thought maybe—but he was already dead."

"Oh, Alex."

"And then Sheriff Kapp showed up. He'd received a telephone tip that something was going down at Devon Hiller's house. He asked me to come in with him, to answer questions. I still wasn't saying much of anything, just that I'd found Devon like that but I had his blood on my sleeve and apparently I even touched the handle of the letter opener because they found my prints on it. The sheriff started insinuating things about you and all I could think about was the murder scene. I'd found the scarf but had I missed something else you left? I confessed there'd been a struggle and he'd fallen. The sheriff was anxious to wrap it all up in record time and he was absolutely sure he had his man."

"You wouldn't let me help you."

"I wanted the investigation to begin and end with me. I thought you would understand what I was doing, why I *had* to do it. Your silence confirmed you did."

"My silence?" Liz said, angry now. "What choice did you give me but silence?"

He shook his head again.

"You didn't give me a chance to explain."

"Explain what? How mad you were? How mad we both were? You and I were prime suspects. Everyone at the house that night heard you threaten your uncle, heard you tell him you'd had enough, that you weren't going to take it anymore."

"I meant I was going to quit my job and stop subjecting myself to his manipulations."

"Dozens of bystanders only heard a threat. You were pregnant. You'd had a miscarriage a few months before and I couldn't let anything happen to you."

"So you told them you did it."

"For once, my family history came in handy. Nobody

ever really expected a Chase man to stay out of trouble for long. I don't think it strained anyone's imagination to picture me as a killer. Logic said it had to be one of us.''

"But, Alex, it wasn't one of us."

He stared at her. "No, it wasn't."

Liz felt her heart thump wildly. Alex reached out and took her hand, kissed her palm, and folded her hand in his. His fingers flicked over her bare finger, absent of her thick gold wedding band. "No," he repeated, "it wasn't."

"You're innocent."

"So are you." His relief was palpable and for the first time she understood the depth of the burden he'd been carrying. He'd thought she'd killed her uncle, he knew he hadn't. He'd given up his freedom and his chance to know his child—all for her. He'd thought she'd been willing to repay this sacrifice by leaving him to suffer the consequences alone. And then she'd asked him for a divorce.

She felt herself lean toward him, she felt him leaning toward her. What came now, a kiss, reconciliation, everything back to the way it was? She pulled away.

His eyes demanded an explanation but she didn't have one to offer. What he'd done was protect her and she felt humbled. But he hadn't trusted her. She'd thought they were a team, but Alex hadn't included her in a decision that would forever change the course of both of their lives—and that of their unborn child. Quite the opposite, he'd gone out of his way to exclude her.

His distrust of the sheriff was old news. It reminded her that Alex had learned, within the boundaries of his highly dysfunctional family, to go it alone. A stint in the army and the years at the fire station had tempered his fierce independent streak so that he'd become comfortable working as part of a team with men he respected. She'd assumed that quality would extend into their marriage, but he'd jumped to a terrible and wrong conclusion this time and he hadn't trusted her when it counted.

That hurt.

More to the heart of the matter, he'd also implicated himself so thoroughly that it might never be made right because Alex was correct—the whole community had reacted to his arrest with a knowing shake of their collective head.

Another Chase man gone wrong.

Only this one hadn't.

Alex stood, and extending a hand, helped Liz to her feet. "Are you okay now?" he asked softly. "Is the baby all right?"

"We're both fine."

"You must know I love you—"

This time she held up a hand to silence him. Her feelings were like tumbleweeds, roaming here and there and everywhere, rootless and brittle. "I can't talk anymore tonight," she mumbled.

"You're exhausted," he said, his voice filled with concern. Taking her hand, he looked at her with eyes so deep and midnight blue she yearned to get lost in them the way she had in the past, lost and found at the same time. He whispered, "You go to bed."

"What about you?"

He glanced around the room then back at her. "I need to think."

She felt a consuming shudder rack her body from the inside out and knew she needed time alone to absorb all this startling new information. For six months she'd thought him a murderer. And worse in some ways, she'd thought he had stopped loving her, stopped needing her. These feelings had never seemed, well, right, but for six months, she'd told herself that her feelings, especially when it came to Alex, were unreliable. All that didn't change in an instant.

She picked up Sinbad who immediately started purring. Lowering her gaze, avoiding Alex's eyes, she said, "When you do get tired, I think it would be best if you slept in the guest room."

She could feel him staring at her pregnancy as though he was wondering if she just wanted the bed to herself for comfort's sake or because she didn't want him that close. She added, "There's a sleeping bag in the closet. All your clothes are packed away in the attic."

"Don't worry about me."

There was so much she wanted to say to him. She didn't know where to start.

He moved to her side, cupped her chin and kissed her. She closed her eyes and concentrated on the moist warmth of his lips, on the undercurrent of desire she could feel pulse between them. It was all she could do to keep from asking him to join her, to hold her, to make love to her, to take away some of the pain they had unwittingly caused each other.

But she didn't. The world had exploded tonight— again. Alex was afraid a new investigation would lead the law to her. She was more afraid that he would once again try to protect her by offering himself up like a sacrificial goat. She didn't want him spending the rest of his life in prison for a crime he didn't commit.

After all, it was just his word that he was innocent, just her word that she was, too. As far as she knew, the only pieces of undiscovered evidence both led back to her: the silk scarf and her late-night visit, the one she'd thought no one knew about.

Most likely, other than the true killer, she was the last one to see Uncle Devon alive.

And that wasn't exactly a comforting thought, either.

LIZ WAS INNOCENT. *He should have known.* She was innocent. Not self-defense, not an accident—innocent.

Of course, the flip side of that was that there was a murderer on the loose. Even worse, there was a murderer on the loose who must have thought they were all but home free. What would happen when that person learned about the hung jury and the new investigation?

Liz's green scarf worried him. How had her uncle ended up with that piece of sand-washed silk wrapped around his fingers? Alex realized he should have asked Liz more about it and he stopped pacing long enough to glance down the hall and consider going to her room right now.

The thought of her snuggled in the bed they'd shared so many times stopped him. There was no way in the world he would be able to leave her side once he was there. Pregnant or not, she was the most sensual woman he'd ever known and he ached for her in his mind, in his body, in his soul.

He needed her.

The dark smudges under her eyes also kept him where he was. It was obvious that the past six months had been as harrowing for her as it had been for him.

Eventually, he made his way down the hall, too drained to put together a coherent thought. The surprise came when he discovered the spare room, so much bigger than his former cell, felt like a prison nonetheless.

For one thing, everything was all changed around.

Gone was the twin bed, the dresser and chairs, the
wooden desk he'd brought from his apartment when they
married. Instead, there was a navy colored futon against
one wall and a glass desk topped with a high-tech computer on the other.

Liz was good with computers. He thought them a giant waste of time better spent outdoors. And how he had
missed the outdoors. Even the short, cool walk from
Dave's truck to Liz's door with the tangy taste of the
sea on his tongue, the crunch of gravel and redwood
fronds under his feet, the roar of the ocean below and
the boughs whipping in the wind above had been sec-
onds of pure bliss. Freedom. Wonderful, messy, beautiful freedom.

He stripped down to his shorts and crawled into the
sleeping bag. The flannel felt good against his skin, comforting somehow, reminding him of all the camping trips
he'd taken with Liz, of the fireside romance that had
taken place once they zipped their bags together and
made love beneath the stars.

He heard the creak of her bedsprings and wondered
if she was as wide-awake as he. The wall was just too
damn thin.

Getting dressed again, he abandoned the sleeping bag
and retreated to the living room but found little comfort.
Memories were everywhere he looked. As lonely as his
cell had been, what had it been like for Liz to be caught
here in an old house full of ghostly reminders?

What in the world was he going to do?

Find the killer, make him or her pay, that's what he
was going to do.

Over and over again, he recalled the night he and Liz
had driven to her uncle's house. Devon Hiller had been
hosting a party celebrating the twentieth anniversary of

his pride and joy, the Harbor Lights Mall. There had been scads of people present. He and Liz had told Devon about the baby in private, but the ensuing explosion had spilled out of the study and into the house. Everyone had heard everything that was said.

Sure, he'd wanted to strike Devon Hiller dead in his tracks. How could he not when Devon's cruel tongue lashed out at the woman he loved? But as Liz fought back, probably for the first time in her life, Alex had stood there, rigid with fury, afraid that if he acted he wouldn't be able to contain himself. When he'd finally looked at Liz he'd been stunned by the expression on her face. It was as though she saw the old man for who he really was, or at least finally understood it. He couldn't wait to get her out of there.

And later, when he'd found Hiller's body, he'd assumed this insight had given his gentle wife the courage to return for a final, private confrontation that had led ultimately to the need to protect herself and her baby.

Restless, Alex roamed the house. He looked at the Homer print of a breaching sailboat on the wall, at the books stacked two deep on the shelves, at the catnip mouse abandoned near Sinbad's water bowl, and once again vowed never to return to prison.

Unless he had to protect Liz.

Who had hated Devon Hiller enough to kill him? Hell, who hadn't? No, that wasn't true. People often hated other people, but not to the point of killing them.

Okay, who kills a man so old and riddled with self-inflicted health problems that he was due to self-destruct within a year anyway? Why take the chance? Why not just wait until the old guy dies of natural causes? According to his will, the only one who stood to benefit from his death was Liz.

Alex watched the sky grow gradually lighter while standing out in back near the bluff. The cold wind of the night before had given way to a light rain which felt great. Cold, wet, great. Seagulls wheeled overhead and the wooden stairs leading down the hillside to the beach below disappeared in swirling mists. Waves crashed against the shore, retreating with a loud swish. A few hours from now, at high tide, there would be no beach, just the relentless surf beating against the huge rocks at the base of the cliff.

Liz had been orphaned days before her eighth birthday when a fire burned her family's home to the ground. Only the fact that Liz was staying at a friend's house had spared her. Her uncle had taken her in, but as soon as she turned twenty-one and inherited her parents' money, she'd bought this place and moved out on her own. Alex imagined that streak of autonomy had irritated the hell out of her uncle but he shouldn't have worried. Liz might have moved ten miles north, but for years after, she'd still worked hard to please the man who had raised her, managing his biggest mall, sweeping up after him when he alienated his employees.

Slowly, Liz was fixing the house up, making it into a home, and though he worried about her spending so much time out here alone, he couldn't deny that there was something very life affirming about living in one of nature's more spectacular pockets. Last spring, they'd talked about building a fenced backyard before the baby came. He made a mental note to start it now.

A movement in the house caught his eye. He turned to see that Liz had come to the glass door and was staring at him, a yellow towel in one hand.

He was still getting used to her ballooned figure. When last he'd seen her, she'd been angular on the outside and soft in the middle. Now she was just the opposite. It made him feel awful that he was responsible for the guarded edge he detected in her.

He had to find out what she remembered about her scarf. If she hadn't left it in her uncle's den, then someone else had taken it there and that someone must have wanted to implicate Liz.

As he crossed the wet ground, he saw her move away from the door, leaving the towel draped over the back of a kitchen chair. He left his wet shoes and the raincoat under the overhang, went inside and dried his short hair as she took a carton of eggs out of the refrigerator. Sinbad, twining his way around her legs, meowed in that strident Siamese cry that always reminded Alex of a small baby.

"Did you sleep okay?" she asked, turning to look at him.

"Fine. You?"

"Fine."

"You look great," he said.

She glanced down at her maternity clothes and protruding belly and smiled wistfully. "Oh, yeah, I'm a real treat. That isn't your shirt, is it? Or your jacket?"

"Dave brought me some of his brother's stuff. Liz, what do you remember about your green scarf?"

She popped slices of bread in the toaster. "Move, Sinbad," she scolded the cat who squeezed his eyes at her and stood his ground. She faced Alex with a troubled expression. "I don't know. I thought about that last night after I went to bed. When had I worn it last, where had I last seen it? But I can't remember. It just seems that I had it and then I didn't have it."

He picked up the cat and rubbed his sable ears. "What about at the party?"

"I don't know. It's been so long ago and so much has happened, I don't remember what I was wearing that night. I do recall that we hadn't changed clothes after work or dressed up or anything. It's important, isn't it?"

"Very. And you were wearing a greenish-blue dress."

She looked thoughtful, then shook her head again. "I know the dress, I used to wear it with your scarf, but I don't remember if I did that night or not. It's no use."

"It'll come to you," he said with confidence, desperate to ease the strain on her face. He put Sinbad down on an empty chair and added, "I notice you have a big old computer in the guest room now. You know how hopeless I am on those things. But maybe you can use it to help us figure out who really killed your uncle."

She bit her lip. "I was thinking. Maybe you should go to Sheriff Kapp or the D.A. and explain this... misunderstanding."

"No."

She was dressed in a pale-blue cotton blouse and loose white sweater, clothes that did nothing to add color to her washed-out complexion. Was she beautiful? Of course, but her beauty was accidental now. With an incredulous tone to her voice, she said, "What do you mean, 'No'?"

"Think about it. A brand-new story, a retraction of my confession, they'll all just think I'm grasping at straws. Worse, the information that you were at your uncle's house later that night to say nothing of the fact that a piece of your clothing was found in his hand will put you under scrutiny, and maybe not just for second degree murder like me. Your scarf might be interpreted as a would-be weapon that suggests premeditation, they might go after the death penalty. Absolutely no way we're ever going to chance it."

"But—"

"I've been thinking, too. I need to figure out who killed your uncle and how to prove it."

"You're not an investigator. We'll hire a really good lawyer—"

"I don't want your name coming into any of this until I know who's responsible."

She jerked open the refrigerator and emerged with the orange juice. He set out small glasses and watched as she poured the juice. "That's very noble, but I repeat, you're not an investigator."

Taking the juice to the table, he called over his shoulder. "That baby you're carrying is mine, Liz." He moved to her side and gently touched her tummy, praying she wouldn't flinch like she had the night before. When she didn't, he left his hand where it was. "I want his or her name to be one he or she will be proud to own. Now that I know you're innocent, I won't rest until I clear that name. That's a promise."

She stared into his eyes and said, "Can you feel it?"

He hadn't the slightest idea what she was talking about. "Feel what?"

She put her hand over his and pressed down a little. "Right here. The baby. Kicking up a storm."

And suddenly he felt a muffled thump against his palm. "Yes," he said, grinning. "Yes." He felt several more soft kicks and then it seemed as though Liz's whole belly kind of shifted to the side.

"You just experienced a rollover," Liz said. "Trust me, it's quite a sensation from the inside."

"I bet it is," he said, longing to lift her blouse and lay his cheek against her stomach. Instead he reluctantly dropped his hand.

"You have to get over worrying about implicating

me, Alex,'' she said as she set their plates on the table. ''We have to tell—''

''No,'' he repeated, and sat down opposite her.

''You still don't trust anyone, do you?''

''I trust you,'' he said.

''But you didn't trust me when it mattered. You didn't give the law a chance. You still won't.''

''You mean that idiot, Kapp.''

''Roger Kapp isn't so bad.''

''He's a dangerous fool. Maybe my poor opinion of him stems from the fact that he was out at my house a lot as I grew up, hassling my brothers. He was a deputy then and liked to throw his weight around. Or maybe it's the way he used you to get to me.''

''Try to put the past behind you. Let's just talk to him—''

''Look, it's my hide we're talking about. And I'm the one who fouled things up. Now, eat something. You need to keep your strength up.''

For the first time since she'd opened the door the night before, she really smiled. Alex drank in the sight—to him more breathtaking than any sunrise—and hoped he'd find a way to make it happen again.

''Tonight we share the same bed,'' he said softly, admiring the lovely curve of her jaw. This new clarity of her features was one of the surprising bonuses of her shorter hair. He could see the long, graceful line of her neck, her sweet earlobes, her golden eyebrows. ''I don't know the rules about sex and pregnancy, but surely being held in a husband's arms is on the approved list,'' he added tenderly.

The smiled faded and she grew increasingly silent. He tried concentrating on the taste of fresh eggs and icy juice. He tried living in the moment, relishing the sounds of the soft rain on the roof, the hum of the refrigerator, the distant thunder of waves. The very fact that he was back in the middle of his own life, seated at his own table, looking at his own wife, was astounding and cause for profound thankfulness. He tried to ignore the black cloud he could feel hovering over them both.

Nothing worked. Liz fed Sinbad bits of egg which he seemed to demand with strident yowls. She folded and refolded her napkin, moved her juice glass from one side of the placemat to the other.

"Remember when you found out you were pregnant?" he asked.

That got her attention. She said, "Yes. Of course."

"You put on that tight red dress with the low, sexy back and bought a bottle of sparkling apple cider. You even soaked off the cider label and replaced it with a champagne label, remember? You made sure we had the evening alone, made a platter of fancy little things to eat, sat me down, mumbled something I couldn't understand and then started fidgeting. In fact, before you finally got the news out, you did everything but reline the kitchen shelves."

She smiled at the memory. "Well, I was nervous."

"I know. And now you're at it again."

She stopped folding her napkin into triangles and looked up at him.

"Besides everything, Liz, what's troubling you?"

"Nothing."

He put his hand over hers. "I'm not an idiot. Come on, fess up, what's wrong?"

She cast him a wary glance and bit her top lip. "I just keep thinking about how you must have hated me."

There was nothing in the world she could have said

that would have astonished him more. "What are you talking about?"

Brushing wayward strands of pale hair from her forehead, she said, "You thought I killed Uncle Devon and then sat by while you took the blame for it."

"No, no, honey. I thought you understood that I understood—"

"You thought I was more worried about myself than I was about you. It makes me feel terrible that you could have thought that of me."

He shook his head, unsure what to say. Why hadn't it occurred to him that his delicate wife would no more stand aside and let him take the blame for something she did than fly to the moon?

"I'm sorry."

Laying her fork aside, gaze averted, she added, "You didn't turn to me when it mattered most. You pushed me and our marriage aside and went it alone. I...I feel as though I can't trust you anymore. I don't want you behind bars for something you didn't do, for trying to protect me, but beyond that I...I don't know. About us, I mean. About our future. I'm sorry."

"You don't mean that," he said.

A single tear rolled down her cheek as she averted her gaze.

She meant it.

Chapter Three

Liz stared at the computer screen and tried to figure out how she was supposed to use it to help find a killer. Overhead, she could hear Alex's footsteps as he moved around the attic looking in boxes. Sinbad must be up there with him, she thought, because every once in a while, she could hear him throw in his two cents via a throaty meow.

Silly as it might seem to non–cat lovers, Sinbad had been her lifeline while Alex was gone. He was someone to come home to, someone who needed her and never complained if she moped about all day in a robe. He ate pretty much anything she fed him, liked to sit for long periods in her lap—back when she had one—and punctuated her remarks with snappy sounds so it seemed he was really listening.

She moved from randomly surfing the Internet to checking her e-mail. She had one message and it was from her friend and co-worker, Ron Boxer. He'd sent it early that morning and a business question was followed by a personal one—did she want to meet him downtown for lunch? Hands poised over the keyboard to explain why she couldn't, she paused.

Why couldn't she? Getting away from everything suddenly sounded like a fantastic idea. She typed a positive response and suggested Ron invite his sister, Emily, to join them. Talking to friends would be good therapy.

An hour later she was still at the computer, finishing the outline for a marketing blitz for the mall. Hiller Properties was a vast and complicated conglomerate, woven together by her uncle and his lawyers. Since her uncle's death, his properties had been tied up, but she was still the one in charge and would be even more invested and involved once the dust settled.

However, after the upcoming office Christmas party, which she felt duty-bound to host, she was off on maternity leave for an indefinite time. Lately, she'd felt herself entertaining ideas of bailing out. To counteract these treasonous thoughts, she'd been working harder than ever.

Of course, there was always the possibility that once the sheriff started digging, someone else would come forward with the news that they'd seen her visiting her uncle late that night. Maybe someone else had seen her car or maybe the maid heard her voice and never mentioned it because what was the point, Alex was guilty? Maybe, despite Alex's best intentions, she'd still wind up in jail!

"Find anything?"

She whirled around in her office chair as Sinbad bounded across the room and landed on the desktop. Papers and pencils went flying as the big cat settled on top of a stack of books and immediately began washing his face with a silky brown paw.

Alex stood in the doorway. He'd put on gray sweats; she almost expected to hear him say he was on the way to the gym. In the background, she heard the tumbling growl of the drier.

"You startled me!"

"Find anything interesting on the computer?"

"I'm not sure where to look. I can't find the Murderers Anonymous site."

Smiling, he said, "I have a few ideas we'll talk about later. Meanwhile, you made a nursery out of my old den."

It was a three bedroom house and she'd chosen the bedroom across the hall for the nursery because of the light. "Yes."

Looking guarded, he said, "If you really won't let me share our bed, then I'd like to throw the sleeping bag in that room."

She gestured at the wall. "But the futon—"

"I don't want to sleep in here. I'll take the futon mattress across the hall and move the crib."

"But this is all set up and ready to go," she protested. She didn't want him changing things. She'd created a nest across the hall and she wanted it to stay the way she'd made it. Why she felt so strongly about it was unclear to her. "It doesn't make sense to drag things around," she mumbled.

"I can't sleep in this room," he said, advancing. He stopped when he was right in front of her, forcing her to look up at him.

"Why?"

He seemed to consider her question as though trying to decide how honest to be. With his free hand, he fondled her hair, one of his fingers drifting down her cheek, across her chin. Every place he touched tingled with awareness. His voice very soft, he said, "Because I can hear you in our old bedroom. I can hear you move. I swear I can hear you breathe. I can picture you in bed and it drives me wild."

It was more of an answer than she had expected, but that shouldn't have surprised her. Alex was not only an arousing man to look at with his smoldering blue eyes, strong athletic body and dark good looks, he also exuded sexual energy, always had, and as long as she'd known him, that focus had been directed at her.

She saw desire on his face now, she felt it emanating from his body, and pregnant or not, it made her ache for his touch, reawakening parts of her that had been dormant for months.

"Whatever you want," she said.

"That way you can work when you want to."

"Good thinking."

"Also, until we have an idea of who really killed your uncle, we need to be cautious. The murderer might very well be someone we know."

Liz felt a tremor move through her body. "I can't believe it's anyone we know," she insisted.

He ran a hand through his hair. "We'll go out to lunch and get a head start on a plan but first I want to stop by the firehouse and return Dave's brother's clothes plus check out the mood there."

"It sounds like a good idea, but I can't go with you."

Alex narrowed his eyes for an instant. "Why not?"

"I already have lunch plans," she said, uncertain why she felt so awkward. She straightened the papers the cat had disturbed. "I made them a long time ago," she lied and mentally slapped herself for doing so. "Anyway—"

"Plans with whom?" Alex asked, backing away a little.

"Business plans," she mumbled.

"Can't you change them?"

"No."

"Can't or won't?"

"Stop pushing me, Alex."

He glowered at her for a second, then said, "Be careful what you say to people."

"What does that mean?"

"All I'm saying is that you and I need to sit down and make plans. We need to figure out who had motive and opportunity. Until we do, let's not divulge more than the fact that I'm going to have a new trial."

"You don't even want me to mention that you're innocent?"

His blue eyes looked intense as he said, "Absolutely not. I know it will be hard for you. People are going to be shocked that you allowed me back in your house."

"You can't blame them."

"It has to be this way. We can't take the chance that Kapp might decide to look elsewhere for the murderer until I can steer him in the right direction. I don't want him considering you."

"You've got to get over protecting me, Alex. I'm a big girl."

"Just be careful," he said, and added, "I'm going to take a shower."

As he left the room, she switched off the computer and went into her room to change clothes, Sinbad on her heels. She didn't want to be in the house while Alex showered. Some of their most intimate moments had started in that shower. Just picturing him standing in it, naked, steam rising around him, his skin glistening wet and slippery to the touch made her feel faint. She felt the overwhelming need to escape the house and Alex and all her old feelings.

RON BOXER had joined the mall staff as the leasing agent eighteen months before. An easy man to like, he'd been friends with both Alex and Liz. After Alex's troubles began and Liz felt so alone, Ron had introduced Liz to his sister, Emily, who had just moved to town following a messy divorce. Emily bought the duplex next to Ron's. Over the months, Ron and Emily had become the big sister and brother Liz had never had.

Ron had already arrived at the narrow Italian restaurant and waved Liz to their favorite table in back. Liz was pleased to see Emily sitting beside him.

Ron was a little shorter than Alex, with hazel eyes and fine brown hair that flopped over his forehead. A fitness nut, he biked to work every morning when the weather permitted. He was good-looking in an all-American way; the female half of the office staff had a crush on him. His sister was in many ways a smaller version of Ron with the same fawn-brown hair and attractive face. She had used her divorce settlement to open a specialty yarn shop in the mall a couple of months ago. Liz knew Ron was in his early thirties and that Emily was a couple of years older.

"We ordered for you," Ron said as he held a chair for Liz. "Iced tea, spinach pie, extra sauce, right?"

"I'm getting too predictable," Liz said, longing for a bowl of minestrone soup instead.

Emily leaned forward. "How is Sinbad?"

"Oh, he's fine. You haven't been over in a few days, you'll have to come pay him a visit," Liz said, and then fell silent. How could she invite friends over with things the way they were? She suddenly realized that when she'd agreed to keep Alex's innocence a secret, she hadn't fully appreciated how difficult it would be.

"Are you feeling okay?" Ron asked as the waitress delivered their drinks.

"You do look a little weary," Emily added.

"I didn't sleep well last night, that's all. I'm fine."

"You should have come over," Emily said with a laugh. "Ron and I were up to all hours moving my furniture around. He seems to think I'm going to win the lottery because he's telling me I should buy myself all new stuff."

Ron smiled. "You need more shelves for all you doodads. Anyway, I just think she should get rid of the castoffs. Most of them came from her marriage."

"Ron is the one stuck in the past," Emily protested. "All he has are the few things Mother left us. There's not much since most went to pay off her last medical bills."

"What's left is sentimental," Ron said. "You must feel that way, too, Liz, about all your uncle's stuff. He had some amazing antiques, didn't he?"

Liz nodded.

"I was just there the one time, but I couldn't believe the quality…and the quantity."

"Uncle Devon was quite a collector," Liz said, her mind only half on their conversation.

"Have you thought about how you're going to dispose of everything after the estate is settled?"

Liz shrugged. "Not really." The fact was that Liz had no clear idea of what to do with her uncle's house or its contents. Sometimes she thought of moving back—it was, after all, the home she'd grown up in—and at other times she never wanted to see the place again. For the moment, the vacant house was under the care of the housekeeper.

"Maybe someday you'll remarry," Emily said. "Your new husband might have the education and taste to appreciate things like antiques."

Liz was still only half listening. She wished the town

newspaper came out in the morning instead of the evening so they'd already know about Alex's hung jury. In the end, it seemed best to just get it over with. Taking a shallow breath, she said, "Alex is home."

Her declaration was met with silence.

Ron finally said, "Alex? As in your husband, Alex?"

"How in the world did he get out of jail? He's a murderer!" Emily added.

Liz bit her lip as she took a sip of iced tea. "It's a little complicated," she said, suddenly wishing she'd said no to lunch. She'd had no idea how emotional she'd feel sitting next to her two friends and how hard it would be to say so little.

The waitress reappeared with a giant round platter and all conversation ceased as she set out the food. Liz stared at her wedge of spinach pie. The smell of the rich red sauce made her queasy and she longed to leave the restaurant and go outside, go home. To Alex...

When the waitress left, Ron spoke in a deep whisper. "Are you saying he was found innocent?"

"Well—"

"I can't believe it," Emily muttered. "What kind of idiots were on that jury? Everyone knows he's guilty."

Ron hunched forward. "Did they decide he didn't do it? If he didn't, who did? This is great news, isn't it?"

These questions, assuming the best of Alex, brought a smile to Liz's lips. "Yes, of course, except it's not that easy. Everything is up in the air. It was a hung jury."

"You must be scared to death he'll come after you," Emily said, her huge eyes filled with alarm.

"Oh, no. Of course not. Listen—"

"But he's a killer!" Emily said. "You need a restraining order to keep him away!"

Ron put a hand on his sister's shoulder. "Emily, let Liz explain."

From over Liz's shoulder came a calm voice. "Maybe I can help."

With a thrill of recognition, Liz looked up to find Alex standing behind her. The thrill quickly degenerated to irritation. Frowning, she said, "Did you follow me here?"

He met her frown with a smile. "I made an educated guess. I know how you feel about Tony-O's spinach pie."

"But I told you this meeting was business. I told you—"

Ron cut in. "Oh, come on, Liz. Maybe the man is hungry. Sit down, Alex, it's good to see you again." Gesturing to his left, he added, "Let me introduce you to my sister, Emily Watts. I think she moved to town after…well, you know."

Alex nodded in Emily's direction as he took off his own jacket, a soft brown leather one that Liz had bought him for his birthday in January. She loved the way it looked on him, loved the feel of it against her cheek when he held her. She had the sudden and overwhelming desire for him to do just that, to hold her, to take her away.

He pulled out the fourth chair. "That looks good," he said, looking at Liz's spinach pie.

She pushed the plate toward him.

"Aren't you hungry?"

"Not really."

Alex took a bite and smiled. "Delicious."

"It must beat jail food," Emily sputtered.

The table grew very still.

"You have to excuse my sister," Ron said. "She

tends to be a little cautious where Liz in concerned. Alex, it's good to see you. I trust there's an explanation. I have to admit I'm dying to hear it.''

"I have to warn you," Emily sputtered, "I won't stand by and watch a confessed murderer harass Liz. She's in no condition—''

"She's pregnant with *my* child," Alex said, his eyes blazing, his voice no longer teasing. "She's *my* wife. I know what condition she's in.''

Ron glanced at his sister. "Calm down. Give the man a chance.''

Liz was secretly thrilled to hear Alex leap to his own defense. As someone who had spent far too many years swallowing her emotions in deference to her uncle's tyranny, she'd always admired the way Alex stood up for himself. He was a man of action. Giving up control and taking the blame for a murder he hadn't committed must be galling.

"Things aren't always as they seem, Emily," Liz said gently. She looked back at Alex and added, "But they're my friends, Alex. I trust them. Please, swear them to secrecy and tell them what's going on.''

She could almost see the wheels turn in Alex's handsome head. "If it means that much to you," he finally said.

"It means that much," she told him, and then excused herself. She knew if she stayed at the table, she'd be inclined to blurt out every detail, and this was Alex's situation to control. She unhooked her coat from the rack on the way out, nodding at people she knew, but desperate for an infusion of fresh air.

Pulling her coat close around her, she stood beneath the gaily striped green-and-white awning and took deep gulps of air suffused with the pungent smells of the sea.

Her frayed nerves and restless stomach slowly began to relax.

This old part of the city hadn't been affected much by her uncle's mall. Gift stores, restaurants and galleries still thrived when the tourists came to town during the summer and now, for the holidays, twinkling lights and garlands of fake greenery gave every storefront a jaunty air. A few blocks east, however, the shopping mall had exacted a huge toll. All these years later, there were still empty buildings. It was hard for a Ma and Pa bicycle shop to compete with any of the huge chain stores.

She sighed deeply. She'd give Alex a few moments to tell Ron and Emily as much as he thought wise, then return.

Looking up the street toward the new library, she instantly spotted the sheriff's car parked half a block up on the other side. She searched the opposite sidewalk. There he was, Sheriff Roger Kapp, standing not a hundred feet away from her, talking to one of his deputies.

Liz felt the instant urge to retreat. Should she go back inside the restaurant? Would Kapp see her if she moved and then would he follow? Did it matter? Alex wasn't an escaped felon. But the thought of a scene in front of Emily and Ron wasn't pleasant. Indecision caught her like a mouse under Sinbad's paw. Naturally, because she didn't want him to, the sheriff looked up and locked gazes with her.

She tried a smile and a nonchalant wave.

He pointed at her.

There was nothing to do but stand there and wait while he sprinted across the street.

The sheriff was a powerfully built middle-aged man with sandy hair just beginning to gray at the temples and a drill sergeant gaze Liz felt sure intimidated the inno-

cent as well as the guilty. He wore his uniform like a
second skin. In deference to the drizzly chill, he also
wore a padded jacket.

Over the years, he'd been a frequent visitor at her
uncle's Victorian estate. It was well known that Devon
Hiller's campaign support had helped win Roger Kapp
the last sheriff's election a few years back. She wondered how Kapp would fare in the upcoming election
without her uncle's backing.

Kapp stopped a few feet away, his gaze traveling her
figure. In her white maternity sweater and slacks, wearing the heavy black coat, she felt like a beached Orca
whale under his careful scrutiny.

"Elizabeth," he said, tipping his hat.

"Sheriff."

"Looks like it's about time for that baby to pop."

She said, "A few more weeks."

"How's everything going for you?"

"Pretty good," she said, wondering if his question
was more complicated than it sounded.

"You know, I was noticing the last time I was at your
place that you don't have a decent lock on your front
door. I know you have that squawking Siamese cat to
warn you when strangers come around, but that cat isn't
a Rottweiler, he can't really protect you."

"No, he'd just purr a robber to death."

"Reason I got to thinking about it all of a sudden is
that your hubby made bail. I suppose you know about
that damn jury."

She diplomatically decided not to mention the fact
that she also knew the mishandling of the original investigation by the sheriff's office had contributed to the
jury's indecision. His insinuation that she needed a lock
to keep Alex away was offensive, but for now she de-

cided to let it slide. She said, "Yes, isn't that wonderful news?"

A frown drew his brows together and when he changed position, she was aware of the creaking sound of his leather holster. "I guess that depends on your point of view."

"I just have a feeling that everything is going to work out great."

"It almost did," he persisted.

Resisting the urge to turn around to make sure Alex wasn't on his way out the door, she added, "Is there something I can do for you, Sheriff?"

"Just a friendly word for an old friend's niece," he said, his gaze never leaving her face. "Alex Chase is rotten through to the core, just like his father and his brothers. It wouldn't surprise me if he turns on you, next."

"Why would he turn on me?"

"Maybe you know something he doesn't want you to talk about."

"Like what?"

"Little details, things you might not even know you know. How about I come out to your place tomorrow afternoon and we'll have ourselves another conversation about the night your uncle died. I'll bring along a few tools and install a decent lock for you while I'm there."

"That's not necessary," she said, thinking fast. She couldn't decide if she should mention Alex was living with her or not. Surely, he already knew, didn't he? Didn't Kapp's deputies keep track of things like that? "I took care of it," she said cautiously.

"Good, glad to hear it. I'll be to your place right after lunch, okay?"

"Fine. I have nothing to hide."

Sheriff Kapp grinned. ''Now, Elizabeth, everyone has something to hide.''

''Do you say that from personal experience, Sheriff?''

Kapp chuckled. ''I swear, there's a little of your uncle in you, after all.''

Liz decided she'd think about his remark later, but she was pretty sure he hadn't meant it as flattery.

His expression grew serious and it seemed to Liz as though he was ready to touch her arm. At the last second, he tucked his hand in his jacket pocket instead. ''If someone is chasing your uncle's fortune,'' he said, ''then you're the next one in line.''

''That's absurd.''

''I hope so. Don't worry, though. We'll have Alex Chase back in custody before you know it.'' With another tip of his hat, he nodded.

Liz watched him sprint back across the street where he hooked up with his deputy and the two of them entered a small cafe on the corner well known for its fish and chips. Relieved that Alex hadn't come outside, she thoughtfully re-entered the restaurant, moving through the tables as quickly as her bulk allowed.

Was it a coincidence that Kapp had shown up on this street when she just happened to be standing there? Since he didn't seem to know Alex was staying at the house, did that mean he was following *her?*

Alex wasn't at the table. She looked around the restaurant and saw him leaning against the brick wall in back, talking on the phone. She also saw the turned heads of nearby diners and knew the fact that Alex had dined at Tony-O's would spread through the small town like a rabid brush fire. Joining Ron and Emily, she took a deep breath. Her stomach had immediately retied itself in a knot.

"You look contemplative," Ron said as she sat down.

"I just ran into Sheriff Kapp."

Emily's sharp intake of breath was followed by a hasty search of the restaurant. Did she expect the long arm of the law to reach right into the restaurant and snatch Alex away? This reaction surprised Liz who thought Emily's reserve about Alex would be a lot harder than this to wear down. "The sheriff?" Emily gasped. "Here?"

"It's okay, Emily. He's gone. I'm so glad you listened to Alex."

"I can imagine how much it meant to you to learn that Alex is innocent," Ron said. "However, frankly, I don't know how much of his story Emily believed."

Emily had recovered her composure. To Liz's dismay she said, "Not very much."

"He told us he's innocent," Ron said.

"What good is the word of a murderer?" Emily insisted.

"*I* believe in him," Liz said gently. "Totally."

"But he confessed. You have to be cautious—"

"He said there were details he couldn't talk about," Ron interrupted. "I don't think he likes Sheriff Kapp much."

"That's true," Liz said, once again appreciating Ron's levelheaded insight. "The sheriff won't rest until Alex is convicted. In fact, he's coming out to my place tomorrow after lunch to interview me again. I know Alex doesn't want me telling the sheriff the truth—I'm just not sure what to do."

"I think you should listen to your husband, Liz," Ron said.

Emily shook her head. "How can you say that? Alex Chase is a murderer."

"He's not," Liz said yet again. Glancing from one to the other, she added, "Don't tell Alex about Kapp, okay? He has enough to worry about right now. He's trying to protect me from everything and everybody."

Emily pointed over Liz's shoulder and said, "Speak of the devil."

Alex put his hands on Liz's shoulders as she turned to gaze up at him. "Are you okay?"

"The fresh air helped."

"Are you hungry?" he added. "Shall I order something for you?"

"No, really, I couldn't eat a bite."

"I just talked to Dave down at the station. Are you ready to go?"

Liz decided she'd rather face Kapp than more of Emily's blatant animosity. She said, "You bet."

Alex put on his jacket and took out his wallet. "Lunch is on me," he said firmly as he laid money on the table. Looking at Ron, he added, "Thanks for listening. I appreciate what a good friend you've been to Liz during these…trying…times."

Ron retrieved Liz's purse from her chair and handed it to her. "Liz is special to a lot of people, Alex."

"And you'll be wise not to forget that," Emily added.

"Emily!" Ron snapped.

Emily looked at Liz. "If you need anything, and I mean *anything,* call me…or Ron."

"I will, thanks."

"She'll be fine," Alex said. "I promise you."

Emily opened her mouth, apparently thought better of what she'd been about to say, and closed it, her attention riveted on her untouched salad.

"You two run along," Ron added. "I'll try to get

through to my hardheaded sister. If there's anything I can do to help, just ask.''

Alex said thanks and Liz promised to call Emily. As Alex took her hand, Liz realized how tempting it was to believe things were eking their way back to normal, and yet that wasn't really true and might never be. Studying the faces of the many acquaintances who watched them leave, she wondered, was the murderer among them? If he or she was, what did they make of Alex's hand wrapped around hers?

''You are aware that your friend Emily is trying to marry you off to her brother, aren't you?'' Alex asked as they stopped in front of Liz's car. She'd swept the street with a frantic glance as they emerged from the restaurant; Kapp's car was still parked across the street but he was apparently still inside the cafe. She breathed a sigh of relief.

Alex's truck was parked a space away. That truck was yet another of his belongings that Liz hadn't gotten around to getting rid of.

She said, ''Don't be silly.''

''Don't be naive. She hates me.''

''She doesn't even know you.''

''Which means she hates me because of what she's heard about me.''

''She and Alex have been staunch allies, Alex.''

''Staunch allies of yours.''

''Whatever.''

''And they both know you filed for a divorce, right?''

They not only knew, but Emily had actively encouraged her. She'd pointed out that Liz was young, she had a baby to consider, a future. Alex was as good as gone—forever.

Liz spared Alex this information. Instead she said,

"Twenty-four hours ago, this entire town was under the impression you were a murderer because you told them you were. Emily doesn't know you well enough to accept your word as quickly as Ron does. You have to give her a while."

"I don't have time to win a popularity contest."

She shook her head.

"I'm sorry," he added with a sigh. "I have a feeling Emily isn't going to be the only one in town who will feel that way about me."

Liz unlocked her car door and slid inside. "Thank you for telling them you're innocent. No matter what, they're friends and I don't know how I could have kept seeing them and talking to them without them knowing."

"Ron is a good listener. I told him just about everything except about your scarf and your late-night visit to your uncle. Those details have to be kept secret, honey. I'll meet you at home after I see Dave. We need to talk."

Liz had a very quick internal dialogue about whether or not to set Alex straight regarding such mundane things as respecting boundaries when this greater issue hung over their heads like smoke hangs over an imploding volcano. She decided she might as well be honest with him. She said, "You shouldn't have followed me today. I told you I was going to a business meeting. You showing up like that made me feel as though you didn't listen to a word I said."

"But it wasn't business."

"That's not the point. I just want you to know that from now on, you need to respect my independence."

One hand on top of the car, the other propped on his denim clad leg, Alex leaned down. His face was so close she could smell his aftershave. It had been months since she'd sniffed this exact odor and the way it came when mixed with his body heat. It made her head swim.

"I have nothing *but* respect for you," he insisted.

She made herself get over the arousing sensation of his proximity. She made herself get over the desire for him that seemed to permeate every inch of her body and grew stronger with each passing moment. "Good. I've been on my own for six months."

"On your own because of me."

"And in some ways, it's been a good thing." At the hurt expression that flashed in his eyes, she added, "Don't get me wrong, I would rather be part of a team than all on my own, but that means I'm an equal partner, not a child."

"I never think of you as a child, honey. You are all woman, every little delicious bit of you."

She nodded. "Well, as long as we understand each other."

"I think we understand each other, don't you?"

She wasn't even sure what he was talking about anymore. Giving up, she returned his smile. "Perfectly."

Chapter Four

Thanks to the phone call, Dave was outside waiting when Alex pulled up in front of Ocean Bluff's only fire station.

"I don't think you'd better come in right now," his friend said as he met Alex a few steps from the truck. He accepted the bag filled with his brother's clothes and tucked it under one arm. Dave himself was a wiry man who barely came up to Alex's chin.

"Battalion Chief Montgomery heard about the new trial but he still thinks you're guilty as hell," Dave added.

"Great," Alex said, looking longingly at the station house, the doors all open. He could see the three red engines parked in the bay, all as shiny as the day they came out of production. He knew the big cardboard box inside to the left was used to collect toys for disadvantaged kids. This place had been his second home for three years; it might never be his to enter again and that thought created still another layer of ache in his heart.

"It's politics," Dave said, glancing over his shoulder. He seemed nervous, which wasn't his normal state by a long shot. Any man who could share the responsibilities of raising three little kids under the age of four, let alone maneuver seventy feet of hook and ladder through the narrow roads of Ocean Bluff, had to have nerves of steel.

"Most of the guys think you got railroaded," Dave added, lowering his voice a notch or two. "The rest think the old man pissed you off to the point where you were justified in stabbing him. Some of them think you should have received a medal or something. But Battalion Chief Montgomery, well, you know how he is."

Cautiously, Alex said, "He's the logical choice for Fire Chief when Purvis steps down next year. He's also as honest as the day is long."

"Plus he and Sheriff Kapp are suddenly buddies."

Alex stared at Dave. "What do you mean?"

"Kapp was here earlier today."

"What did he want?"

"I don't know. Montgomery doesn't exactly confide in me." He looked over his shoulder again. His behavior made Alex jumpy and he found his gaze straying to the towering brick building, too.

"Listen," Dave said, his voice barely more than a whisper. "I'll ask around. Meanwhile, this is a lousy spot to hold a serious conversation. I'm off tomorrow. Why don't you come by the house? Ginny is taking the kids Christmas shopping so we'll have a little privacy."

"Sounds good," Alex said. "There are a few things I'd like to explain to you."

Dave nodded tersely and backed up a few steps, effectively cutting short Alex's inclination to clap him on the back or shake his hand.

Alex drove off wondering what was going on. Dave had said Chief Montgomery and Kapp were buddies. Did it matter? Alex couldn't see a connection or that even if there was one it pertained to him, but it was bothersome, nevertheless.

Well, no matter what Dave dug up, telling him the truth about the night Devon Hiller died would feel great. Even talking to Ron had been a relief. Emily—well, Emily was another matter.

Just how much sway did that fiercely protective woman have over his wife? he wondered. Hopefully, not too much because she was going to be one tough nut to crack. Would he try for Liz's sake? Absolutely.

What wouldn't he do for Liz's sake? After high school, after years apart, they'd been lucky enough to find one another again. He'd known immediately he still loved her. The miracle occurred when he discovered she still loved him.

Would she really leave him when and if this was ever resolved? Once before, he'd felt it all slip away from him. Those weeks of sitting in his cell had been a nightmare. Then the trial, the divorce papers, the hopelessness—

When Liz had told him last night that she hadn't killed her uncle, he'd felt a surge of hope he was not going to relinquish. Liz loved him, he knew she did. She was just feeling the shock of having her husband back, looking out for her. He understood how hard-won this new independence of hers was. She would have to learn how to balance being self-reliant *and* protected by the man who loved her because he wasn't going to go away.

He pulled up beside Liz's car. The rain had stopped and the sun was struggling to get through the high, wispy gray clouds. He spent a second looking at the grove of towering redwood trees that dwarfed the single story white house and felt the sense of peace he always felt when he knew he would see Liz within moments.

As soon as he got out of the truck he heard himself hailed by Harry Idle, an apt name for a man who seemed to do very little except watch satellite television and keep track of his only neighbor's comings and goings. Alex wasn't too fond of Idle, but he walked out toward the fence to meet him as the older man sauntered across the country road.

"I heard on the television that they let you go," Idle said as he came to a halt. The balding sixty-year-old had put on a few pounds since the last time Alex had seen him and after that bit of mild exertion, was breathing heavily. His weight was probably pushing three hundred and he smoked like a burning building.

Alex said, "For the time being."

"I figure you did the community a favor by killing Devon Hiller."

Should he protest or get away? That one was a no-brainer. "Well, see you around, Harry."

But Harry was just getting wound up. Leaning against the mailbox post, he added, "That man ruined half this town when he put in that shopping mall. I had a nice little shoe store until Devon Hiller came along. Couldn't afford to relocate at his fancy-schmancy mall so it went down the tubes. I haven't had a decent job since. That's when the Mrs. left me, too. And now, all these years later, my little girl is in a drug rehab program for the third time, all because our family got busted up by that tyrant. Downtown used to bustle. Now it's dead. That's all because of Devon Hiller. I'm just sorry someone didn't put an end to that geezer twenty years ago."

"I really do have to run," Alex said.

"Can't tell you how many times I thought of doing it myself," Harry said, adding with a vaudevillian wink, "and I'm not the only one thought that way." Pounding Alex on the back as though they were coconspirators, Harry lumbered back across the road.

ALEX FOUND Liz at the table, spooning canned soup into her mouth in such dainty little sips that it made his heart flip in his chest. Raised in a family of men, spending his adult years around still more men, the feminine way she had of doing everything from applying lipstick to painting her toenails always fascinated him.

She looked up and smiled. "Hunger finally got the best of me," she said. "Don't let Sinbad out, okay?"

Using his foot, he gently nudged the cat back inside before closing the door. "I've been meaning to ask you. Since when don't you let the cat out?"

She shrugged and averted her gaze and he suddenly understood. The answer was simple: *since he went away.* "How did everything go down at the station?" she asked.

He sat down opposite her. "Okay. Did you know there was a certain degree of animosity among the locals when your uncle built his first mall?"

She nodded. "Of course. I was pretty young, but over the years I heard things."

"And what about when he built subsequent malls?"

"They were smaller, just strip malls, really. I don't even know if many people realized he was behind them."

"It's a small town—I bet lots of people knew. And I bet some little businesses got shoved aside, right?"

"Probably." She frowned and added, "For every business Uncle Devon helped go under, two new ones started. He brought jobs and opportunities into the community. And after the malls, he was involved with land development. Half the houses on the south end of town are there because of him."

"You're defending him," he said softly.

"Weird, huh? Well, I'm not really defending the way he did things or the way he didn't care who he hurt."

"And I'm not concerned with the ethics of growth and all that right now. What I am wondering is how many former business owners with a grudge had the opportunity to kill your uncle?"

Liz blinked. "Oh."

"Maybe you could get together some figures on the computer or something."

"Or something. I have to warn you that I find it rather amazing what information noncomputer people think computer people can ascertain with the flip of a switch and a few pounded keys. It doesn't always work that way."

"You'll make it work," he said with complete confidence.

"Maybe. Remember those boxes my uncle had us take home a month or so before he died? They're in the garage. He said they were full of my stuff, but you never know, there might be something in one of them that will help."

"We'll look."

"And I'll get a list of everyone who went out of business within a year of the mall opening. Then we'll dig a little further and see what happened to them next."

"Harry Idle's wife left him."

Liz smiled. "Can you blame her?"

"The point is that he blames your uncle."

"Harry Idle?"

"His daughter has been in and out of rehab. The man thinks his life would be perfect if your uncle had left well enough alone. He may be right."

"Are you saying that Harry Idle stabbed my uncle?"

"What I'm really saying is that where there's one disgruntled former shopkeeper, there may be more."

"But would they wait two decades to exact their revenge?"

"Didn't the newest strip mall open just last winter? There are undoubtedly new grudges afloat. Anyway, it's a place to start."

"I'll check everything I can think of," she said as she took her empty soup bowl to the sink, Sinbad following and meowing. As Liz shook kibble into a bowl and set it before the cat, Alex reached for a pad of paper and a pen.

"What are you doing?"

"I'm going to work up a sequence of events. Your uncle was alive when you left. Do you remember if he was smoking a cigar?"

"I don't think so. I don't remember any smoke."

"There was a smoldering cigar in the ashtray when I got there. I saw your car, what, maybe ten minutes before I found him. Fifteen, tops."

"How did you get into the house?"

"I knocked, but when no one answered I tried the knob. I didn't see how he could be asleep because I knew you'd just left and you'd told me he suffered from terrible insomnia. The door was open. His housekeeper, who told the sheriff she slept through everything, said he always locked his doors."

"I don't remember locking it after I left," Liz said. "Of course, I was too upset with him to care much one way or another."

"Who else had a key?"

"Just me. And the housekeeper and Uncle Devon. He was pretty careful about things like that."

"Then maybe the killer was already inside the house

when you were there and left the door open when he or she left after the murder.'' He felt a sudden jolt of worry. Had Liz been inside the house with a killer? Would that person now wonder what she'd seen?

"I know the sheriff didn't find any broken windows," he continued, trying to hide this worry from Liz. "Unfortunately, half the town had access to the house that night thanks to your uncle's party. We need a guest list."

"That *is* on the computer," Liz said.

"Good. We'll cross-reference that list with the new one you compile of out-of-work former businesspeople and see what comes up."

"Do you really think—"

"I don't know," he interrupted. "I just don't know. I'm also wondering who phoned in that timely tip. It wasn't me or you or the housekeeper."

"Was it the murderer?"

"I think it must have been. My lawyer said it came from the public telephone at the Four Corners Market, less than a mile from your uncle's house. It was anonymous."

"How did the sheriff explain that?"

Alex shrugged. "Some good Samaritan said he heard yelling and grew concerned when it stopped abruptly. He or she, they couldn't tell if it was a man or a woman for sure, said they heard it as they were walking their dog."

"Yelling so loud that a person on the road could hear it, but not the housekeeper?"

"She sleeps above the garage, not in the house."

"That's true. Plus she plays a radio all night tuned into a San Francisco talk show. She's addicted to it." Liz bit her lip. "I was thinking about what you said, how you found Uncle Devon in front of his desk. If he walked around the desk by his own volition and took the letter opener with him, doesn't that mean that whoever came into his study that night made him nervous or afraid?"

"That's a good point. I had to come up with a story for the sheriff that explained the physical evidence in such a way that it was believable that I murdered the old man, but that doesn't make my account accurate."

"And what story did you come up with?"

"I kept it simple. I told him that your uncle and I argued, that your uncle got angry, picked up the letter opener and tried to attack me and stabbed himself instead. It didn't go over very well because I outweighed him by fifty pounds, was fifty years younger and didn't have a scratch on me."

"I think it more likely that whoever entered his den frightened him."

"Hard to picture the old buzzard frightened of anyone, isn't it?"

"Yes. But if that happened, then it was premeditated."

"Especially since your scarf ended up in his hands. Someone must have brought that scarf into your uncle's den, intending to use it, to make it look as though you killed him with it. Keep that in mind, Liz. We're looking for a cold-blooded killer who wanted you blamed."

"Then maybe someone killed Uncle Devon as a way of getting rid of me."

"But you're the only one who stands to gain a penny from his estate."

"Then there must be another motive we haven't discovered yet," she said. She looked upset which wasn't too surprising considering the topic they were discussing.

Alex got to his feet. "How are you feeling?" he asked, pulling her close.

"A little tired. Don't worry, I'm always a little tired lately."

"I can't help but worry," he said softly. "And I need to apologize to you. I didn't really follow you today, I just saw your car out in front of Tony-O's and couldn't resist the temptation to see you."

She touched his cheek. He trapped her warm fingers with his own. "I realize what you've been through," she said. "I don't want to make things any harder than they are."

"You've been through just as much."

"I know you want to hear me say everything will go back to normal. That I'll go back to the way I was. I wish I could."

"I don't want you to go back to anything," he told her, "except loving me."

She bit her lip. She wasn't going to say it, he knew that. She wasn't ready, she was still too scared that she'd be giving up something of herself if she admitted she couldn't live without him.

He lowered his face to hers, half expecting her to push him away, but she didn't. Instead, she focused on his mouth with an intensity that excited him into an instant erection. When their lips touched, he felt it in his groin.

As he parted her lips with the tip of his tongue, their teeth clicked against each other in their eagerness to consume, to be consumed. In the very old days, back in high school, a kiss like this would have led to agonizing frustration. More recently, it would have led to bed. But now it encapsulated them in a sort of time warp. The moment they separated, it would be over, and Liz would walk away. He didn't know how he could bear it.

She felt different as he pressed against her. Gone was the slender shape that had molded to his with such an ancient grace. He didn't mind. In fact, he yearned to see this Liz naked, to run his hands over her ripe curves. He yearned for intimacy that went beyond a kiss or even lovemaking, the intimacy of the past where her body had been more familiar by far than his own.

But he knew he had to earn that intimacy. With a flurry of small kisses, he struggled to calm himself. He wanted her to want him in the same damn-the-torpedoes way he wanted her. Completely. Devoutly. Eternally.

"I love you," he whispered against her cheek, licking her earlobe, delighting in the way she shivered in his arms. "I know you love me."

They each took a step back, their gazes still connected. After a deep sigh, Liz said, "I better get to work on those lists."

Liz HEADED for her computer but the nursery door was ajar and she found herself in that room instead. Her head was spinning, her body was tingling, she felt totally alive, confused and out of breath.

Weak sunlight spilled through the window, dousing the crib with filtered light. The glowing effect was enhanced by the soft yellow paint she'd chosen for the walls. For the moment, this room was perfect, and as she sat in the newly purchased white rocker, she remembered why she needed to be strong.

Not for herself. For her baby.

From the top of the changing table, she hooked a crocheted teddy bear that Emily had given her and held it against her chest. Within weeks, Alex's baby would fill her arms. In a moment of instinctual insight, she knew she was carrying his son, and she knew he would have his father's blue eyes.

Alex's voice came from the doorway. "I have that list of dates," he said.

She swallowed a lump and said, "Great."

He didn't move. He stared at her from across the room and didn't say a word. His gaze enflamed her. The thought of losing him again made her heart hurt.

She thought about Kapp and his impending visit. She wanted to tell Alex, but something held her tongue. She'd noticed Alex had a habit of getting irrational when the sheriff's name came up, understandable after all he'd been through. But she couldn't help wishing she could convince him....

Softly, she said, "Alex, please, let's take all of this to the sheriff. He's not really a bad man—"

His answer sounded weary. "No."

"But Kapp—"

"Is a jerk. He's been to the fire station, no doubt he'll want to come here. When he contacts you, tell him we'll meet him at his office, okay? I don't want him in this house."

Tossing aside the crocheted bear, Liz stood, her fear getting the best of her. "You've got to be more reasonable, Alex."

"Me? I'm always reasonable."

"Ha!"

He took a step toward her. "You're trembling. What are you afraid of, honey?"

"I'm afraid we'll fail, I'm afraid you'll go back to jail or I will. I don't understand how you can be so distrustful—"

Another flash of irritation. "And I don't understand how you can be so trusting. Why would Kapp believe me after I confessed? You said it yourself, until twenty-four hours ago, everyone believed I was a murderer because I told them I was. It's too late to change my story without the evidence to back it up. And I won't risk you.''

''We could try—''

''How do you know for sure that Kapp himself isn't in on your uncle's murder?''

''That's ridiculous. They were friends—''

''Friends? Think about it. In all the years you knew him, did your uncle really ever have a friend?''

''Well, no—''

''Exactly. He had associates. He had flunkies.''

''But Sheriff Kapp—''

''Kapp owes his election to your uncle's money and support. He has his own agenda, Liz.''

''If he owes his election to my uncle how can you now say he wanted my uncle dead? It doesn't make any sense.''

''Nothing makes sense. What worries me is that deep in your heart, you have the unshakable belief that the white hats always win.'' With that inane comment, he turned and left her. She could hear him walk back down the hall. She stooped awkwardly, picked up the bear and brushed his whiskers back into shape with shaking fingers.

She would not let Alex go to prison again, not without a fight. He was worried about protecting her—well, she was equally worried about protecting him.

Kapp would be here tomorrow. If she got Alex out of the house for the duration of the interview, then she could feel Kapp out, so to say, decide if it was safe to tell him the truth. Surely Kapp would never suspect her of such a terrible crime. Surely he would be open to the possibility that Alex was innocent. He was, after all, a lawman. He would want the truth above all else.

Alex would be furious.

Alex need never know.

If she was subtle enough, even Kapp wouldn't know what she was doing unless she decided to trust him. He might be a lout, but he was an honest one, wasn't he?

What if he's as crooked as Alex thinks he is?

No. Alex was wrong about Kapp, she felt it in her bones. Okay, he was right about one thing, Kapp could be a little creepy and she didn't relish spending time alone with him. Tough.

Could she trade on Kapp's feelings of loyalty to her uncle to make him see he was hounding the wrong man and that if he didn't look elsewhere, her uncle's true killer would get away with murder?

More to the point, she couldn't imagine an interview in this small house with both Alex and Kapp in attendance, nor did she want to go to Kapp's office where he would have the home court advantage. The tension and distrust between the two men would suffocate her in either location. She couldn't let Alex take all the chances and she couldn't stop thinking for herself just because it was so tempting to rely on his strength. His judgment wasn't always crystal clear—he was only human and he hated Roger Kapp.

She began plotting diversions for Alex.

Nothing ventured, nothing risked, nothing gained.

Right?

Chapter Five

There was a giant clock in Alex's brain, ticking away the moments of his freedom with a relentless momentum that showed no signs of abating. If anything, it was getting worse. What had he accomplished so far? He'd irritated Liz half a dozen times and talked to Dave and that was about it.

You discovered your wife isn't a murderer, intentional or otherwise, he told himself.

All night long, he'd dozed in his soon-to-be-born baby's room, waking with a start every time fatigue claimed him, sometimes laying there for a long while before realizing where he was. The only thing he'd known for sure was that he wasn't in jail. It was too dark and too quiet. In jail it was never either of those things.

Nor was he in his own bed next to his own wife.

He thrust the post hole digger into the earth and wrenched it free, depositing the soil in a pile beside the hole. He'd been doing this since daybreak, or more accurately, since the dense fog grew light enough to suggest daylight. He didn't like the fog. He wanted to see the world clearly, not through a curtain of gray, moist air.

With strong arms, he hefted the digger again and deepened the hole, some of his frustration dissipating with the force of his actions, his brain whirling as he tried to decide what to do next.

LIZ AWOKE with Sinbad tugging on a nightgown button. As she gently batted him away, he licked her fingers and began purring, rubbing her hand with his chin, the sharp edge of one fang grazing the side of her finger.

"You silly old cat," she murmured.

His purr was warm and reassuring, but he soon grew bored with their game. After she let him out of the room, she dressed in maternity jeans and a bulky red sweater to ward off the chill.

As she attempted to subdue her hair, she heard a rhythmic thumping noise coming from the back of the house and realized she'd been hearing it off and on for quite a while. Looking out the window, she found fog so thick it all but obscured Alex's tall, strong figure. He was digging holes. He had started the fence. In December. In the foggy cold.

For a second, she recalled planning that fence, him marching off the exterior perimeter, her wrapped in an intoxicating cloak of impending joy. She could remember wondering if there was anything in the world more wonderful than carrying the baby of the man you adored and being absolutely certain that he adored you, too.

As Sinbad tore into a can of Seafood Fancy, she went outside. Alex and she had passed the night before in virtual silence, Liz working on the computer, Alex hovering nearby, both tense, it seemed, and both too stubborn to make the first move to resolve anything.

But now it was a new day and Liz had a new problem—she had to come up with a plausible excuse to get

Alex out of the house for the duration of Sheriff Kapp's visit.

"You've started the fence," she said as she stopped in front of him.

His eyes were gray, like the fog, as though stress had bled the blue right out of his irises. He smiled down at her, and as usual, his gaze made her feel desirable despite the fact that as she'd clomped through the damp grass, she'd felt like the *Queen Mary* churning through a heavy Atlantic swell.

"I thought it better safe than sorry," he said, pulling off his work gloves and running a hand through his damp hair.

She felt a huge lump lodge in her throat. "You mean if you have to go back to jail again."

"It's a possibility," he said softly. "We can't ignore it."

"Is that why you installed the chain on the front door last night after I went to bed?"

"Actually, I did it this morning. I should have done it long ago."

Shrugging, she looked in the direction of the ocean, and said, "I remember the first night I spent in this house. I'd just moved in and one of those spring storms came through where everything happens at once. Wind, rain, lightning, thunder—it was incredible. The house almost vibrated."

"It must have scared you to death."

"As a matter of fact, it put me right to sleep."

"Someone else would have wondered what they'd gotten themselves into."

"We've weathered our fair share of storms in this house, too," she said. "They've never seemed to bother you much."

"Are you speaking metaphorically?" he asked, smiling.

"No, I'm being literal."

"Then I'll remind you I've never been through a storm in this old house when I was here alone. I always had you."

His words hung in the air between them. She couldn't help but consider the metaphor aspect of their discussion now that he'd pointed it out. She said, "Listen, Alex, about yesterday afternoon—"

"I'm sorry about the way I acted," he said, beating her to the punch. "I've been a little…tense."

"We're both tense," she said, touching his shoulder. He put his free hand over hers and their eyes locked.

"Just being together after months of not even seeing one another takes some getting used to, doesn't it?" he said.

What an opening for suggesting time apart! Before she could actually think of a way to go about using it, he added, "Dave said he was going to spend yesterday afternoon asking around the station to see if he could get a handle on what was going on between Chief Montgomery and Sheriff Kapp. He asked me to come by his house today. Will it interfere with your plans if I go over there around lunchtime?"

She went from relieved to suspicious, just like that. Sure, she wanted him to disappear for a couple of hours, but why was he suddenly so anxious to escape her? About to protest, she finally came to her senses. He'd just handed her what she wanted and she was complaining? Was this what a guilty conscience did to you?

"No problem," she said.

THE PHONE RANG a few minutes after Alex left. It was Kapp's assistant explaining there'd been a change of plans. The woman sounded apologetic as she asked Liz to meet the sheriff at his office.

How about that for fate? No way Alex could walk in on an interview held at Kapp's office and she could explain going there when she told him she'd received a call after he left. She readily agreed, but as she drove, had to admit she was still unsure how to go about finding out if the sheriff was open to considering Alex's innocence. She'd have to wing it, think on her feet, have catlike reflexes! Laughing at this image of herself, she pulled into a parking space.

The building was singularly unattractive, a square box composed of beige stucco, crisscrossing ramps and iron railings. Liz walked through the front door and found her way to the sheriff's office where she was met by a young deputy with flaming red hair and a sparse mustache. He looked baffled by Liz's announcement that she'd come to see Sheriff Kapp.

Glancing at his watch, the deputy said, "Uh, Mrs. Chase? I thought he was going to drop by your place. Wasn't that the plan?"

"His assistant called and changed the place of the meeting," Liz explained.

"I haven't heard a word about a change and Belle Carter just went out to lunch with her fiancé," the deputy said. "She won't be back for at least an hour."

Liz looked at the big wall clock and sighed. Mix-ups like this one weren't all that unusual in business situations and she understood that sooner or later it would be explained, but still, it was a nuisance.

"I can page the sheriff if you like," the deputy offered.

"Good idea."

Liz stood by as the deputy tracked down the sheriff. By the flush that stole over the young man's face as he mostly held the receiver to his ear and listened, she guessed the sheriff wasn't happy. By the time the youthful deputy returned to the counter, he'd developed a nervous tic in his left eye. "Sheriff Kapp said he stopped by your place fifteen minutes ago. He sounded a little…tweaked."

Liz shrugged. The foul-up was on the sheriff's end and she felt no responsibility.

"He said he's on the other side of town now. He'll swing by your place later today."

"Okay," she said with a resigned sigh. A subtle little interview with the sheriff didn't seem to be in the cards. No doubt Alex would be home by the time the sheriff arrived and everything she'd tried to avoid would happen. Perhaps it was inevitable that Alex and Kapp face each other, and perhaps even preferable that it take place in the privacy of their home instead of in an office.

She was exceedingly relieved to find no sign of either Alex's truck or the sheriff's car in the driveway. At least she'd have a few moments to get her thoughts in order. She contemplated making cookies so the house would smell homey. If it soothed the qualms of prospective buyers, might it not also work on testosterone-driven male adversaries?

She was digging out the supplies for chocolate chip cookies when she finally realized she hadn't seen any sign of Sinbad since coming through the door. She searched the house from one end to the other, assuming she'd find him stretched out under a bed or lurking in the back of a closet until she noticed the bathroom window ajar.

Alex must have left the window open when he took

his shower! She grabbed a piece of cheese to use as bait. Since Sinbad had spent the first year of his life outside, she reasoned that his being out there now wasn't too big of a deal. Still, she'd feel better once she got him back inside.

The first place she checked was the warm hood of her own vehicle. She found not so much as a single damp footprint. She walked around the outside of the house, calling his name and the ubiquitous "kitty, kitty," but there was no answering meow and no sign of his dark mask. Eventually, she wandered out to the area where Alex had started the fence. It was possible the curious cat had watched the construction from the window and was now checking it out for himself.

She searched the few holes that didn't have poles sticking out at slanted angles awaiting backfill, each time expecting to find two blue eyes staring up at her, each time finding nothing. Her route led past the bluff and at last, over the faraway sound of the waves crashing against the rocks below, she heard a plaintive cry that stopped her in her tracks.

"Sinbad?"

A single strident cry scaled the cliff. Sinbad, the stinker, sounding more like an infant in distress than a cat. Clutching the stair railing with both hands, she called again, peering into the fog, preparing herself for his long dark shape to dash past her feet.

But he didn't come. Instead, another haunting cry echoed like faraway thunder. Liz studied the stairs, but the wooden structure disappeared into the fog ten feet down the cliff. She glanced back at the house, willing Alex to come through the back door.

The desire to lean on Alex to solve even this most trivial of problems appalled her. When had she become such a class-A wimp? Until the other day, she'd taken care of herself for months and this was no time to turn into a simpering female. The beach stairs were safe— Alex himself had reinforced them two summers before— and she'd been up and down them a hundred times since then. She was wearing walking shoes and jeans, she still had Sinbad's cheese to coax him out of whatever little shelter he'd found, and by the sound of the surf, high tide was imminent.

Sinbad was playing with her. He did things like this all the time. She took off down the stairs.

There were eighty-five steps in all, she knew this as she'd counted them once. There were four landings and three turns, one at twenty-five steps, another at forty, and the last twenty steps shy of the bottom. In this way, the stairs zigzagged their way down the cliff to the last landing which hovered above the giant rocks at the base. When the tide was out, it was a simple matter of jumping from the last landing to the rocks to the gravel beach. When the tide was in, it was wise to head for high ground as the beach all but disappeared.

The first twenty-five steps were relatively easy. Though Liz repeatedly called the cat's name, he was suddenly quiet. She made the switchback and started down the next stage, still calling. The waves were now louder and the clinging fog made the stairs and the railing wet. Her fingers were cold and she wished she'd thought about gloves. She took it slow, always aware of her new shape and altered center of gravity, determined to find out why Sinbad wasn't dashing up to meet her without risking her baby's safety. "It's okay," she murmured, and patting her tummy added, "Mommy is being very, very careful."

Visibility got worse as she proceeded downwards. By

the time she reached the second landing, she could barely see five feet ahead. She paused and leaned against the railing, calling Sinbad. At last he answered with another strangled cry. Fumbling in her pocket, she found the cheese, but the distress so evident in the cat's garbling made it clear a snack wasn't going to help. Was something wrong with him? Dropping the cheese, relying on the railing to guide and support her, she took another step and another, scanning the cliff side and the stairs below.

Where was the cat?

Another noise, this one even closer by, but almost drowned out by the crashing surf. She was down far enough that she could actually feel the occasional stinging drop of spray. Slowly, she kept descending until her feet hit the second to last landing. She peered downward and felt a leap of relief when she saw Sinbad's dark face, four steps below. As she scolded him for playing games with her, she noticed the peculiar tilt of his body and a piece of what appeared to be twine encircling his neck.

A halfhearted reprimand died on her lips. Something was wrong. His eyes looked wild, his fur was damp. He meowed in such a heartrending way that she scrambled to get to him quickly. He looked like a tangle of wet fur with two blazing eyes.

The twine had gouged into his fur, wearing a path right down to his skin which looked raw, even from this distance, and provided evidence of how desperately the cat had struggled to free himself. She stepped over his prone shape and down so that she could work on the twine which appeared to be knotted over and over. The stairs creaked. Trying to sound soothing, she talked to him as her cold fingers struggled with the knots. He seemed to know she was there to help for he stayed very still.

At last the final knot came undone and Liz threw the twine toward the beach below. She expected the cat to dash past her up the stairs, but he stayed right where he was and growled. She touched him and he spat.

Alarmed by his odd behavior, sure now that he was injured, she lifted him, trying not to react to the low ominous growl that rumbled in his body. She suddenly realized his back right leg was hurt. Gently, she cradled him in the bulk of her sweater pulled away from her body to form a makeshift sling. She resettled her weight. The stairs seemed to sway, but she barely noticed.

Staring at Sinbad with her heart in her throat, she touched his head and he nuzzled her. His nose was oddly dry and his body trembled. She whispered calming words as her fingers grazed his throat and she felt the vibrations of a deep, quiet purr.

Frantic to get him to the vet, she put her weight on the stair he'd been occupying. At once, she heard a loud crack and the wood groaned. She tried stepping back, but it was too late. Her weight had proven to be a catalyst and the ruined stair dropped away into thin air, taking the steps closer to the beach with it. Liz grabbed with one hand for the landing. As it swung away, she found herself thrown forward. Sinbad screeched and clawed her belly through the loose weave of her sweater. Reaching with one hand, she found a railing to grasp, but that too began to creak and slip, slamming her against the face of the cliff. The rocks twenty feet below were invisible in the fog, but she knew they were there, and she knew how deadly they would be if she fell. Her fingernails scratched the dirt and rocks, searching for something to hold onto, some way to move to safety,

knowing that there was precious little hope of doing
either.

Desperate, terrified, she whispered Alex's name.

ALEX STARED at Dave and said, "Is he sure about this?"

Dave nodded. "Mike Sinclair had an appointment to
talk to Montgomery. You know how Montgomery has
those two doors leading into his office? Well, one was
slightly ajar, so Mike assumed it was okay to enter. He
says the chief was standing behind his desk, mad as a
hornet. Sheriff Kapp was standing on the other side. Before either one of them noticed Mike, he heard Chief
Montgomery accuse Kapp of trying to blackmail him."

"Mike heard the actual word 'blackmail'?"

"That's what he says."

"Blackmail," Alex mused with more than a little
glee.

"Mike said he won't swear to anything."

"There's nothing to swear to," Alex said. "The
chief's accusation just gives me a place to start looking.
If Kapp is into blackmail, maybe he tried it on Hiller."

"And maybe Hiller refused to pay up so Kapp killed
him."

"Maybe." Alex wanted to get back to Liz, to tell her
about Kapp. He'd been gone just a little over two hours
but it felt like two weeks.

"Thanks for the information and the sandwich," he
told Dave.

"No problem, buddy." Dave extended a hand and
added, "Tell me when I can talk to the guys at the station and tell them what you've told me."

"Not yet," Alex said. "Wait."

"Whatever you say. It's good to have you back."

"Yeah. Now all I have to do is figure out how to stay back."

ALEX WALKED in the front door. He almost called out Liz's name, but the house was so quiet, he realized she must be napping.

He glanced down the hall and saw that her door was open, which seemed odd. Or perhaps that open door signified an invitation. He shed his jacket and walked down the hall with light footsteps in case she was asleep, hoping she wasn't, hoping she'd welcome him…

He peeked through the doorway. The bed was neatly made.

He called her name. He called Sinbad. He searched the house, finding her coat on its hook inside the front door, her purse on the chair where she usually left it, a package of walnuts and some chocolate chips sitting on the drainboard, an open window in the bathroom. It was the only window in the house that didn't have a screen. He closed the window, curious now, and let himself out the back door.

Thanks to the fog, it was difficult to see any distance, but a quick walk around the yard assured him she wasn't there. He recalled her mentioning her uncle's boxes so he searched the garage and then opened the door to the attic. No Liz, no Sinbad.

This was getting spooky. Might Liz have ridden into town with a friend? Wouldn't she have left him a note? Wouldn't she have taken her coat and purse? Would she walk across the road to Harry Idle's house? Why? And what about Sinbad, what about the open window?

He found himself out in the back again, and this time the bluff drew him like a magnet. It was impossible to tell if she'd come this way and it was still too foggy to see the beach below. He called her name. He heard a faint answer and his heart flooded with relief and then, as she screamed, with panic.

He raced down the stairs, his mind filled with horrible images. He pushed them aside as he negotiated the landings and switchbacks, expecting to see her appear in the fog at any given moment, the victim, perhaps, of a twisted ankle or a cramp. He kept yelling her name, but after that scream he hadn't heard a sound except the waves hitting the rocks. Dread and fear bit at his heels like two malevolent dogs.

Not Liz. Not the baby. Not hurt. No.

The second to last landing was just ahead. The moment his foot hit it, the whole thing swayed and he skidded to a stop, hopping back as the creak of wood competed with the sound of the surf and the whole thing looked ready to plunge into the sea. Rails and steps dangled like the broken limbs of damaged trees after a storm. Most importantly, Liz, plastered precariously against the cliff, one hand gripping a tuft of long weeds, one leg wrapped around a piece of swaying railing, was trapped.

"Alex!" she cried.

His head cleared as he surveyed the scene and weighed his options. He didn't think she could last long enough in that position to wait for a rescue team. He knew what had to be done and he knew it had to be done quickly.

"I'm going to get a rope. Can you hold on a little longer?"

"I…I think so."

"Just hold on. I'll be right back."

"Hurry."

"I'll be right back."

Leaving her like that was about the hardest thing he'd ever done, but attempting to rescue her without a rope was stupid. Thankfully, he could picture a long, thick coil of three-quarter-inch nylon rope hanging in the garage right where he'd placed it over a year before. He took the steps two and three at a time, arriving at the top gasping for air but running.

Where was Liz's cell phone? Should he waste time searching for it and calling for help? He didn't have time and he let the thought go as he raced into the garage.

The rope was where it was supposed to be. He looped it over his shoulder, comforted by the heaviness of it. There had to be at least a hundred feet. He grabbed his leather gloves off the workbench at the last moment. Within minutes, he was back across the yard, pulling on the gloves.

He'd fished for salmon off the coast many times, and he'd seen the beach stairs from that vantage point more than once. He knew the first landing was more or less above the third landing, slightly off to the left, perfect. Pausing at the top of the bluff to tie off an end of the rope to one of the cement pillars that formed the anchor for the stairs, he gathered up the rest and started down.

As he descended, he calculated distance and angles. If only the fog would clear! Wrapping the rope around a stanchion and securing it with a clove knot, he tied a bowline loop to act as a seat and crawled between the railings, pushing himself away from the cliff with his legs, paying out rope through his tightly gloved hands.

Muscles honed first in the army, then in firehouse workouts and lastly with self-imposed training at the county jail came to his aid as he carefully made his way down the cliff face, letting out rope as needed, careful not to dislodge any more dirt and rocks than necessary.

He called Liz's name and felt his heart practically launch itself into orbit when she answered. Within a few minutes, he caught sight of her bright red sweater. Soon after he began the task of moving into perfect position, maneuvering himself below and to the right of her.

The world came together when he felt his arms go around her and knew that her fate no longer depended on a clump of tenacious weeds and a piece of rotten wood. He buried his face in her damp hair and felt her whole body shiver.

"It took you long enough," she mumbled, looking at him over her shoulder. Her eyes were huge and green and wet. Salt encrusted tears trailed down her dirt smudged cheeks. He was busy looping the rope around her which proved more difficult than he'd anticipated.

"Don't let go of that weed yet, sweetheart, but move your other arm. I can't get the rope around you."

"I'm holding Sinbad. He's hurt. In fact, I'm not even sure he's still alive."

"Then turn slowly toward me. It's okay, I've got a loop of rope under your leg, let go of the wood. I've got you."

She did exactly as he asked. The wood she'd been depending on swayed back toward the stairs and broke away, falling into the fog, crashing onto the rocks below, a reminder of what could have happened and might still happen if he wasn't sure and quick and strong enough to prevent it.

The ache in his shoulders disappeared.

By the time she'd moved to his side, the cat swaddled in her sweater and ominously still, he'd secured the ropes.

"I knew you'd come for me," she said.

"I'll always come for you."

Their lips met in a soft kiss that mingled tears and fog and brine. It was a moment he wished he could freeze and save and lock away because it was pure, untainted by anything but need. "Let's get out of here," he said huskily.

"Sounds good." She sniffed and squared her shoulders. "What do I do?"

"Hold onto me and follow my example. I'm going to need to use both hands to pull us up this rope." Hand over hand, using his legs to help, he started the arduous process of scaling the cliff. Liz helped as much as she could. It took a lifetime or two, but eventually, the first landing came into view. He helped her climb onto the structure, praying it was in better condition than the mess at the bottom. Then he pulled himself through the railing and plopped down beside her.

Casting him a look he would never forget, she murmured, "You saved me."

He couldn't think of an answer so he kissed her again.

She carefully folded back her sweater.

Sinbad lay ominously still in the nest of red wool, his eyes closed, his neck raw, his mouth slightly open and his side moving up and down with shallow, rapid breaths. "His back leg is hurt," she said softly.

"Looks as though he's in shock," Alex said, untangling Liz's feet from the rope. He stared hard at her tear-stained face and added, "First things first. Are you okay? How about the baby?"

"I feel okay. It doesn't seem to have affected either one of us. I'll go see my doctor, but not until after the cat is taken care of," she added firmly as he helped her stand. "I'm fine, Sinbad isn't."

There was no arguing with her and for that matter, she did look and act as though she'd survived everything very well. He'd keep a close eye on her for signs that an adrenaline rush wasn't the only explanation for her current vigor. He helped her into his truck, then went inside and finally found her cell phone in her office, grabbed a thick blanket for Sinbad and hit the road. By the time they got to the vet's office, everyone there was prepared for their arrival and Sinbad was whisked away like a patient in an emergency room, which was exactly what he was.

Alex and Liz sat side by side on the green vinyl couch in the waiting room, and for the first time, Alex got a good look at his wife.

Her hands were scratched and dirty, the nails broken, bits of weed and rock clung to her sleeves, dangled from her hair. Her gaze never left the door to the examination room.

"He's going to be fine," Alex said, removing a piece of damp moss from her shoulder. "He's young and healthy."

"Did you see his neck?"

"Yes."

"How did he get tied up in that twine?"

"What twine?"

"There was twine around his neck, knotted twine."

Alex gently tugged a small twig from her hair, too stunned to speak. Liz studied his eyes, and then the ordeal finally seemed to hit her full force, and she dissolved into body-wracking sobs. He felt his rotting staircase theory crumble away. When the tears subsided, she began explaining the sequence of events that had preceded the catastrophe, and he felt an even greater surge of alarm.

He had a million questions to ask her, starting with the window and ending with the stairs, but just then the door opened and their vet came into the waiting room. Alex had never seen a vet actually come out to talk to a patient's owners. Was this good or bad? He mentally crossed his fingers, as much for Liz as for Sinbad, and took Liz's cold hand into his.

"How did this happen?" the vet asked. A sidelong glance at him suggested she'd seen last night's newspaper and recognized him as the man with the hung jury, the man the police were determined to bring to justice. She wore a small pin on her smock engraved with the name, Victoria Kippling, DVM. She was almost as tall as Alex, slender and pretty with dark brown hair and eyes.

"I don't know," Liz said. "I can't figure out how he broke his leg and then ended up tied to a stair. Maybe he fell, but then that doesn't explain the twine...."

The vet shook her head. "*He* didn't break his leg," she said. "At least, I don't think so."

"It's not broken?"

"Yes, it's broken, but not in such a way that suggests he had much to do with it. The right femur suffered a point of impact fracture. There's a lot of bruising. I can only think of one way that could have happened that wouldn't have incurred additional injuries. If a dog had caught him, for instance, you'd expect to see puncture marks or if he got tangled in a machine, you'd find abrasions and cuts. With a car, his nails would be frayed. There was none of that."

Alex met her gaze. "So what do you think happened?"

She stared right into his eyes and said, "Frankly, I suspect a human kicked him. I think they aimed at his hind quarters. The femur is tucked up right against the belly."

Her voice left little doubt about which human she thought capable of this deed. Liz gasped and Alex turned his attention to her. "It's okay, honey. We'll figure this out," he assured her.

"I hope you do," the vet said.

Alex was thinking fast and hard. If someone tied something around the cat's neck to keep him from running away, then someone had staged this incident.

"Sinbad must have fought like crazy to get free," the vet continued. "It's amazing he didn't choke to death."

Liz's eyes were wide with alarm. She leaned her head against Alex's shoulder and he felt her tremble.

"It's okay," he repeated into her soft hair.

Liz said, "Is Sinbad going to make it?"

Touching Liz's arm, the vet said, "I've started him on antibiotics and sedated him. I've treated the gouges on his neck. He's been X-rayed. After you leave, we'll operate to set the bone and secure it with a pin. He'll be kept very still and warm. I'm cautiously optimistic at this point. Why don't you call in the morning?"

Liz dissolved into more tears. The vet let them go back and see Sinbad, which calmed Liz down. The cat's side rose and fell slowly and if you didn't look at the raw wound around his neck, he appeared to be sleeping peacefully.

Alex felt his heart wrench at the brutality of the act that had been perpetuated on the little animal and worried sick about why it was done. What was to be gained but to get one of them to go down those stairs, and how could anyone have anticipated the stairs giving way unless they'd been rigged to do so? The evil behind such a plot was numbing. He could feel Kippling's eyes on him, but he didn't care. Let her think what she wanted.

Finally, she moved closer and spoke so softly only Alex could hear her.

"I'll take good care of the cat," she said. Nodding in Liz's direction, she added, "You take good care of *her.*"

"Do whatever you can to save Sinbad. He means the world to my wife."

The vet smiled. "About before, about the way I thought it might be you, I'm sorry. I was upset, but—"

"Forget it."

The vet nodded, squeezed Liz's hand and left. Soon after, Alex coaxed Liz away from Sinbad's side. Within minutes, they pulled up in front of Liz's doctor's office. By the time they straggled home with a clean bill of health for Liz and the baby, it was dark.

Alex unlocked the front door and a small card fell to the porch. He took it inside and checked it out. Liz was taking off her shoes by using the toe of one foot to dislodge the heel of the other, holding on to the doorjamb for balance. She looked at him curiously. "What's that?"

As he read, a cold spot formed in his chest. "Sheriff Kapp's business card."

The look on her face caused the chilled spot to spread. He flipped the card over. "There's a handwritten note on the back. Kapp says he's sorry he missed you both times today. He asks that you call him tomorrow."

Liz swore under her breath.

Flicking the card with a finger, he said, "You want to tell me what's going on?"

"Not particularly—"

"Damn it Liz—"

"Calm down. I'll explain everything, just let me wash up first."

He looked at her bedraggled figure and concern for

her well-being pushed aside some of his anger. ''I'll heat a can of soup while you shower,'' he told her though his own stomach was now as twisted as a country road.

She nodded and disappeared down the hall.

Chapter Six

Liz ate without appetite. The ordeal on the cliff followed by a hot shower had left her incredibly sleepy but she knew she owed Alex an explanation. Halfway through the clam chowder, she caught him staring at her. Might as well get it over with.

"I was going to meet the sheriff here at the house," she began, halfheartedly crumbling a cracker into her soup. "I didn't tell you because I knew you'd come unglued. I can handle Roger Kapp and I can handle you but I don't think anyone can handle you and Kapp at the same time. Certainly not me and certainly not in my condition. So I kind of lied about it. There, are you happy?"

"I thought we agreed that you wouldn't see Kapp alone," Alex said, his voice a controlled slow burn.

"No," she said, setting aside her spoon. "That was your idea. I didn't agree to it."

"But you didn't disagree."

"Honestly, Alex—"

"Because you almost died today, Liz. If I hadn't come home—"

"I know," she snapped, and then softening her voice,

added, ''but that had nothing to do with meeting Roger.''

''After what Dave told me about him—''

''What? What did Dave tell you?''

Alex stopped pacing long enough to look at her. ''One of the guys walked in on Kapp and Chief Montgomery. He heard the chief accuse Kapp of blackmail.''

She shrugged. ''Maybe you and your friends are being too literal.''

''What do you mean?''

''I mean maybe he used it as an expression. Maybe Kapp said something mildly annoying and the chief said, 'Are you trying to blackmail me?' Like that.''

''Apparently their body language made it clear how serious Kapp took the accusation. I don't think they were playing around. The point is, maybe he blackmailed your uncle, too.''

''Oh.''

''I wonder if that's why your uncle backed Kapp during his campaign for sheriff. I could swear I recall him complaining about Kapp before and after he was elected but he sure was gung-ho for the guy during the campaign.''

''You're right. And now Roger is running for sheriff again and Uncle Devon is dead. What does that mean?''

''Well, your uncle can't hurt Kapp's chances by endorsing someone else, that's for sure. Tell me about the sheriff's intended visit. Tell me how he arranged it and why he said he missed you twice today.''

Doing her best to ignore the irritable edge in his voice, she told him about meeting Kapp outside the restaurant, about her frustration with Alex for refusing to ask anyone for help, about her certainty that Kapp wasn't a crook and how he'd ultimately be interested in the truth.

As she spoke, Alex looked at her like she was the most naive woman to ever walk the face of the earth. Maybe she was.

Then she told him about the sheriff's office rescheduling the appointment that day. The rest he knew.

"So Kapp reschedules, thus making sure that you were away from the house. He uses that time to kidnap our cat. The stairs could have been rigged days ago."

"Then you didn't leave the bathroom window open?"

"No. I'll check the outside tomorrow to see if I can tell if it was jimmied. Anyway, after Kapp kidnaps our cat and breaks Sinbad's leg, he tampers with the stairs. Everyone knows what a softy you are for Sinbad. Then he pretends to be across town when he's probably hiking back to his car—who's to know where he really is? You come home, do exactly what he had planned, you die."

"Why?"

"Why what?"

"Why does he want me dead? That doesn't make any sense. And hiking around to his car seems dangerous—anyone could see him and how would he explain it?"

Alex had plopped down on a chair by now and he ran a hand through his hair. He shook his head.

"Suppose the sheriff is guilty of this crime," she continued. "What if what he really wanted was for you to climb down the stairs instead of me?"

"The only reason the man would want either one of us dead is to cover up his murder of your uncle and when he killed your uncle—"

"If he killed my uncle—"

"*If* he killed your uncle, he took pains to frame *you*. Remember the scarf."

Liz rubbed her eyes. "Maybe."

"I think the first step is for me to go down those stairs

tomorrow morning and see if I can tell for sure if someone tampered with them.''

"Isn't it dangerous?"

He grinned. "Probably. I'll use my handy dandy rope.
If the stairs have been messed with, then I guess you're
right, I guess we better tell the cops.''

Liz said, "No."

Now he looked startled. "What?"

"The sheriff tried to scare me by making me think
you were after my uncle's money and that you might try
to hurt me. If he's innocent, his first thought is going to
be that you did this. If he's guilty, then he'll make sure
it looks like you did it because right now, an attempted
murder charge would be a nice way for him to get rid
of you again.''

"There's your safety to consider," he said firmly.

"Let me win this one," she said, rubbing her eyes
again. The stress of the day was beginning to take its
toll. "Promise me you won't go down that cliff until I'm
awake and can help you," she said, rising.

He stood as well and smiling, smoothed a lock of hair
away from her face. "You look bushed."

"I am."

"In the future, we have to work together, Liz. Everything depends on figuring this out and finding a way to
prove it. When I think about what could have happened
if I hadn't gotten here in time—''

She put her fingers against his lips. "But you did. You
saved me.''

He kissed her fingers and looked at her in such a way
that she felt her insides melt. He'd always had a way
with her and she was pretty sure he knew it. But he
didn't push his advantage and she was half relieved and
half saddened.

He said, "You resent my having saved you, don't you?"

"Don't be crazy. If you hadn't come along, I probably would have fallen and broken my neck. I can't imagine what would have happened to our baby."

He nodded, but there was a look in his eyes she couldn't identify.

"I thanked you," she said softly. "I meant it."

"I know you did. But part of you resents needing me."

Part of her was afraid that through no fault of his own, he wouldn't be around to be needed, so maybe he was right, maybe part of her resisted becoming too dependent on him. She bit her lip.

"It's okay," he said. "I think I understand. But I'm not going away. Just remember that."

"It's not that easy and you know it," she said.

He grinned the old Alex grin. "I know. Good night, try not to worry."

"What do I have to worry about? Almost dying today? Sinbad living through the night? Or maybe about which one of us is going to wind up in jail for killing my uncle?"

He shook his head.

Long after she'd slipped into bed, she heard him prowling the house, inside and out, checking windows and doors. His concern both frightened and comforted her. She fell asleep wishing he'd knock on her door, or maybe just break it down, wishing he'd demand she let him in, taking the decision to be wise and cautious away from her, putting her destiny in his hands where in her heart of hearts, she knew it belonged.

She fell asleep with tears in her eyes.

ALEX PULLED UP the rope that still dangled over the edge of the cliff and checked every inch of it. It wasn't enough that it appeared to be just as he left it the night before. He didn't trust that whomever had plotted the first "accident" hadn't come back during the night to wreak more havoc.

It looked okay. Within minutes, he was scaling the side of the bluff, using muscles now sore from the exertion of the day before. By the time he pulled himself back up to the first landing, he knew for sure that Liz's misadventure had been no accident.

He'd already discovered scratch marks on the trim outside the bathroom window and now this. Fury flared in his gut. Someone had tried to kill Liz. She must know something about her uncle's murder that the true killer was afraid would come out during a new investigation. She was in danger because of the new trial. If anything happened to her because of him—

Well, it wouldn't. He wouldn't let it.

He quickly made his way up to the top of the cliff where he found Liz just as he'd left her, wrapped in a coat against the drizzly winter day, arms wrapped around herself. She looked very pregnant and very vulnerable. He surmounted his desire to run to her, to wrap her in his arms and protect her from who knew who or for what reason....

"It's obvious someone sawed through the underpinning down there," he told her as he worked the snug leather gloves off his hands and shoved them in his back pocket.

Liz wrinkled her brow. She looked completely washed-out to him, almost wan, and he wished he could dare tell her to spend the day resting. He knew she wouldn't; it was probable that she couldn't, given the events of the past twenty-four hours. She was on edge, and frankly, she had every right to be so. He crossed mental fingers that her call to the vet's office would result in good news.

"If I had been…hurt…wouldn't the authorities have checked for signs of sabotage?" she asked. "Wouldn't they have investigated?"

"Maybe the investigation would have been conducted by the sheriff's office and maybe the sheriff knew he could control the outcome," Alex said, knowing that he had no real proof that Kapp had had anything to do with it.

"I guess…"

A new thought entered his mind and refused to budge. "Or maybe they would have found just what they expected to find," he said, alarm rising in his throat. He took off for the garage, Liz behind him.

He found what he was looking for laying carelessly on his workbench, an old chisel with white paint chips covering the metal tip. He stared at it like it was a bomb which he expected the would-be assassin had intended it to be.

Liz caught up with him as his gaze lifted to the peg board hanging on the wall behind the work bench, to the two wood-cutting saws he kept there. Sure enough, the larger of the two had fresh wood caught in its teeth. A sprinkle of sawdust had been dislodged when the saw was placed back on its hooks and lay scattered across the cluttered bench.

"What—" Liz said, but then it must have struck her what she was looking at. "Your tools," she whispered.

"If the police were here investigating, they would find paint that matched the trim on the bathroom window right here on *my* chisel and sawdust from the underpinning of the beach stairs caught in *my* saw. It would look as though I jimmied the window and booby-trapped the stairs, and then tried to make it look like an accident. I would look guilty.''

He reached for the chisel, but Liz caught his hand. ''Is it all right to touch it? What about fingerprints?''

''If there are any fingerprints on these tools, you can bet the farm they're mine. More likely, they've been wiped clean. Whoever did all this would have worn gloves.'' He recalled the gloves he'd grabbed from this bench the day before, the same ones that were now stuffed in the rear pocket of his jeans. He took them out now and stared at them, recalling how he'd had to all but peel them off his hands a few minutes before.

''Are these yours?'' he asked Liz.

She looked confused. ''No, they're yours.''

He pulled one on again and flexed his fingers. Either his hands had grown since yesterday morning when he'd dug the fence post holes or the gloves had shrunk. ''I don't think so,'' he said, taking the one off again and searching for a label of some kind. There was no identifying tag in either glove.

Was he wrong? Had they always been tight? Had wearing them out in the damp affected the leather? Or had the maniac who had rigged the stairs and broken Sinbad's leg brought them along?

Then why leave them behind?

He spent the next several minutes looking for his own gloves, which meant he scoured the garage, searched out by the fence project as well as inside his truck, and all through the house. Back in the garage, he stared at the gloves on his workbench. They were either his or the would-be killer had taken the wrong pair.

They had to be his.

"What about the twine?" Liz said. "I threw the original bit down the bluff. It's probably been washed away by now. But you don't have twine out here, do you?"

He shook his head, then stopped, considering. Rummaging around in a drawer beneath his table saw, he found a spool of twine left over from the garden two years before.

"It's green," Liz said.

"It sure is."

"The twine around Sinbad's neck was natural colored." She hugged herself and added, "Alex, I'm scared."

He put an arm around her slender shoulders. "Nothing is going to happen to you, sweetheart. I won't let it."

"It's not me I'm scared for."

He kissed her hair. The honey colored strands were damp and felt cool against his lips. "Let's go inside," he said. "Let's call the vet and see how Sinbad is doing. Come on, you're freezing. I'll make coffee."

"Or hot chocolate?" she asked, looking up at him under a sweep of dark lashes. Her green eyes looked huge, and for a second he flashed back to the day before when she'd looked just like this as she glanced at him over her shoulder, the two of them dangling from a long piece of three-quarter-inch nylon rope.

He tried to think of someplace he could send her where she'd be safe until he figured out what was going on. She could stay with Emily.

Except, how would he protect her if she wasn't by his side, day…and night?

"Hot chocolate it is," he said.

"But first I need to call the vet," she added, glancing at her watch. "It's nine o'clock, they should be open now."

BEFORE SHE GOT a call in to the vet, Ron Boxer called. Ever sensitive, he reacted to the stress even Liz could hear in her own voice. "Did I catch you at a bad time?" he asked. "Has something happened?"

"No, no." She was surprised by how much she wanted to confide in him, but one look at Alex heating milk for her hot chocolate dampened the desire to spill her guts. She and Alex needed to discuss what information they shared before she said a word to anyone.

Ron pressed her. "Are you sick, are you hurt? Is it Alex, is something wrong?"

"Everything is fine," she assured him. "As you know, this is a pretty difficult time around here, but we're coping." She suddenly thought of Alex's observation about Emily trying to match her up with Ron and added a little self-consciously, "We're working together. Me, Alex and Sinbad. We're fine. What's up?"

He gracefully let the matter go. "Considering everything else, this is going to seem trivial, but I was wondering about your plans for after you give birth. Jane said you weren't coming back to work after the baby is born, at least not for a few months. I've got a franchised sporting goods outlet interested in the big empty department store space at the south end of the mall. Should I bring this up at our monthly meeting? Will you be here in January?"

Jane Ridgeway was Liz's head of marketing. "Jane can handle it. I won't be back in January though I'll be in touch via e-mail and the phone and can come in if someone really needs me. Go ahead and work out the details with Jane."

"Good enough. Get some rest."

With that good advice, he hung up and almost immediately the vet's office called. Liz talked to Dr. Kippling for a few moments, then gravitated to Alex and the delicious chocolate mixture he had concocted.

"Hmm, I love a man who can cook," she murmured as he poured the hot chocolate into a mug and handed it to her.

"That's me. Master cook, specialties coffee, soup and hot chocolate. What did Ron want and what did the vet have to say?"

She told him about Ron's question, then added, "Dr. Kippling says Sinbad looks better this morning. She set his leg and said he licked a little food off the technician's finger. If he keeps improving this way, we should be able to bring him home in a couple of days."

Alex leaned against the counter, his hands wrapped around a mug of coffee. "He's a tough little bugger."

Liz felt herself smile for the first time in what seemed like days. He took care of that with his next statement.

"Someone is worried about what you know, so worried that they're willing to risk everything to get you out of the picture."

She felt a shudder go through her that the steaming chocolate couldn't touch. He was right, she knew this.

"I've been thinking about it. It would be entirely too dangerous for someone to go down the stairs from this bluff. We could have seen him—or her. But someone could have come along the beach at low tide and climbed up to do the dirty work."

"How would they get your tools?"

"The garage is unlocked. I've only been back two days and frankly, I don't recall noticing either the saw or the chisel."

"What did you use when you installed the chain on the front door the other night?"

"I used the tools out of the little box you keep in the

hall closet for fix-it projects. Except I went into the garage for the cordless drill, but that wasn't on the workbench. Even if it was, I'm not sure I would have noticed anything missing. I left it midproject last spring when I was arrested. I hadn't put things away properly."

"I didn't have the heart to straighten it up after…while you were gone," she said. "I was going to. Ron offered to help me, but after boxing up your clothes and moving out your furniture, I just couldn't—"

He put a warm hand on her shoulder. "I'm glad you couldn't. Anyway, the point is that the saw and chisel could have been missing for weeks or just hours and neither one of us would know."

"So, maybe someone took the tools, then walked along the beach and sabotaged the stairs, then came here while we were both gone, jimmied the window, replaced the tools, hurt Sinbad and tied him to the stairs for me to find."

"Either that or they took the saw weeks ago and got the idea to jimmy the window with our chisel when they came to use the cat as bait. So, who knew we'd be gone?"

"Well, the sheriff—"

"Exactly."

Liz shook her head. "He's not the only one. Dave knew you were coming to his house."

"Why would Dave—"

"All I'm saying is that there were other people who knew some of our plans and may I remind you that the sheriff is the one who offered to install a chain on my door? Would he have done that if he was running around stealing your tools?"

"What better way to case out the garage and see what's out there? Maybe he was formulating a plan."

"You're hopeless. Okay, the sheriff knew about me leaving, Dave knew about you—"

"How about Ron and Emily?"

"They knew the sheriff was coming, but they didn't know he changed his plans and called me into his office. And they didn't know about you."

"I hate to say anything that might give Kapp a break, but do we even know if he was the one who changed the original meeting place from here to his office?"

"I guess we don't."

"Exactly. Take Harry Idle, lurking over there across the road, looking out his window. He sees me leave, he sees you at home, he disguises his voice and calls you away, he comes over here—"

"Wait a second. I can't picture Harry Idle messing with stairs and windows and cats. And he's got huge hands."

"You're thinking of the gloves. You're right."

"Exactly. Plus, how would he know I was expecting the sheriff?"

"Kapp knew he was coming, of course, and so did Ron and Emily and probably half the sheriff's department. He could have heard it from a buddy in the department."

Liz shook her head. "I don't know. And neither the sheriff or Ron or Emily knew *you* were going anywhere."

"This isn't helping. How about your scarf? Have you remembered when you saw it last?"

"I'm afraid not. I keep trying. It's like I have a mental block."

"We need to find out for sure if the sheriff was behind the call that changed your meeting from here to there and we need to see if there's anything incriminating about the sheriff in those boxes you brought home from your uncle's house before he died.''

"I think they're just boxes of my school records and things he didn't want to store anymore.''

"Maybe so, but since the rest of his stuff is still tied up, they're all we have. I'll go dust off those boxes and bring them inside where it's warm. We'll go through them together.''

"And I'll call the sheriff's assistant and make sure it was she who called here,'' Liz said.

"I DIDN'T CALL YOU,'' the young woman said adamantly once Liz had reached her. "I've already been grilled by the sheriff about this, Mrs. Chase. I didn't change anyone's plans and I don't know who did. And I don't take too many long lunches, I don't care what that pip-squeak deputy says. If he'd get a life of his own, he wouldn't have to tattle about mine.''

Liz related this information to Alex, speculating that since the sheriff had questioned Belle Carter himself, he was innocent.

"Or just covering his tracks,'' Alex said, piling the last of five boxes near the kitchen table. They each took a chair and opened a box.

"Good grief, he saved these?'' Liz said as the first bundle she touched turned out to be a dozen or so old report cards. "I never dreamed.''

"He also saved the programs from your recitals,'' Alex said, lifting out a stack of papers. "I didn't know you took ballet. You look damn cute in your tutu.''

"Let me see.'' Alex handed over a picture of her in a pink tutu standing arm and arm with another girl dressed in lilac. "Oh—this is Carmen,'' she said, gently touching the other child's face. "She was my best friend.

She had the most beautiful long, dark hair. Sometimes, she'd let me braid it. I haven't thought about her in years.''

"And you never told me you play the piano," Alex added as he produced a recital card.

"I don't. Uncle Devon insisted I try, but I guess he came to my one and only recital and heard how hopeless I was because the next day the piano disappeared from the house and he never mentioned lessons again. I think my nanny at the time cried with relief.''

He lifted out additional papers, all semi-yellowed with age. "I thought you said your uncle didn't have anything to do with you when you were little. He sure kept a lot of stuff.''

"The nannies probably collected it," Liz said as she found several drawings she didn't recall making. Her initials were on the papers, though, and since most featured a small house being consumed with red and orange crayon fire, she assumed she'd been working out the deaths of her parents.

The realization that she'd coped with their loss by re-creating their deaths this way made her feel a pang of sorrow for the little girl who had gone from beloved only child to orphan in the time it took a fire to rage through her home. At first, she could remember wishing she'd been with them when it happened. Not because she had a death wish, but because she was convinced she could have saved them. Later, she'd realized that wasn't a likely scenario; in all likelihood, her life would have ended with theirs.

How ironic that she should fall in love with a fireman of all people. She looked at Alex and found him staring at the drawings in her hands. Their eyes met and he smiled at her.

She sighed back a flood of tears and set the drawings aside. "Let's try different boxes."

The next two held more memorabilia including pictures of Liz with her parents, pictures taken years before their deaths when Liz was a toddler with plump legs and arms and white-blonde hair. She'd never seen the pictures before and was startled by how much she'd grown to resemble her mother and how handsome her father had been.

"I don't think I can take too much more of this stroll down memory lane," Liz said.

Alex propped the last box on top of one of the others and cut it open. "There's just the one more. We might as well finish the job. I'll do it, you sit there and look pretty."

"It'll be easier to search through the box than manage looking pretty," she said. "My ankles are swollen, I have no lap to speak of, my fingernails are all cracked and chipped and I slept on my hair wrong."

"You look perfect to me," Alex said, laying aside the box flaps, and damn if he didn't manage to sound sincere.

This box was slightly different from the others. While the top layer held scraps of Liz's past, the bottom of the box was filled with correspondence, grouped in separate stacks and bound with string. Her uncle's name seemed to be on every envelope.

"The man never threw anything away," Alex said as he thumbed through the letters. "There isn't a postmark here that isn't over twenty years old."

"I'll go through them later," Liz said, standing and stretching. "Maybe my parents wrote to my uncle once in a while and maybe he kept their letters. If so, I'd like to read them."

"You don't know much about them, do you?"

"Very little. The fire destroyed everything and Uncle Devon was never what you could call chatty. He turned my care over to a nanny who quit after a year or so because he was so nasty to her. After that, there was a whole string of nannies, one after the other, all leaving when his belligerence wore them down."

A stack of papers on the table caught her attention; she'd forgotten to return the drawings to their box and she picked them up now, looking again at the raging crayon fires, noticing for the first time the two little stick figures caught in the waxy flames.

"What an awful way to die," she whispered.

Beside her, Alex said, "There are no good ways to die, honey." He kissed her cheek and added, "Which brings us back to yesterday's incident. Why don't you call the sheriff and invite him out here? I want to hear what he has to say for himself."

"But you and he are like firecrackers when you're together."

"I know, I know. I'll make you a deal. I'll be in the house, but I won't barge into the interview unless he tries something."

"Like clubbing me over the head?"

He laughed softly. "Something like that, though hopefully nothing quite so drastic."

"You're wrong about the sheriff, but I'll go ahead and arrange it."

"Good."

Liz yawned into her hand. "Another long day and it's only half over."

Alex trailed a finger down her cheek. "You could take a nap," he said, his eyes suddenly brimming with mischief.

Ah, the memories, of lazy afternoons making love, napping, reading, making love again. So many memories...

"I can't go to sleep at night if I nap during the day," she said, pretending she didn't know what really lay behind his suggestion, pretending that the touch of his finger on her face didn't have her aching for his touch in other, more sensitive areas. Last night, she'd wanted him to break down the door. Today, she was trying to keep her distance. She felt a continual pull toward him while at the same time fearing it. If she was this confused about her feelings, she couldn't imagine the mixed signals she must be sending him.

"I read somewhere that if you lay down without sleeping, you're resting your body, and that if you lay down and go to sleep, you're resting both your body and your mind. But there are ways to lay down and close your eyes and rest neither. We used to be pretty damn good at it."

"I know," she whispered, "but I'm not ready for that kind of—"

"Intimacy." There was a note of irony in his voice, and his eyes narrowed.

She nodded miserably. She'd let him save her, but not love her. How messed up was that? And in this scary time, could she deny she needed him in every way imaginable? Or that he needed her?

His expression softened again, as though he understood how torn she was and didn't want to add to her pain. He said, "Well, then, as an alternative, how about I bring down some of those Christmas boxes I found in the attic? The holidays are just a couple of weeks away."

"What with everything that's been going on, I forgot all about it."

"I grew up in a house where no one put up anything. Mom had split and Dad was usually in jail or sleeping it off somewhere. My brothers had problems of their own, so it was usually just me and a television special. I don't want that for our child, even if he or she isn't technically here to celebrate with us."

"Of course not." What he didn't say but what Liz understood was that this might be the last Christmas he spent in his home with his baby, born or unborn, the last Christmas they all spent together.

No! she screamed internally.

But you don't have control. You can go to the sheriff and tell him about your scarf and your late-night visit and Alex could still end up behind bars.

"While you get the boxes, I'll go buy a tree—" she said, but he cut her off with a jingle of his truck keys.

"From now on, you aren't going anywhere without me. Where you go, I go. From now on you and I are more or less joined at the hip. Tell me what obligations you have ahead in the next few days."

She shook her head. "Nothing important—"

"What about your annual office Christmas party? Won't you be responsible for it this year now that your uncle is…gone?"

"Yes, but I'll beg off—"

"No. Don't do that. I'll go with you."

"Why?"

"Like I said, where you go, I—"

"I mean why do you want me to go to it? I can get someone else to stand around and hand out bonuses and congratulate everyone that we managed to pull through another year without losing more than ten percent of our leases. My assistant, Jane, can do it or Ron—''

"But if we're there, we can ask questions. We can ferret out information. Maybe there's someone within the management team at the mall who hated your uncle enough to kill him.''

"I thought you had Sheriff Kapp pinpointed for that dubious distinction.''

"I like to keep my options open. Where is the soirée being held this year?''

"The Egret Inn.''

"Hmm, ritzy,'' he said with a glint in his eye. They'd dined just a few times at the Egret Inn because Alex was right, the place was ritzy and expensive and exclusive and all the rest. She studied the floor in lieu of looking at her feet which she hadn't been able to see in about two months, and said, "Alex, beyond our attempts at sleuthing, that party is likely to be kind of uncomfortable for you. People love to gossip—''

"Let them. All I care about is finding Devon Hiller's murderer and the fiend who almost killed you. Period. A little gossip can't hurt me.''

She nodded. He was right. Gossip couldn't hurt them. Falling off cliffs—now that could.

Chapter Seven

After the stress of the day, walking around parking lots crowded with cut evergreen trees seemed like a veritable walk in the woods. It began raining midway through their search, but it was a relatively mild rain for December, and Liz had brought an umbrella.

They stood beneath it, side by side, as a good-natured teenager straightened a dozen different trees for their perusal. They finally chose a Nobel Pine and Alex strapped it into the back of the truck. They made one more stop and Liz waited in the truck while Alex went inside a wireless phone company and signed up for a cell phone. By the time they finally arrived home, Liz was starving. As Alex secured the tree in the metal stand, she made a plate of sandwiches which they ate as they decorated the tree.

In the end, it took up most of a corner and Liz felt a melancholy streak for Sinbad who would have loved the process. She couldn't wait to get him home and see how he'd react to the red balls and twinkling green lights. Hopefully his cast would keep him from scaling the tree and bringing it crashing to the ground.

The fact was that, thanks to the tree, the living room had assumed a magical radiance. Looking up at the star on the very top, Liz realized the warm glow of hope had replaced the icy despair she'd been feeling for days.

But it was late and she was tired and she didn't know what Alex had meant when he said joined at the hip. He cleared that up as he locked doors, turned off the lights and started down the hall.

"I'm sleeping in our bedroom," he said firmly, almost backing her against the wall. "I can bunk out on the floor or in a chair, that's up to you, and I don't expect anything from you, but I am going to be in the same room with you. Someone tried to kill you yesterday."

She said, "Okay."

He seemed surprised by her submission.

"Don't look so stunned. I'm not a complete idiot. Someone tried to kill me yesterday. I think sleeping with a big, strong fireman sounds like a great idea."

"So, all I am to you is Mr. Fireman?"

"Yep," she lied.

He kissed her forehead. "It's a start," he said.

ALEX WATCHED Liz demurely take her nightgown into the bathroom to change. She looked as nervous as a new bride.

By the time she emerged, swathed from throat to ankle in pink flannel, he had bunked out on the chair in the corner, fully dressed, his booted feet up on a stool he'd brought from her office, an afghan thrown over his legs.

Mr. Fireman, safe in his corner…

"You can sleep in the bed," she said softly.

And how he yearned to do so. But not like this. A man had his pride. He wanted her to want him. She'd refused him earlier and nothing had changed except her fatigue level. He said, "I don't plan on sleeping much."

She came to his side and he took her outstretched

hand. Resisting the urge to tug her onto his lap, he kissed her palm. She smelled like roses and looked like a pink angel with tousled hair. She brought his hand to her lips and kissed his fingers, then released him.

She moved to her side of the bed, her movements so different than before and yet so familiar. As she settled under the blankets and turned off the light, he realized he loved her with a ferocity that almost scared him. He kept seeing the flames in her drawings juxtaposed on top of the image of her clinging to the cliff wall. It was all he could do not to bundle her away to safety.

But they couldn't leave unless they were willing to spend the rest of their lives running, and he wasn't. There was a time and a place to make a stand and if it wasn't here and now for their baby's sake, then when? So he stayed in his chair and planned on keeping his eyes open.

HE AWOKE sometime later and lay in the dark, listening. Somewhere nearby, a dog barked.

He got up slowly and quietly, checking on Liz whose regular, deep breathing reassured him. He heard another noise and more barking and took off down the hall. Additional sounds came from outside, footsteps, something else. Without pausing to grab a weapon, he pulled open the front door as headlights across the road blazed on. Blinded momentarily by the lights, he heard the gunning of an engine, the spinning of tires. He ran toward the road as a car took off toward town.

His first thought was to follow the car. Yanking the keys out of his pocket, he climbed into the truck and started the engine, whipping out of the driveway, just missing the mailbox. Red taillights were visible on top of the hill and he pushed down on the accelerator, determined to catch up with that car.

Another thought struck him as he crested the hill.

Was this a diversion to get Liz alone in the house?

He pulled over to the side of the road, watched for a second as the taillights disappeared around a bend, pounded the steering wheel with a fist. Then he turned the truck around. He was back in his own driveway in record time.

He unlocked the front door. The trip down the hall seemed endless. He threw on the bedroom light.

The bed was empty. His heart stopped.

The bathroom door opened and his beautiful wife stood blinking at him, rubbing her tummy, half-asleep.

"What's going on?" she said drowsily.

Alex's heart jump-started back into action, skittering around in his chest like a drop of cold water in a hot pan, bouncing and dancing and damn near evaporating. He managed to say, "Nothing, honey, go back to bed."

She smiled and nodded and hit the sheets again, never fully awake. He checked to make sure the window was locked, then turned off the light and went back outside.

Okay, the car had pulled away from in front of Harry Idle's house in such a way that suggested it was up to no good. A late-night visitor? But he'd heard footsteps. Could he have heard them from all the way over at Harry's house?

Doubtful.

He finally noticed the rain had stopped. There was no moon to speak of, but a bevy of stars glittered in the night sky. As he walked along his own front path, he thought that his footfalls on the gravel encrusted redwood duff produced a sound similar to one he'd heard.

He thought back and recalled another sound before the footsteps. Not the dog, something else.

He went back for a flashlight, then returned outside. The garage door was closed but not locked. Had they left it open again? He raised it now and then closed it, pretty sure the sound he'd heard had been the muffled thud of the heavy wooden door hitting the cement. Opening it again, he shined the flashlight over the contents of the garage. Everything looked just as it had earlier that night. Liz's uncle's boxes in one corner, old furniture in the other, newly cleaned saw hanging in its proper place over the workbench.

The workbench. Here too, nothing looked any different, though the cluttered condition of the surface made certainty a dicey issue at best. Nevertheless, his gaze drifted over the cans of spray paint and the row of old coffee cans used for storing nails and screws. Curled pieces of sandpaper vied for space with soft red rags and scraps of wood. The leather gloves lay on top of it all.

The gloves.

He propped the flashlight on top of the vise and tugged on the left glove.

It fit. Not tight, just right, a good fit for a man with big hands. The right one was a perfect fit as well. And even more telling, there was a narrow brown tag sewn into the seam on both gloves. Of course, the brand he bought always had that tag, he just hadn't remembered it until that moment.

"They're not the same gloves as earlier today, are they?" Liz asked from the open door.

She'd put on a robe and slipped her feet into moccasins. Her hands were clasped together under her chin. Even in the semidark, her eyes looked huge.

"No," he said, putting the gloves down. "No, they're not the same."

"Someone was in our garage."

"Yes."

She looked like she might faint. In a heartbeat, he was at her side.

"I'm okay," she said. "It's just the thought of someone coming in the dark, sneaking around in our garage. It makes me feel…"

"Let's go back to bed."

As he followed her inside, locking doors as he went, he thought about the gloves and the anonymous trespasser. It had to be the same person who had sabotaged the stairs and so cruelly broken Sinbad's leg. It seemed to Alex that this nameless monster was taking increasingly dangerous chances—he or she had left their own gloves behind and then he or she had almost been caught exchanging them.

He had to be ready to pounce at the next mistake.

"Don't leave me," Liz said as she climbed into bed, reaching out with pleading eyes.

"No chance of that," he said, and grabbed the afghan. He stretched out next to her, on top of the comforter, flinging the afghan over him. He had no intention of undressing and snuggling beneath warm blankets with his very desirable wife. If anything else was going to happen tonight, he wanted to be ready.

Besides, she hadn't invited him to snuggle. Instead, she reached for his hand and held onto him as though she was dangerously afloat and he was the only tether that kept her from drifting away.

He told the parts of his body that spontaneously reacted to the warmth of her nearby body, the softness of her hand, the sweetness of her expelled breath, to take a hike. He lay awake with eyes wide open for hours.

"I CAN'T EXPLAIN the mix-up the other day," Roger Kapp said as Liz invited him inside. While Alex and she had rehearsed what she'd say, she knew there was no way she could actually control the conversation with the sheriff. He was a strong-willed man and wouldn't take direction from her.

"It must have been somebody's idea of a joke," Kapp added. He took up an inordinate amount of room. Not as tall or broad shouldered as Alex, he had an imposing way of standing.

"It would seem so," she said uneasily. "I made coffee, Sheriff. Would you like a cup?"

Two mugs sat on the table in front of the chair she chose, the one across from the Christmas tree. He took the proffered cup. She didn't intend to drink hers. The last thing in the world she needed was caffeine.

"Sit down, please," she said.

He stood for a second, as though trying to decide if he wanted to sit. Liz knew him well enough to know he coveted authority and she reasoned that he was probably a little uncomfortable interviewing her on her own turf. Too many variables, too many unknowns.

Alex had said the sheriff would notice every detail of the room and he was right about that. It seemed the sheriff's gaze never stopped moving and that he took in every little thing, including the new chain on the front door, the stack of cardboard boxes Alex had piled near the Christmas tree and his work boots lined up carefully by the front door.

"So, Chase is living with you," Kapp said as he finally decided to sit down. His voice held a note of scorn.

"He's my husband," she said softly.

Kapp shook his head. "You're a brave woman, Elizabeth. A man like that can't be trusted. I take it he's around here somewhere."

"He's in the office, working."

"And where's that Siamese cat of yours?"

She felt her throat constrict. Was mentioning Sinbad's absence a threat? Was Alex right, had Roger Kapp set the trap on the stairs? She said, "He's at the vet's."

"Hope he's okay."

"He's fine," she said, heart racing. She took a deep breath and pushed away the fear she recognized as a knee-jerk reaction to her own imagination. Roger Kapp wasn't going to hurt her with Alex in the next room and, for that matter, perhaps he was just making polite chit-chat. The key to this situation was self-control. She added, "He broke his leg."

Kapp furrowed his brow. He'd taken his hat off when he entered the house and she noticed his sandy hair lay flat against his skull. Still, he had a large head and dark gray eyes and he looked at her now as though divining the truth from the recesses of her mind.

"Sorry to hear that. We need to go over the night Devon was killed. If you'd feel more comfortable doing this away from your…house…I'd be happy to drive you into my office."

"I'm fine right here," she said, adding, "I have to warn you that I don't have anything new to add to my original statement."

He produced a notepad. "Just tell it all to me again."

She launched into her story, again omitting her late-night visit, not mentioning the scarf, still uncertain that it wouldn't be wise to do both.

It occurred to her how she could broach the subject

of her uncle's boxes. "Go ahead and set your cup on one of those cardboard boxes right there beside you," she said. "You can't hurt them. They're Uncle Devon's."

He looked at the boxes and then at her, then at the boxes again. "I didn't think his possessions had been released yet," he said slowly. "I thought his estate was still tied up."

"It is, but he gave me these boxes a month or so before he was killed," she said. "They're full of correspondence." She didn't add that all of it seemed to be over twenty years old. Instead, she watched his eyes like Alex had cautioned her to do, and sure enough, the sheriff did look uneasy.

"Funny he'd give that kind of stuff to you," Kapp said.

She shrugged. "I was his only relative, Sheriff. Eventually I'll see everything he owned, won't I? There's the wall safe in his home office and all his safety deposit boxes. The man never threw a thing away. I've just started going through these boxes. They're full of some very interesting documents."

He said, "Documents?"

Deciding on a forthright approach, she said, "It appears you were blackmailing him."

His glance darted back to the boxes, then he stood abruptly. The cup flew from his knee and shattered on the floor. He knelt at once. "I'm sorry—" he began, but stopped. Standing up, the broken china and puddle of coffee still at his feet, he said, "What did you say?"

"You were blackmailing him," she repeated, nodding discreetly at the boxes. "You blackmailed him into supporting your run for sheriff."

She waited for his protest. After all, it wasn't as

though she had any real proof and it wasn't as though a huge part of her didn't suspect Kapp's guilt existed solely in Alex's head. But the sheriff stood there nervously rubbing his forehead, seemingly speechless, apparently unable to dissemble, to deny, to evade.

She found herself thinking, *Alex and his friends are right: Roger Kapp is—was—a blackmailer!*

Equally stunning was the realization that her uncle had been susceptible to coercion, he'd had something to hide.

The next thought left her reeling. *What?* What had Uncle Devon had to hide?

Kapp finally said, "That's ridiculous."

It was too late. With a burst of anger, she stood. "Did you hurt my cat, too? Did you try to hurt me? Did you break into my house last night?" Suddenly remembering to check his hands, she glanced down and saw that he had ordinary sized hands for a man, smaller than Alex's, bigger than hers.

The gloves that had inadvertently been left behind, then stolen back in the dead of the night would fit this man.

He backed toward the door. "I don't know what you're talking about," he said. "If you're in the middle of a crime wave, ask yourself when it started. I bet everything was fine until you invited Alex Chase back into your house, right? He's after something and it doesn't take a genius to figure out what. Watch your step, be careful."

"You blackmailed my uncle," she said calmly which wasn't easy given how anxious she felt. "What did you have on him? Did he get tired of paying, did he refuse to help you with your re-election campaign? I know how he was, I bet he decided you could go public with whatever you had on him. I bet he dared you to do it.''

The sheriff rallied. ''You're upset,'' he said condescendingly.

''Damn right, I'm upset.''

''Why don't you file charges against Chase, why don't you face the truth about the man?'' With that, he grabbed his hat and coat from the chair by the door where Liz had put them. Turning one last time, he said, ''I don't need your permission to investigate your uncle's den again to see if there's something there we missed the first time. I know you keep the housekeeper on to take care of the place, so as a courtesy, I'm telling you that next week we'll be going back out there. You might want to alert her. I won't be here again until I come to arrest your husband for murder. And this time, I promise, it will stick.''

''Promises, promises,'' Alex said. As he strode into the room, Liz looked from one man to the other, their differences startling in such close proximity. One sandy colored from head to foot, sturdy, officious but presently flushed, the other darker, steamier, broader in shoulder, slimmer in hips…and more in control. This was something she'd always admired about Alex, whether flying up and down a basketball court or fighting an inferno— he responded to ultimate danger with a powerful sense of authority that was as intimidating as it was comforting. It all depended on whether you were for him or against him.

''You!'' Sheriff Kapp bellowed.

''Listen to me, Kapp,'' Alex said. ''Liz doesn't have one single piece of incriminating evidence against you. Those boxes are filled with childhood papers and some very old letters, most of which predate all of us. I asked her to insinuate that she had the goods on you, just to gauge your reaction, which was, by the way, interesting. I'm telling you this—'' and here he paused to squeeze Liz's shoulder ''—so that you understand she poses no threat to you.''

''Threat?'' Kapp said, eyebrows all but shooting right off his high forehead.

''You're guilty as hell and you know it,'' Alex said. ''You blackmailed Devon Hiller. I don't know why, but I'd bet my last dime that you did.''

Kapp stared hard at Alex, then shook his head. ''So you've changed your story,'' he said. ''Now you're innocent and I'm the bad guy? What about your confession, Chase?''

Liz held her breath, wondering how Alex would respond. She knew he was still adamant about not implicating her and she suspected that even if it meant he spent the next thirty years in prison, he'd stay that way.

She said, ''Alex is innocent, Sheriff.''

She felt Alex's body tense as the sheriff's invasive glare went from him to her. Kapp seemed to consider her statement before saying, ''The only reason I can think of for a man to confess to a murder he didn't commit, is to protect someone he thinks did.''

''I can think of other reasons,'' Alex said.

Liz stood there quietly. She felt trapped between two pit bulls. Throwing a scrap to either of them seemed foolhardy so she kept her mouth shut.

Alex said, ''Just out of curiosity, Sheriff, do you have an alibi for the night Devon Hiller was murdered?''

Kapp smirked. ''You may hoodwink Elizabeth with your innocent talk, but I'm not falling for this little game you're playing. Not that I need one, but of course I have an alibi and no, I won't discuss what it is with the likes of you.''

Alex dropped his hand and stepped forward. ''You know when you said that you wouldn't be back here again without a warrant for my arrest? I think that's a good idea.''

''It's up to you whether I come back or not,'' Kapp said with a sinister gleam in his eyes. ''Any more shenanigans and Elizabeth might decide to cut her losses. Who could blame her?''

He tugged on his hat and was gone.

Liz buried her face in her hands. She felt Alex's arms surround her. She pushed herself away. Wiping tears from her eyes with shaky fingers, she said, ''These aren't tears of fear, Alex. These are tears of frustration. Sheriff Kapp is positive you not only killed Uncle Devon but that you're a threat to me.''

Alex tilted her chin with a finger and kissed her lips.

She wasn't finished. ''I shouldn't have accused him of trying to hurt me because now he knows something happened to me, and he thinks you did it.'' Peering into his eyes, she added, ''If something else happens to me, you'll be in terrible trouble.''

His eyes suddenly hard and bright, he whispered, ''If something else happens to you, I won't care what kind of trouble I'm in.''

''But the sheriff thinks—''

''Let him think what he wants to think.''

''I can't stand the way he acts like he's so much better than you. I want him to know you're innocent. You didn't want me to tell him anything else, but—''

''What's done is done and the look on his face was worth it.''

''We need to figure this out soon,'' Liz said. ''If Kapp

was blackmailing my uncle then that means my uncle did something he was ashamed of or something illegal, something that might have driven the sheriff to murder. But we don't know that for sure. Perhaps if we can figure out what Kapp had on Uncle Devon, we can figure out who else wanted him dead.''

''Unless it all begins and ends with Kapp,'' Alex said stubbornly.

She shook her head and stared at him. Those incredible eyes, that defiant stance, the way he moved, the way he stood! She looked away at last, and desperate for a diversion, said, ''Let's go visit Sinbad.''

ALEX LINED a basket with a royal-blue towel and set it in a blocked off corner of the kitchen. As he passed the cold fireplace, he wished Liz was more comfortable with fire because he had a feeling the cat would crave warmth during his long convalescence, but her fear of it was too deep for him to excise. He'd tried, way back in high school when the school had set a bonfire before a homecoming game. Though he'd coaxed and cajoled, she wouldn't go near it. Later that night she'd explained about her parents and he could still recall the profound sorrow he'd felt on her behalf.

His mother had walked out on him and his brothers when Alex was five years old. His father had abdicated parenthood by crawling into a bottle. *Her* parents were dead. Even as a kid, even hurting from all the blows life had dealt him, he'd known her situation was worse than his. Maybe his mother would come back someday, maybe his father would stop drinking and shape up. There was no such maybe for Liz.

When they met again after he'd become a fireman, he'd been almost certain his profession would bother her to the point where he'd have to make a choice: her or the fire department. She'd surprised him by accepting what he did though she didn't like to hear stories about tragedies.

Then again, who did? The whole point of being a fireman was to prevent tragedies.

He walked down the hall to their bedroom. He liked to think of it that way though he was still keeping his distance, waiting for her to break down and beg him to ravish her. He'd missed so much of her pregnancy that she was like a foreigner to him in some ways, speaking a different language at times, sporting a different body, thinking thoughts that baffled him, keeping him at arm's length.

The vet had sent a recovering Sinbad home with them and he found the cat and Liz not in their bedroom, but in her office. Liz was sitting at her desk. The cat was lying in a big box, his azure eyes still dazed. His hind leg was shaved from the operation that had included inserting a pin into the broken bone to keep it in place while it healed. The cat made a noise like a strangled lion as Alex approached.

He sat on his heels and scratched Sinbad's head, amazed to hear a hoarse purr. You had to hand it to the little guy. Some human had hurt him this way and yet he was still willing to trust. Every time Alex saw the shaved fur, the stitches, he thought about how close he'd come to losing Liz. Every time he thought of the cruelty involved in willfully breaking the cat's leg and winding twine around his neck, he wondered what else the person who had done this was capable of.

"How's he doing?" he asked Liz.

"He's still kind of dopey," she said, swiveling in her chair to face him.

"I made him a basket and stuck it in the warmest corner of the kitchen, near the heater vent."

"Good. I've been busy, too." She took a piece of paper out of the printer. "I compiled the list of displaced shopkeepers we talked about. When I compared them to the guest list for Uncle Devon's party, I found six names that matched. Two are very elderly people who didn't make it to the party because they're residents in a local nursing home and one is a woman who, at the time, was in the middle of a three month tour of Europe."

"And the others?"

"Well, one of them is Harry Idle, believe it or not. Did he mention being invited to the party?"

"No. Odd."

"Highly. The other two are women who ran a kitchen supply store at the corner of Fourth and Main umpteen years ago. It went belly-up when Uncle Devon opened the Harbor Lights Mall. They signed a lease to open a similar store at the mall just a few months ago, so I guess he invited them to the party because they were in negotiations at the time. I can check them out further."

"What about the new strip mall? Any disgruntled people from that invited to your uncle's party?"

"That mall went up on a piece of land that had been for sale forever. Uncle Devon got a great price and then it was rezoned and he built the mall. Four stores opened up. Three of them were established businesses anxious to move to a new and better location. The fourth is a grocery outlet in a part of town without one, so while it will have an impact, it's not like it's unexpected competition. It's hard to see that anyone suffered too greatly from that mall."

"Okay. Well, I'll give Harry the third degree about why he never mentioned being at that party. I'd also like to know if he heard the car last night. Maybe he saw something that would help pin down the identity of the driver.''

She caught his hand. ''Alex, we haven't talked about what the sheriff said. If he's going to recheck my uncle's study—''

''Don't worry, he won't find your scarf. I rolled it up and hid it in that little spot you showed me when we were in high school.''

''Good. Still, if he's going to look the place over, I'd like to, too.''

''Have you been there since—''

''Uncle Devon's murder? No.'' She shivered and added, ''The housekeeper takes care of things.''

He let it drop.

He picked up the cat as gingerly as possible, and with Liz on his heels, carried him back to the kitchen. Sinbad accepted the basket with a surprisingly demure meow as Liz filled food and water bowls and set them inside the makeshift enclosure alongside his commode. Eventually, he made an attempt to get comfortable which seemed like a good omen.

''He'll be fine,'' Alex said.

''I know.''

He couldn't take his eyes off the stitches.

Liz put her arms around him from the back and nuzzled his neck. She wasn't tight against him, the baby precluded that, but her spontaneous show of affection made his heart soar. ''It was sweet of you to make him his own little bed,'' she said.

''I'm a sweet guy,'' he said, gripping her hands and turning to face her.

''Unless you're Harry Idle. Poor Harry.''

''Poor Harry, my foot.''

"Thank you for taking such good care of me," she said softly.

"My pleasure."

"I owe you so much. I owe you my life."

He kissed her lips. For once, she didn't pull away or pursue their interrupted conversation. He kissed her again and again until he felt her lips dissolve into spun sugar and his own body throb. Her fingers dug into his back as he loosened his grip and held her face between his hands. Her eyes were half-closed and the eager yet sensual look on her face made her so sexy that breathing became a chore.

"My precious, precious, love," he whispered, kissing her eyelids, her earlobes, her chin.

She melted against him as much as a woman as pregnant as she was could. She didn't pull away or tell him she wasn't sure…. He wondered if he could lift her and her precious little bit of cargo into his arms and decided that hell, yes, he could pick her up and carry her to Canada if need be.

He tasted salt on his lips and opened his eyes. Hers were still closed, but two tears had escaped, had slipped by her defenses, leaving moist trails across her cheeks, down her throat and that's what he'd tasted.

For an eternity, he held his breath and in the quiet recesses of his mind, he heard her words. *I owe you so much,* she'd said, *I owe you my life* and then she'd offered herself to him after days of restraint.

He made himself say, "This isn't the time, sweetheart."

Her eyes fluttered open, the lashes slightly damp. "It isn't?"

"No."

"I know I'm not the same—"

"It's not you," he said softly, trailing one hand down her neck, across her full breasts, caressing her rounded belly. How could she doubt his need for her, his attraction to her? He added, "You're perfect."

"It's everything else?"

"It's everything else."

She rested her head against his shoulder while he wondered if he was as dumb as a fence post or just plain crazy. But she was crying and that seemed wrong, that seemed sad, and when he kissed her sadness was the last emotion he felt. Did she think she owed him her body because he'd saved her? Did some part of her fear he wouldn't be there for her if she wasn't there for him?

At least they were coming closer together, at least it seemed they were in the same book if not on the same page, and holding her like this felt pretty damn good. He kissed her hairline and was entertaining second thoughts about the conclusions he'd reached when the phone rang. She lifted her head and stared into his eyes, hers dry now. She seemed as reluctant as he to sever this tie. It rang again and Sinbad yowled.

"If it bothers you so much, answer it yourself," Alex growled at the cat, but the spell was broken and Liz drifted away with a final glance at him from over her shoulder that sent his libido into a futile overdrive. He went outside to find Harry Idle.

Chapter Eight

"I want to know if you're mad at me," Emily said, her voice both defensive and agitated.

Liz shifted the phone into her right hand and said, "Oh, Emily, no, of course not."

"Because you haven't called. Ron told me I was rude to your husband the other day."

Liz sat down on a kitchen chair and peered through the window for a sign of Alex. All she could see from that angle were the bare branches of an apple tree. "I've been so busy, I'm sorry I haven't called," she said. "And don't worry about Alex. He understands that you were…surprised…when he showed up at the restaurant."

"I was!" Emily agreed. "I thought he was locked away for good. I guess I kind of overreacted because of my own miserable marriage, but I know I shouldn't judge every male by my own ex. Ron says you love Alex. He says if Alex says he's innocent, I should listen."

"How kind of Ron," Liz said, wondering anew why Alex had pushed her away a few moments ago. She'd been ready, more than ready, damn near brimming with pent-up emotion and desire, but he'd retreated. She knew him well enough to know he must have had a compelling reason.

Whatever it was, she was thankful. She needed to keep a level head, she needed to think, not feel, not react, not lead him on, not hurt him any more than she already had. Making love to him would have been a mistake, it would have been a promise she wasn't sure she could keep.

"Ron asked me to come with him to the party on Saturday night," Emily continued, and Liz struggled to pay attention. "I don't want to go if it would upset you or…your husband. I know this party is really for the office staff and not the store owners—"

"Emily, please, I hope you decide to be Ron's guest. It will be a wonderful opportunity for you and Alex to get to know each other better. Come." Her attention was once again diverted because she'd gone to stand in front of the living room window and had found Alex across the street, talking to Harry Idle. Okay, talking *at* Harry Idle. She said, "Listen, Em, I really do have to go."

"But I haven't even asked you how everything is going. How are you feeling? How is Sinbad?"

"I'm doing well and he came home today."

"Home? Home from where?"

Liz suddenly realized that she'd not told anyone about Sinbad. At first she hadn't known how much to share and then events kept piling up. Reluctant to get into it but feeling guilty that she'd shut out a good friend, she said, "Sinbad was injured on our beach stairs the other day. He broke his leg." At the sound of Emily's inhaled breath, Liz hastened to add, "He's okay, Emily, really he is. I mean, he will be once he heals."

"The poor baby," Emily said. She'd always had a soft spot for the cat.

Liz's gaze drifted to Sinbad who was asleep and looked moderately comfortable on his blue towel. "You know what a little tyrant he can be. It's strange having him so quiet."

"Alex must have been shocked when he found him."

"Well, Alex didn't exactly find Sinbad. I did."

Another gasp and a cry of alarm. "You! Liz, what in the world were you doing on those rickety stairs?"

"Saving the cat," Liz said, wishing she'd kept her mouth shut. She wanted to protest the word "rickety," too, but kept quiet. "I'm sorry, Emily, but the rest of the story is going to have to wait, okay?"

"I can't believe you kept this from me! I can't believe Alex let you go down the those stairs by yourself! That just seems irresponsible to me. Did you tell Ron about this?"

Liz bristled at this comment and all its implications. She said, "Not yet. There hasn't been time."

"You used to make time for your friends," Emily said quietly.

"Em, I have to go. I'll see you tomorrow night."

As Emily finally hung up, Liz felt ashamed of herself. Emily had been a rock during the past few months and now Liz felt suddenly impatient with her friend's passive-aggressive tendencies. Emily had always been this way. Why hadn't it bothered Liz before? She chastised herself and promised that she'd be more patient in the future.

Meanwhile, why was Alex poking Harry Idle in the chest?

"WHY THE HELL didn't you call me?" Alex demanded.

Harry spread his hands. "How was I supposed to know you had problems last night?"

Alex told himself to calm down. He knew he shouldn't have jabbed at Harry's tempting midsection—he blamed frustration for his lapse. "So you just happened to look out the window at two in the morning, saw a strange car outside and someone opening our garage and thought, 'Oh, hey, just a burglar at the Chase house, no big deal'?"

"I told you," Harry said, eyeing Alex warily. "I saw the car on my way to the bathroom and thought maybe someone had broken down or got a flat tire and then on my way back to bed, I saw someone lift your garage door but I didn't put the two together and I didn't know that it wasn't you over there getting in your garage and since when is that cause for alarm?"

Alex took a deep breath. If Harry had only called, maybe Alex could have caught this shadowy someone. He said, "How about the car? Did you notice anything particular about it like the make or color or maybe the license plate?"

"It was just a dark car, that's all."

The sheriff's car was white with a black and gold stripe and a big insignia on the door. On the other hand, if the sheriff had mischief or worse on his mind, would he have used an official car?

"Did you look outside when it peeled out of here?"

"I must have been back asleep by then. Didn't hear a thing."

Alex said, "Why did Devon Hiller invite you to the party celebrating his mall's twentieth anniversary party?"

Harry took a moment to think as he produced a crumpled pack of cigarettes from his shirt pocket and lit one up. The ritual of popping a cigarette in his mouth, flicking a lighter, forming a small weather screen—all this focused Alex's attention on Harry's hands. It was impossible not to notice how big they were. No way could this man have stuffed those paws into the missing gloves.

As the acrid smoke drifted upward, Harry said, "I go out sometimes with the gal who does his gardening. She wangled me an invite. Truth is, I wanted to go to that party and see where the old goat lived. Pretty fancy place he had. We left early so I missed your little woman telling him off. I ate as much as I could hold, drank a whole bottle of his champagne and left. Must have been cheap champagne, too, 'cause it gave me a hell of a hangover.''

"When we talked the other day, why didn't you tell me you were there?"

"You didn't ask," Harry said as if explaining something elementary. He took a puff and added, "It's cold out here. I know it's not noon yet, but come on inside and I'll make us a couple of hot toddies."

"I don't drink, Harry. I'm sorry I got so steamed and…er, poked you."

"That's okay." Dropping the half-burned cigarette to the ground and grinding it out with the heel of his boot, he added, "Least you didn't stab me, right?" He followed this awful joke with a hearty laugh that started a coughing spasm.

Alex grumbled a goodbye and went home.

It HAD BEEN almost a month since Liz had actually been to the mall, choosing to take care of business by computer or over the telephone instead. The truth was that she had been having less and less to do with the place, giving Jane Ridgeway increasing responsibilities.

As canned music filled her head, she felt the same indecision she always felt. This mall and her uncle's house were pieces of her life, huge pieces in which she'd invested a lot of time and effort. It didn't seem right to abandon them to strangers, to sell out, to move on. It didn't seem right to turn her back on the two things that had formed the continuity of her existence.

And yet, sometimes she ached to do just that.

Alex had decided to stay in the food court with a couple of tacos and his cell phone. He had a list of friends to call with his new number, so Liz felt no need to rush. Apparently, Alex didn't think she was in any danger while roaming around inside the mall with a few hundred anxious shoppers. Obviously, he'd never tried to cut through the line waiting for hot cinnamon rolls.

At the Santa station, the mall split in two directions, and she followed the tiled floor to the right, feeling guilty that she didn't foray to the left wing first to look in on Emily. Well, she'd see both Emily and Ron tomorrow night, she reasoned, and once this whole ordeal was over, she'd be the best friend they ever had.

Meanwhile, she spotted two members of her security department posing as shoppers, watching for shoplifters. Way to go, team!

The new kitchen store was up and running and looked to be doing a rousing business. Liz knew how vital it was to the store's success to take advantage of holiday sales and judging by the lines, things were looking good.

She walked between rows of gadgets, pausing for a second to eye a potato masher, not because she needed one but because the thought of mashed potatoes reawakened the hunger the cinnamon rolls had kindled.

"May I help you find something?" a pleasant woman in her early fifties asked. She was artificially blond, plump and pink, a candy confection of a woman. She studied Liz for a second and added, "Aren't you Elizabeth Chase?"

Liz admitted she was. She recognized the other woman as Marie Poe, half of the team who had opened the store. Ron had introduced them to Liz when they came in to sign their lease.

"If you're not too busy, I'd like to talk to you and Doris. Is she here?"

Marie looked over her shoulder. "She's behind the cash register."

"You're really busy," Liz said. "This doesn't concern mall business, so maybe I should come back—"

Marie patted Liz's tummy. "Honey, you don't look as though you have coming back in you. I'll get one of my daughters to stand in for Doris. Excuse the pun, but we'll wrap while we rap. Hold on."

Marie disappeared into the crowd and Liz made her way to the back of the store, pausing only slightly to look at a gizmo that promised to puree everything from apples to zucchini, creating natural, healthy baby food. Hmm—.

Within a few moments, the two co-owners showed up. They produced a stool for Liz while they stood around a butcher block table normally used for cooking demonstrations, but commandeered now for a wrapping station. They both immediately chose what appeared to be already purchased gifts and tore off sheets of their trademark glossy red paper. Liz asked them about the night her uncle died.

"Oh, dear, such a shock," Marie said as she folded and taped the end papers over a huge box that held a food processor. "Doris and I left right after the altercation between you and your uncle and your husband." She looked embarrassed and glanced at her partner.

''Exactly at nine forty-five,'' Doris said. She had embraced her gray hair, cut it short, wore it severe. The lines on her face suggested she was a lifetime smoker. ''The cops pinned us down on this right after it happened,'' she said. ''Marie, hand me that tape.''

Liz bit her lip as she thought. That put them at the party and potentially on scene. Who was to say if they left when they said they did? They were obviously close and might cover for each other or even commit a crime together.

But what about her scarf? Could she have left it at her uncle's house? Might they or someone else have used it simply because it was handy? It didn't explain the sabotaged stairs, but maybe the two events weren't connected.

Thinking now of motive, she said, ''I think I remember you guys had a store downtown several years ago.''

''Kitchens Etc.,'' Doris said, slapping a silver seal on the finished product, attaching the receipt and starting in on another.

''The funny thing is,'' Marie added, ''your uncle more or less killed our business, didn't he, Doris?''

''He opened up this mall and no one came downtown anymore.''

''I hated him back then,'' Marie said. ''It wasn't bad enough he took all our business away, but he was so dadburned nasty about it.'' She appeared to suddenly realize to whom she was talking and turned as red as the wrapping paper. ''I'm sorry. I know he was your uncle. Especially since your husband killed him, you must have a lot of sad feelings about…everything.''

''Marie,'' Doris said. ''Honestly.''

''It's okay,'' Liz told them. ''You were at the party,

you heard the words we exchanged. And, as a matter of fact, my husband had nothing to do with his death.''

Boy, did that feel good to say. She could see curiosity written on both of their faces. They'd have to live with it; she shouldn't have mentioned Alex's innocence to them and she wasn't going to compound the damage by explaining herself.

''The thing is,'' Marie said as she chose a set of steak knives as her next project, ''that both of us gave up working when we went belly-up. Doris went back to school and got her business degree and then opened Landers Title Company. I started having babies, five of them in eight years. Best time of my life. So, by the time Doris sold her business for a tidy profit and I inherited a small trust from my father, we realized how much we owed your uncle for forcing us to take different paths that ultimately led us right back to the beginning. We actually got along with him pretty good this time around. After all, he did own the mall, or he did until he died. Isn't that right, Doris?''

Doris shrugged.

Liz wondered at the shrug but said, ''I don't suppose you saw something at the party, something, oh, I don't know, suspicious or out of place?''

Marie said, ''Besides the big fight?''

Doris added, ''The only person we knew was the leasing agent, Ron Boxer.''

''And his sister,'' Marie said.

Frowning, Liz said, ''Emily Watts wasn't at the party.''

Doris nodded. ''That's what I keep telling *her*.''

''And *I* keep telling *her*,'' Marie said, ''that she was. Oh, don't get me wrong, I didn't know it was Emily at the time. We hadn't actually met. That didn't happen until later when she opened the yarn shop and started attending the store manager's meetings. It took me a few minutes to remember where I'd seen her before."

"You asked Emily and she told you she wasn't there," Doris insisted.

"But I saw her admiring that fantastic curio cabinet in your uncle's study. You remember the one, Liz."

"I remember it," Liz said. As soon as her uncle's estate was settled once and for all, she would have to catalogue his possessions. The thought was staggering— her uncle had been quite a collector.

For now, she made a note to ask Emily about the party, but it seemed to her that Marie must be mistaken, just as Doris said she was. Still, it wouldn't hurt to clear it up.

Liz put a hold on the gadget that pureed baby food and left the store, making her way past the Santa and the crowd of wiggling children waiting to sit in his lap, past the athletic shoe store and the card shop, stopping for a second to admire the array of lovely green and red satin dresses she was still months from being able to squeeze into, moving at last to Nature's Knits.

Emily's store was one of the narrow ones, most of the front taken up by a large window and a glass door. The window was filled with knitted articles of clothing and toys, all done in beautiful rich colors seemingly plucked from the earth, the air, the sea. In deference to the season, a few crocheted white snowflakes the size of dinner plates were suspended in among the sweaters and caps.

A newcomer to Emily's staff was behind the counter, wrapping a gift for an elderly man who leaned on his cane. They both looked up when Liz entered. The man smiled and the woman nodded a greeting. She had a pierced bottom lip and spiked orange hair and couldn't have looked more out of place in a store specializing in vegetable-dyed yarns than if she'd just fallen off a spaceship. When Liz asked to speak with Emily, the girl shrugged.

"The boss left early," the salesgirl said as she taped the plain brown paper in place. Liz knew Emily liked to keep her wrappings simple to complement the earthy theme of her store. It made the wild-looking clerk's presence that much more interesting.

"I can tell her you came by if you want to write your name down," the woman said as she bound the package with several twists of twine, fastened a cinnamon stick on top with a casual bow, and stuck a green-and-gold store sticker in place. She presented it to the man who tucked it beneath one arm.

Liz couldn't stop staring at the bolt of twine. Natural colored twine.

Her head said twine was everywhere and nine-tenths of it had to be this color.

Her heart skipped a few beats.

"Want to leave a message?"

"Uh, no," Liz said. "No thanks."

She turned to leave, and then, feeling like a traitor to her friend, picked up two skeins of beet-dyed yarn and asked for them to be gift wrapped.

USING TWENTY FEET of his trusty rope, Alex dropped from the last remaining landing onto the rocks below. He knew he didn't have a lot of daylight left to find the piece of twine Liz had thrown toward the beach, but he had to try.

He flashed on the image of her approaching through the food court, her face so pale it was almost translucent.

She'd frantically told him about Emily being at her uncle's party—maybe—and the twine in the yarn shop.

He'd told her twine was everywhere, and it was. But if he could find the piece that had been used on Sinbad, they could compare it to Emily's, a sample of which Liz had procured by having something wrapped. He had no illusions of being able to declare unequivocally that it was the very same twine from the very same spool that had been used to anchor Sinbad to the stairs; his hope was that the differences would be vast enough to show that it *wasn't* the same.

Time was ticking away.

Liz was inside the house with the doors locked. She'd protested him coming to the beach alone; he'd circumnavigated her worries by waiting until, exhausted, she'd fallen asleep. He'd left her safe in their bedroom.

He scampered over the rocks and despite everything, felt a sense of joy and freedom at being this close to the cold Pacific Ocean. Icy spray tingled on his skin. The wind blew through his hair, its fingers cold and invigorating. Waves broke on the rocky beach and washed away with a rumble he loved. He came across a wide rock hidden by the curve of the land and recalled the moonlit night he and Liz had made love on the spur of the moment, seduced by the sounds and smells of the sea, seduced by their love for each other.

He turned his back on the past. The future was where he was headed, where he was determined to spend his life, not locked away in a cell, locked away from everything and everyone he cared about, locked into memories as his only comfort.

Taking a flashlight out of his pocket, he began searching each nook and cranny. Twine was so lightweight; the wind might have blown it anywhere, the rain might have driven it into a tiny crevice, the currents might have carried it north or south or halfway to Japan. It seemed an impossible task to find one little bit of twine.

And so it proved to be. He gave up as daylight faded everything to shades of gray and even the white rope he needed to climb to get back to the landing above began to disappear. He climbed up the big rocks and over a stranded section of stairs that had yet to be washed away. It was then he saw something flutter in the wind.

A twelve inch piece of string—no, twine—was wrapped around one of the rail supports, caught on a contorted nail. It was too short to be the piece he was looking for, but too coincidental to be unrelated. Perhaps Sinbad had chewed this piece free before Liz came along. He spent a few moments untwisting it, crammed it in his pocket and grabbed his rope for the ascent up the cliff.

Yanking it hard, anxious to see Liz, he staggered backward as the whole length came hurdling toward him.

LIZ AWOKE with a start. The house was twilight dark and silent. She glanced at the digital alarm clock and saw that it was after five o'clock.

The last thing she remembered was Alex rifling through drawers, searching for the flashlight he'd had just the night before. Apparently, she'd fallen asleep, and as the baby kicked and rolled inside her, she sat up, angry with herself for leaving Alex alone to go down to the beach on a fool's errand.

Now, after a rest, the twine at Emily's store seemed more a coincidence than some ominous portent of doom pointing a shaky finger at Emily of all people. Liz slipped on a sweater and made her way down the familiar hall and into the kitchen without turning on lights, anxious to keep her night vision intact. Sinbad yowled from his basket and she stopped to pet him and assure him how beautiful he was despite the raw wounds on his shaved neck and the ugly shaved area surrounding the stitches on his hip.

"I'll feed you in a few minutes," she assured him as she let herself out the back door and made her way carefully across the damp grass toward the bluff, expecting to see Alex's flashlight at any moment, heralding his return. Halfway there, she heard a noise behind her and jumped.

A shadow seemed to move in among all the other shadows. She stared into the gloom, straining to hear something that would explain away what had startled her: a neighbor's dog, a...well, a neighbor's dog.

"Alex?" she called.

A dark shape seemed to dispatch itself from the recesses of the back of her house and move toward her, silent and ominous. Liz felt her heartbeat accelerate and the desire to run was quelled only by the knowledge that running from anyone in her present condition was all but pointless. Still, she poised ready for flight.

She said "Alex," again, hopeful, but knowing he would never come at her like this. "Who's there?" she demanded, her hands unconsciously protecting her belly.

The shadow stepped close enough that she finally saw the shape of a man—a big man. Harry Idle's voice carried over the thumping roar of her heart.

"Liz?"

She almost crumbled with relief. "What are you doing out here, Harry?"

He moved very close, so close in fact, that she could detect the odor of stale cigarette smoke on his clothes.

"Your house is dark," he said, coming another step closer. Liz backed away. "What are you doing out here in the dark by yourself?" he added. "I'm surprised Alex lets you wander around like this. You could fall right off that cliff and kill yourself."

Outrage at his sexist remark fled in the face of a growing feeling of alarm. She said, "Why are you in our backyard?"

"I'm looking for you," Harry said, advancing as she retreated. "You know, you shouldn't be out here alone. It's dangerous. There might be someone out here in the dark, someone who wants to hurt you."

Like him?

"I think you should leave," she said, fighting to keep her teeth from chattering with fear. The bluff wasn't far away—the sound of the waves was more distinct and the edge more perilous. She couldn't keep backing up without looking where she was going and she couldn't afford to take her eyes off his face.

He grabbed her arm. "You'd better come with me."

She twisted free and tried to turn, but her feet slipped on the grass. She ended up on her hands and knees, twisting as much as she could to face her attacker.

Harry loomed over her, hands plucking at her sweater. She screamed and the next thing she knew, a light appeared, a man yelled, Harry disappeared and Ron leaned down beside her.

"Liz," he said, "are you hurt? Here, take my hand, come on now, get up slowly, be careful."

He pulled her to her feet. Liz felt like crying, not from pain but from relief. She held onto Ron's arm, swallowing her tears, facing Harry, shaking with outrage.

Ron said, "What in the hell were you doing to her?"

"I wasn't doing nothing," Harry insisted.

Liz tugged at Ron's arm. "I can't find Alex," she gasped.

Ron flashed his light on Harry who covered his face with his hands. "What did you do to Alex?" he said, his voice low and threatening.

"I didn't do anything to anybody," Harry said. "I was just looking out for her. You're here now, I'm leaving."

"Wait a minute," Liz said. "What do you mean that you were just looking out for me?"

"Your lights were all off and I thought I saw someone on your porch. I was going to call the cops but I thought I'd take a quick look for myself. You startled the hell out of me."

"Why didn't you just tell me this?" Liz demanded. "Why did you act so threatening?"

"I didn't act threatening."

"The hell you didn't," Ron said.

"I'm not taking any more of this," Harry said and turned to leave. Ron reached out as if to stop him, but Liz pulled him back. "Never mind Harry, Ron. Alex went to the beach a long time ago. The stairs are broken two thirds of the way down. He might have slipped or—"

"Stay here," Ron said as he started down the beach stairs.

She called, "Be careful," as she looked over her shoulder to make sure Harry Idle had really left.

ALEX TIED a waterlogged piece of driftwood to the end of the rope and, swinging it into the gloom above, aimed for the landing and the rail surrounding it. He'd been stuck on the beach for half an hour now. Every once in a while, the stick would thud on the landing and seem to catch, but it always came back and, a couple of times, damn near brained him.

He knew he was in no real danger. The tide was low and if need be he could hike down the beach and eventually find a gully or another way up the bluff. It would take a few hours, but it was doable. Only the potential of what was happening to Liz kept him swinging the rope.

Wasn't this one of the main reasons he'd bought that damn phone? What was the point of having the blasted thing if he forgot to carry it?

He'd examined the end of the rope with his flashlight and knew it hadn't been cut. Someone had loosened it or perhaps the knot he'd tied had worked itself open. That one was hard to believe. If there was one thing he knew about, it was tying knots and he'd bet a bundle that his had stayed in place.

He looked up when he heard the pounding on the stairs that signified someone was coming. A zigzagging light heralded help on the way, and he hoped against hope that it wasn't Liz, not so pregnant, not in the dark. Still, if she was on the stairs it meant she wasn't trapped in the house with a homicidal maniac, right?

"Liz?" he yelled.

A voice yelled back. A man's voice. "Are you hurt?" The light had stopped on the last landing.

"Is that you, Ron?"

"Yeah, it's me. Don't worry, Liz is fine."

Thank heavens. He said, "I'm going to throw up a rope. Loop it around the stanchion up there. Tie it off. Watch out for the stick tied to the end of it."

"You got it."

Within a few moments, he was at the landing, Ron's extended hand a welcome help as he climbed onto the wooden platform. He clapped Ron on the back, damn near hugged him. "Liz is okay?" were the first words he spoke.

"She's fine. When I got here, I found someone named Harry hassling her—"

Alex was off like a shot. Ron had left Liz alone with Harry lurking about? He took the stairs at breakneck speed, no easy task in the dark. He found Liz at the top, a small dark shape with a distinctive side profile, his wife and his baby—his life—and he ran to her, to them, gathering her into his arms, kissing the side of her head, holding her as close as he could.

"You okay? Ron said Harry—"

"I'm all right," she interrupted, but her voice sounded shaky.

Cupping her cheeks, he kissed her forehead. "What happened to you? You took so long, I was coming to see if you were hurt—"

"Trouble with the rope," he said.

Ron appeared just then and they all straggled toward the back of the house.

Ron said, "What in the devil is going on around here?"

Alex opened the door and switched on a light. Sinbad meowed and blinked his blue eyes. Ron leaned over the barricade to pat the cat and looked up at them.

"Emily came into my office this afternoon, very worried about Liz because of a phone conversation the two of them had had this morning. She said something about Liz finding Sinbad on the beach stairs…well, you know how cautious Emily is, how she worries about…things. I thought she was overreacting, but I agreed to come out here after work and check on you guys."

As he straightened up, he stared hard at each of them

in turn. "I tried calling from the car but no one was home. I didn't think much of it until I got here and found all the lights off and both your cars parked out front. As I was knocking on the door, I heard Liz scream. Harry was standing over her. It looked as though he was hurting her."

Alex felt a quake inside. Harry mauling Liz? He wanted to march across the street and tear Harry into bite-size pieces of fish food. As a matter of fact, what a dandy idea. He started moving toward the door, but Ron stepped in front of him.

"Better get out of my way," Alex said softly.

"Not until you calm down," Ron said.

Liz reached for his hand and he met her gaze. "I've been going over and over Harry's actions. I don't know, maybe I misinterpreted things. He said he saw someone over here and he was worried that you'd be mad at him again, so he came to investigate and maybe I startled him as much as he startled me."

Unwilling to cut Harry Idle one iota of slack, Alex thought of the intruder's car racing away in the middle of the night; it had been parked in front of Harry's house. He thought of Harry's two-decade-old grudge against Devon Hiller. He and Liz had more or less ruled Harry out because of the size of his hands as compared to the gloves and maybe even more because of his physical condition, which made the idea of him vandalizing the stairway seem ludicrous.

But what if Harry wasn't working alone?

What if he was in cahoots with the woman he said did Hiller's gardening, the one who had wangled him an invitation to the fateful party, the one who must be in pretty good physical condition to do her job. Or maybe someone else, maybe someone who worked at the mall and carried the same hatred in his or her heart that Harry did.

"I don't think he was really trying to hurt me," Liz said.

"Sorry, Liz, but I don't agree," Ron said.

Alex agreed with Ron, but he didn't say anything. Instead, his mind wrapped around the fact that, as usual, there wasn't a thing they could pin on anyone. He couldn't swear his knot hadn't come undone by itself, Liz couldn't swear Harry had done anything more than unwittingly frighten her.

They were still at square one.

Liz patted Ron's arm. "I'm fine," she told him. "I know Emily is worried about me, but please, reassure her I'm doing great."

Ron was not to be deterred. "And Sinbad," he said, eyebrows raised. "What happened to Sinbad, Liz?"

"His leg—"

"How about his neck? Come on, you can trust me, what happened to the little guy?"

Alex fought not to resent the familiar, friendly way Ron cajoled Liz and the smile that curved her lips in response. He made a mental bet with himself that Liz would hesitantly try to reassure Ron. He knew she hated the secrecy, the operating on a need-to-know basis that made such sense to him. The truth was a big issue with her, as was trust; she'd resented Alex for not trusting her when it counted most and he just couldn't see her turning away from that position when it concerned Ron. Ron had been the one she had depended on while he was away and Alex could sense her struggle with the desire to re-establish this cozy relationship that must have brought her such comfort.

He felt a spasm of jealousy followed by a sigh of sorrow.

And then, just as Alex expected her to launch into an explanation, she leaned back against him, just a little bit, hardly noticeable, but he felt the subtle shift of her weight and the warmth of her body as it grazed his. Her words supported her body language, as she spoke softly but firmly.

"It's like we said, Ron. Sinbad had a terrible accident, that's all."

Alex felt a swell of satisfaction.

Ron shook his head. "Listen," he said, serious now, gazing at them without a hint of humor in his eyes. "Sooner or later, this is all going to get to be too much for you guys. I don't know what's going on, but I do know that something is wrong that goes beyond Alex getting ready for a new trial. I hope you guys don't wait too long to ask for help." He looked directly into Alex's eyes and added, "I know something about allowing yourself to become…isolated. It can be dangerous. Not just for yourself, but for others. I—well, let's just say I have some experience in this facet of life. When you need to talk, I'll be here for you."

As Liz saw Ron to the door, Alex considered Ron's warning. Was he right? Was Alex jeopardizing Liz by not going to some law enforcement official, perhaps going so far as to bypass the sheriff if that were possible?

There other things to consider as well. The cat's situation and the sabotaged stairs weren't an accident. The stolen gloves, ditto. He had to consider the possibility that tonight, his rope *hadn't* come undone on its own, that Harry *had* seen someone lurking around the house. If it was true, there was a question begging to be asked:

How many more times could Liz's attacker screw things up?

Didn't the law of averages suggest that sooner or later, he or she would get it right, that sooner or later, Liz would die?

Why? What did she know?

Or was it something else?

Chapter Nine

As Ron's taillights disappeared down the road, Liz caught Alex's arm and said, "Did you find it?"

He extracted a piece of twine from his pocket and together they hurried back inside the house. As Alex headed to the bright lights of the kitchen, Liz retrieved the package she'd brought home from Emily's store.

The differences between the two samples of twine were immediately obvious. The twine from the beach stairs was the color of oats, that from the yarn shop, molasses. They were a different gauge as well, the stair twine being much sturdier and thicker.

"They're different," Liz said as she sank down on a kitchen chair, flooded with relief. "Emily had nothing to do with any of this."

Alex sat down opposite her and took her hands in his. He juggled them thoughtfully, as though weighing one against the other. "It would appear that way," he said at last.

"But…" she prompted, hearing it in his voice.

He released her hands and sat back in his chair. "But does it really mean anything?"

"I don't understand—"

"I mean, so what if the twines don't match? You and

I have a spool of green twine in the garage, a length of natural color in my glove compartment that came wrapped around something or other, and I found a bit of yellowish stuff in the junk drawer in the kitchen. Twine is twine and yet it isn't.''

She sighed deeply. He was right.

''I know it's next to impossible to imagine your friend, Emily, as some kind of fiend.''

''Yes, it is.''

''Or corruptible.''

Liz nodded, but as she did, she realized something had been tugging at her memory, something all these recent thoughts of Emily had brought to mind. Feeling her way, she said, ''I keep thinking about that day at Tony-O's. You were using the phone at the back of the restaurant. I came inside after talking to Sheriff Kapp. I was upset and when Ron asked why, I mentioned running into the sheriff. You should have seen Emily's face, Alex. Her eyes got wide and she looked all around the place. I thought she was worried about you, but then it became clear that Emily couldn't care less if Kapp nabbed you or not.''

''She's a sweetheart,'' he said dryly.

''I think the look of abject fear was for herself, not for you.''

''Why?''

''I can't imagine.''

''Maybe she has a trunkful of old parking violations.''

''Maybe she robbed a bank back in San Francisco before she moved up here.''

''Maybe she's in a witness relocation program.''

''With her brother?''

They smiled at each other, the playful banter relieving

some of the tension that had been building for the past hour or so.

"And what did you make of Ron's warning?" Alex added.

"You mean his comment about isolation, about knowing how it could work against you in the long run. Maybe it had to do with the time he spent caring for his dying mother. I've heard caregivers can become very isolated."

Alex's brow furrowed. "Liz, what do you really know about Ron? Or Emily, for that matter?"

"Well, we've both known Ron for eighteen months but for most of that time, he was simply another employee. Thanks to a background check before I hired him, I know where he used to work and that his former employers gave him good references. Since we've become friends, I've learned that he nursed his mother through a fatal illness and that his sister was involved in a messy divorce. I don't know much about Emily because I wasn't working much when she applied for a lease. She filled out the usual forms and Jane Ridgeway ran the background check and approved the lease. It was all slightly irregular, but my uncle had just died and I was on bed rest and you—"

"It's okay," he said, covering her hand with his own.

She looked at his lean, strong hand and fought the desire to put her head down on top of it. When he'd held her out in the yard, she'd felt so safe, his heart thumping because of the way he'd run up the stairs to make certain she was all right, his hands and lips incredibly hot and protective. He was constantly putting her welfare above his own.

Alex said, "Ron and Emily rallied to your side during

an extremely difficult time. I know you feel bad for even suspecting them, but we have to suspect everyone.''

''I've been a miserably selfish friend to both Ron and Emily,'' she said. ''I know so little about them and I've all but ignored them since you came home.'' The thought struck her like a bolt of lightning. If Alex ever had to go away again, she wouldn't be worthy of their friendship.

It couldn't be one of them. Why in the world would either one want to kill her uncle and implicate her? Now Roger Kapp, he was a different story. He might have been blackmailing her uncle; that might have led to murder and then a plan to frame her that Alex spoiled by confessing, but worked even better as he hated Alex. And then there was Harry Idle. Perhaps he got together with an old crony or his landscaping honey and plotted a savage revenge for Devon Hiller's tyranny. But could Ron or Emily or any one of the thirty people who would attend the staff Christmas party the next night do such things? It was inconceivable.

Suddenly ravenous, Liz rummaged in the refrigerator as Alex fed Sinbad, crooning over the little beast as though he was a baby. She hadn't been to the store in so long there was precious little to eat. She finally found a couple of servings of frozen onion soup in the freezer and popped them in the oven. An hour later, they sat down to steaming bowls of fragrant broth topped with croutons and stringy cheese.

''Delicious,'' Liz said.

''After dinner, I want to go across the street and talk to Harry,'' Alex said as he studied his soup. ''Don't worry,'' he added, a glint in his eye. ''I'm plenty calm now. I want to hear his explanation about his presence in our yard before he has time to embroider his story.''

Their eyes met as he added, "Why don't you come with me?"

She was only too happy to comply. It seemed nothing good ever happened when they were apart.

HARRY'S INADEQUATE porch light was on as usual and his car was parked in its customary spot in the driveway. A string of solid red lights draped forlornly across the front of the house brought little Christmas cheer and even less additional light. While the living room drapes were closed, Alex could hear the sounds of a television inside.

Holding Liz's hand and pointing out the cracked brick in the walkway, Alex knocked on the door, waited and knocked again. Beside him, teeth chattering, Liz rang the bell. It was cold enough that their condensed breath formed halos around their heads.

"He's in there," Alex said, knocking again.

"Maybe he just doesn't want to talk to us," Liz said.

"Tough. Have you ever been inside his house?"

"A couple of months ago. I made him macaroni and cheese when he had a sinus infection. This door opens into his living room."

After additional knocks brought no response, Alex tried the doorknob which twisted easily in his hand. They both peeked through a modest crack and saw the edge of an upholstered blue chair and a man's legs and feet, the latter encased in brown socks. Several apparently empty beer cans littered the floor.

Alex called out, "Harry? You in there? Can we come in and talk to you?"

There was no answer, nor did the feet stir.

Alex pushed the door the rest of the way open.

"Do you think we should do this?" Liz whispered.

"Absolutely. If Harry drank himself into a stupor, he might need help. Trust me, I have a lot of experience with this. My dad passed out almost every night."

In the flickering blue light of the television, they found Harry Idle sitting in his chair, eyes closed, chin touching his barrel chest, one hand wrapped around a beer can. He was wearing a dingy gray sweater and black jeans, a striped blue-and-green knitted afghan thrown haphazardly across his lap as though he'd settled down for a night of drinking and TV. Alex immediately crossed the room, stepping over and around the cans, bending down next to the chair as Liz switched on a light and turned off the television.

The memories this scenario brought back to Alex were all sharp and unpleasant. "Harry?" he said, touching the older man's shoulder. Harry slumped even further.

Liz was suddenly beside him, awkwardly bending down and retrieving something from the floor beside the chair. "It's a prescription bottle," she said breathlessly. "For a sedative. Alex, it's empty."

And suddenly it was clear to Alex that this wasn't a case of drunkenness but something far worse. He swept his finger through Harry's mouth, checking for an obstruction in his airway. Lowering his head, Alex felt the slightest exhalation against his cheek. He checked Harry's wrist for a pulse and when that wasn't satisfactory, put two fingers against his neck. The pulse was there but reedy at best.

"Call for an ambulance, tell them possible drug overdose," he said as he gently pulled Harry onto the floor. "Read them the information off the prescription bottle," he added, as he tilted Harry's chin back and began ventilating. His only concern was to keep Harry Idle breathing until the experts arrived.

He was barely aware of Liz dialing 9-1-1.

As Liz dressed for the mall staff Christmas party, she heard Alex on the phone with the hospital, trying to get additional news on Harry's condition. Judging from his end of the conversation, he wasn't meeting with much success.

She'd bought her dress over the Internet and until this moment, had never actually tried it on. Looking in the mirror, she found that it fit all right, but that the midnight-blue color was much darker than it had appeared on the computer monitor. In addition, she thought as she tugged at the long sleeves, the velvet material was heavy and cloying. She pulled up on the neckline, rather startled by the new swelling fullness of her breasts.

Alex and she had spent the night before in the same bed, but once again, he'd not undressed or gotten under the covers. She felt safe with him so close—safe and frustrated. The day-to-day tension between them was lessening, but at night, lying in the dark and hearing him breathe, feeling the weight of his body on the blankets next to her, being so close and yet so far away, the tension built to the point where she found sleeping damn near impossible. She wanted him to go back to the futon mattress and stop taunting her with what she knew she shouldn't have; on the other hand, she didn't want him to move an inch farther away.

He gave her room to dress in privacy, he barely touched her, yet he was kind and attentive. Was it finding poor Harry on death's doorstep that had distracted him or was it something deeper and more terrible? Had they really grown so far apart? When and if they finally figured out what was going on, would they have a marriage to salvage?

She applied lipstick and turned as Alex entered the room. Somehow he'd managed to put more color on his face in a few days of foggy, rainy freedom than she had during the entire week of their tropical honeymoon. The dashing tuxedo she'd bought him last Christmas and which fit him now better than ever, didn't hurt his swashbuckling dark good looks, either.

He looked like James Bond.

She looked like Miss Moneypenny's washed-out kid sister. Correction, pregnant kid sister.

"You look stunning," Alex said as he stroked her hand. She waited for him to pull her into his arms, but he didn't. "I've always heard that pregnant women glow but I never believed it before tonight. Your face is radiant."

As always, he managed to infuse his voice with sincerity. The man was amazing. Or nearsighted.

She said, "What did the hospital say about Harry?"

"Not much," he told her. He moved to his bureau and snapped on his watch. "Same as this morning," he added. "Harry's in a drug-induced coma, except now they report that his daughter is at the hospital with him."

"I'm glad his daughter came."

"So am I. She can keep an eye on Harry."

"What do you mean, keep an eye on Harry?"

He moved back beside her. "I mean that maybe Harry had a little help taking those pills."

"I looked for a suicide note last night."

"So did I, after the paramedics came and took over. But the sheriff's car was there this morning. There's little chance now that there'll be any proof left to find."

Liz frowned. "Why would the sheriff—"

"Because maybe Sheriff Roger Kapp is the figure Harry swore he saw. Maybe he was still in the shadows and heard Harry tell you and Ron Boxer all about it. Maybe Kapp was afraid Harry would recall more as time went by.'' He ran a hand through his hair and added, ''I guess I'm going to have to bite the bullet and talk to the sheriff.''

''Do you want me to—''

''No way. I'll go see him.''

''If there's any question that Harry didn't swallow those pills on his own, the sheriff will find a way to blame you whether or not he's the one who did it. You know that, don't you?''

''And he'll have Ron Boxer to testify that I was mad enough to do it, too.''

''But you never left my side,'' Liz said as she tried to fasten a small diamond solitaire.

Alex took the chain from her. As he secured it, his hands grazed the back of her neck and their eyes met in the reflection of the mirror.

There's love between us, she found herself thinking. *Deep, abiding love. The only question is whether or not it will be enough.*

He seemed to read her mind, for he lowered his head and kissed the nape of her neck and she closed her eyes.

''Let's go,'' he whispered, his breath tickling her skin, sending shivers, causing all sorts of trouble within her.

She opened her eyes and nodded.

AN HOUR LATER, they pulled up under the awning in front of the Egret Inn. Built to overlook the bay, the structure was as glistening white and as ethereal-looking as its namesake, many of whom nested in the tall trees nearby.

Alex had to more or less pull her from her car and as Liz let him grab hold of her arm and yank, she realized the low-riding sports car would have to go. It was one thing for her to need the jaws of life to get out of the thing; it wouldn't be long before she'd need a vehicle with a back seat big enough to hold a baby car seat and a trunk large enough to carry a stroller and heaven knew what else.

The valet parking attendant whizzed away in her car as Alex opened the tall etched glass door and ushered her inside. He took her coat and gave it to an attendant. Squeezing her hand, he said, "I'll take care of everything, honey, you just do your normal stuff and I'll skulk around in the shadows asking probing questions, okay?"

She knew he intended to lighten the mood with playful talk, but there were edges of truth in what he said that made her too nervous to appreciate his efforts. She usually enjoyed these parties, but this was the first time since her uncle died that she'd attended one and never before as the host.

"Try not to worry," he said.

"That's a tall order to fill, Alex. Everything seems to be falling apart around us. If Harry tried to kill himself, does that mean he regretted trying to hurt me or killing my uncle or was he just depressed because the winter TV schedule is so lousy?"

"We don't know for sure what happened to Harry. Maybe he got drunk and took the last couple of sleeping pills without realizing what he was doing. Without access to his toxicology reports, we're in the dark."

"So what do we do?"

"I'll go to the hospital and talk to the sheriff or maybe Harry's daughter, but for tonight, we proceed as planned."

"Which means while you're trying to find motive and opportunity to prove one of my employees murdered my uncle, I'm supposed to hand out Christmas bonuses.'' She realized she was whining as she added, ''I hate doing this in such a public way. I think they should be sent via the mail or given out at work.''

''So why do it this way?'' Alex asked.

Liz frowned for a second. ''It's always been done this way.''

''Because your uncle liked lording his power over everyone else. You don't feel comfortable with that.''

She smiled. ''You're right, I don't. Okay, next year if I'm still in charge, I'll do it my way.''

''Good enough.''

They entered the designated room which momentarily brought a sense of peace to Liz's overburdened mind and heart. The golden paneling highlighted the centerpiece, three large trees of staggered heights, each decked out with pure yellow lights and white birds, the snowy-looking ground around their trunks twinkling with glittering pine cones. Several round tables circled the trees and the white china, gold tableware and crystal goblets shimmered and sparkled.

''It looks beautiful,'' Liz said.

''Very classy,'' Alex agreed, then frowned and whispered, ''Head's up, three o'clock.''

Liz smiled at the use of their old code for approaching disaster, and turned to the three o'clock position in time to see Emily headed their way.

''Be nice,'' she whispered out the side of her mouth.

Alex leaned down and nuzzled her ear. ''I'm always nice,'' he said with a nibble.

ALEX TOOK one last deep breath of Liz's heavenly scent, and raised his head. Surprise, surprise, Emily scowled at him.

Liz put a little distance between herself and him which annoyed the hell out of him. She was acting a little odd tonight which he thought perfectly understandable given the circumstances—Harry's condition and the fact that they'd found him, the uncomfortable position of ''boss lady'' she'd had to assume—but he was determined to stick to their agenda and question the people around him. People who had worked closely with Devon Hiller, people who might have grown to resent and hate him enough to kill him.

His resolve was strengthened by his desire to avoid talking to Emily. Alex didn't know for sure why Emily was so protective of Liz but he suspected it was for one of two reasons. The first was relatively easy to take: Emily wasn't convinced that Alex wasn't a murderer pulling a fast con on his guileless wife. Hence, she felt protective and would back down once she accepted the fact he was innocent.

The second was harder: Emily wanted Liz as a sister-in-law. If he didn't figure out this mess and save his own skin, it seemed possible that sooner or later, Emily would get her wish. Not right away, but someday. How could he blame his beautiful wife for wanting someone with whom to share her life? She knew Ron, she liked him. How could he deny her a contented and happy future?

How could he stand living if it ever happened? How could he bear another man, any other man, making love to *his* wife, fathering *his* child? He'd rather be dead.

Liz and Emily hugged and Emily spared him a quick smile with all the brilliance of a thoroughly doused fire. Turning to Liz, her voice scolding, she said, ''I can't believe you went down those beach stairs. That's so dangerous. You must be more careful. Promise me if you need anything, anything at all, you'll call Ron and not strike out on your own. You can depend on him.''

Alex had the urge to punch Emily in the mouth. Honestly, his desire to pummel everyone he met was getting out of hand. He met Liz's gaze and recognized a pleading look that asked him to be tolerant, so he tried a different approach.

''That's a stunning necklace you're wearing, Emily.'' What woman didn't like a compliment? It was the truth, too. From a thick gold chain hung an enameled gold pendant of a prancing horse with pearls dangling from hoofs, tail and jeweled saddle. It looked museum quality and truly striking against Emily's green dress. With a sideways glance at Liz, Emily tucked it beneath her neckline.

So much for conciliation.

Liz said, ''I was at the mall yesterday, Em. You weren't in your store.''

''I went out to do some shopping,'' Emily said, more or less turning her back on Alex. Her rudeness brought out a stubborn streak in Alex and he resolved to stay by Liz's side until Emily wandered away.

Liz turned so that Alex was once again included in the group. She said, ''Were you buying your dress? It looks new. It's lovely.''

''Do you like it? Green is my favorite color, but this shade is never easy to find. I had to go to Myers Junction to that little boutique.''

''Which one?''

Emily bit her bottom lip and shrugged. ''I'm not sure.''

''It's very becoming but I thought I saw something like it in a window close to your own store,'' Liz added, frowning.

"Oh, yeah." Emily lowered her voice but Alex caught her next words. "I don't much care for Alicia O'Donnell. She's a snob. I don't like to shop in her store."

Liz nodded and Alex realized he wasn't the only person Emily didn't approve of.

Meanwhile, Liz seemed determined to sleuth. "I saw Marie Poe and Doris Landers when I went into their store to buy a machine that purees baby food. I won't need it for several months, but I thought I'd like to have it on hand. Anyway, Marie told me that she saw you at my uncle's party. She said that you were in his den, by the curio case. I didn't know you had attended."

Emily rolled her eyes and said, "I didn't. I hadn't even moved to town yet. What would I be doing at your uncle's party?"

"I thought maybe you came with Ron."

"Marie told me this same story when we met for the first time at a store manager's meeting. I told her then she was mistaken, but Marie is a space cadet, if you know what I mean. It's a good thing she teamed up with Doris. I can't imagine Marie is capable of running anything but her mouth."

Liz didn't say a word. If this was typical Emily, Alex thought to himself, she couldn't have many friends. She seemed to be a bitter woman with a nasty streak and a third reason for her distrust of him came to mind—she was jealous of Liz's shifting alliance from Emily back to himself. Liz was the kindest woman Alex had ever known—it was her most outstanding trait as far as he was concerned. No doubt she had put up with Emily's snide comments out of compassion and now Emily was terrified to lose her one friend in this town.

Could Emily have orchestrated the events at their

house to sway Liz away from him? Might the incidents that occurred after he came home be unrelated to Devon Hiller's murder? Did Emily hate him enough to somehow rig the stairs so that he would fall and then be appalled to discover that it was Liz who had come close to dying and not him?

He eyed her with this in mind and thought it possible. The woman was young and healthy and though she didn't look particularly athletic, she didn't look weak and incapable, either. It was a little bit of a stretch to imagine her using Sinbad as bait, but no more so than imagining Harry Idle concocting a plot of evildoing that required actual exertion or Sheriff Kapp framing Liz for murder.

So many unknowns.

As the mall maintenance superintendent sidled up to Liz, and Emily turned her attention to another couple, Alex started making his rounds. It was awkward, to say the least, as everyone there knew exactly who he was and of what he'd been accused. Okay, and to what he'd confessed. He persevered but discovered only that Devon Hiller had had few wholehearted admirers and that Liz was well liked. Neither revelation came as much of a surprise.

During a splendid sit-down seafood dinner, he asked still more questions of the man and woman on either side of him. She was someone new on the staff, excited about her job in advertising. Her husband worked out of town and wasn't much of a talker. Neither of them had a single interesting insight when it came to the death of Devon Hiller. Giving up on sleuthing, he cast longing looks at his gorgeous wife who sat at another table, surrounded by people who seemed to hang on her every word. It suddenly dawned on Alex that Liz would soon become a very wealthy and powerful woman, attracting people impressed by such things.

Better they should be impressed by her generous spirit.

Ron approached him right after Liz had distributed the Christmas bonus checks. He held the long envelope in one hand. "This will come in handy," he said with a smile. "Your wife is more generous than her uncle."

"Yes, she is," Alex agreed.

"Not that I wouldn't like to be in the position of never having to worry about another nickel," Ron added. "A life of leisure would give me more time to pursue my hobbies."

Alex nodded, but couldn't really empathize. These months of professional inactivity where he'd been downright ostracized by the fire department had been terrible for him. Liz had enough money to keep them both comfortable, but that wasn't the point. He missed getting a paycheck with his name on it, missed going to work, missed his cohorts and the work they did together. He would gladly trade this party and tuxedo for a three alarm fire and his turnouts.

To Ron, he replied politely, "I guess I don't know what your hobbies are."

"Well, I know you're quite the sportsman," Ron said. "Liz talks about how you hike and climb and play ball. Me, I like biking. Races sometimes, but mostly just touring. It's great to be out on the road. Sometimes I go south past Myers Junction, down to Fern Glen. Lots of antique shops down that way which happens to be my second passion. It's a pricey hobby, though, so I mostly look and dream."

"You're a real renaissance man."

Ron nodded in Liz's direction. "That's what your

wife says, too." Lowering his voice, he added, "Listen, how is she really doing?"

Alex stifled a wave of jealousy. He'd expected the conversation to drift to Liz but that didn't mean he liked it. He said, "She's doing well."

"Not too upset about last night?"

"You mean Harry Idle attacking her?" When Ron nodded, Alex realized that he didn't know about Harry's destiny with a stomach pump. Alex added, "No, she's fine. Thanks, by the way, for rescuing us both."

Ron waved away the thanks as he tucked the bonus envelope in the inside pocket of his jacket. "Just glad I could help. Say, I'd like to talk to you about something," he added.

Alex steeled himself for some kind of intimate discussion concerning Liz. He said, "Sure."

"It's about Emily," Ron said, staring down at his shoes.

While Alex didn't want to talk about Liz, he wanted to talk about Emily even less. Swallowing a sigh, he said, "What's up?"

"My sister is, well, she's gotten it into her head that I'm interested in Liz. Romantically, that is." Ron looked up, seemingly stuck for words. Suddenly attentive, Alex waited for Ron to continue.

"I admit, I do find your wife extremely appealing. What man wouldn't? And for a time there, I thought that she and I might, well, you know. I'm aware that Emily encouraged Liz to file for divorce. I want you to know I didn't know Emily had a thing to do with that until just recently. I gather Liz and you are reconciled."

Alex managed a nod. Liz had never said a word to him about Emily's involvement with her decision to seek a divorce. Confused and feeling oddly betrayed, he muttered, ''We aren't worrying about this right now. There are other, larger, concerns.''

''No kidding,'' Ron said. ''I'll try to get Emily to cool it a little. She gets a bee in her bonnet and there's no stopping her.'' Ron laughed, and added, ''There's a phrase I haven't heard since my mother died. I bet I've never actually used it before. Wonder where it came from.''

''Just imagine how agitated but determined to do something about it you would be if there was a bee trapped in your hat,'' Alex said. He forced a smile. He'd been under the impression that Liz was oblivious to Emily's fantasies concerning Ron. If Liz knew all about it, did that mean she had been or might even still be interested in Ron?

His head said, *No way.*

But she'd cried when she kissed him.

His heart didn't know what to say.

And what about Ron? Was he putting out feelers, trying to discern if Liz might be available sometime soon? Was he in love with her or with her coming wealth? Why was he telling Alex all this, putting his sister in a bad light, admitting that if things were different, he'd pursue Liz? Could Ron be behind the murder and the last few days of trouble for some mysterious reason?

Alex felt as though he was beginning to see kitty kickers and assassins behind every tree. He glanced down at Ron's hands. Deciding to try the direct approach, he said, ''Your hands aren't as big as mine.''

Ron wrinkled his brow and glanced at his hands, then at Alex's hands. ''I guess,'' he said, clearly stumped by what this had to do with anything.

Alex sighed to himself. *Nothing, that's what.*

And following on the heels of that discouragement

came a newfound determination. Christmas was coming. He was tired of feeling bleak, his baby was due in less than three weeks. He needed real information. He needed to know more about Ron Boxer and everyone else who had attended that party. He needed to know what—or who—had pushed Harry Idle over the edge; he needed to understand the nature of Sheriff Kapp's blackmail scheme and how it may have backfired into murder; he needed to see Devon Hiller's house again, his den, retrieve Liz's scarf, try to find a clue there that he and the sheriff had both missed or that the sheriff had inadvertently left when—and if—he set the stage to frame Liz.

And, too, there was the issue of the upcoming retrial. His lawyer had left messages; he wanted an appointment to discuss "strategy."

What strategy? Lacking positive proof to clear himself without implicating Liz, there could be no strategy.

There was a lot to do, there wasn't a lot of time.

Chapter Ten

While Alex went to the hospital to try to talk to Harry or his daughter, Liz flicked on the computer. He'd checked all the locks before he went and made her promise not to leave the house alone. It promised to be a very long day following a very long night.

Alex had been restless when they got home, pacing the hall long after she fell into bed. He'd been up before her this morning, out working on the fence with a vengeance, as though he thought he might have to leave it for good at any moment. It scared her to see him so focused, so determined, as though he was worried that time was running out.

After breakfast, he'd announced they were stepping up the pace and that included researching the backgrounds of everyone remotely connected to Devon Hiller. She'd had to point out they didn't have the time or resources for all that.

In the end, they'd agreed to concentrate on people who had worked for Devon Hiller as mall staff employees and on those who held leases for the smaller, more personal stores; those employed by her uncle for private services such as housecleaning and grounds maintenance; the sheriff; Harry Idle and his daughter.

As she had easy access to the employment records from the mall, that's where she started. Though her main interest was in ruling out Ron and Emily, she made herself start alphabetically.

Ron's name came up third, and she reviewed the facts. He'd been born in the San Francisco Bay area, just as he'd told her. He'd attended college there and held several jobs before moving to Ocean Bluff and coming to work for Harbor Lights Mall eighteen months before, citing personal reasons for the relocation, which Liz knew meant his mother's death. If there was anything wrong with his employment record it was simply that he'd held so many jobs which sometimes indicated a person who had difficulty getting along with fellow workers. She could remember asking him about it and believing him when he told her that during his mother's protracted illness, he'd lost jobs due to taking time off. As his mother was no longer alive, he was anxious to settle down.

He was a conscientious employee whom everyone seemed to like and a dependable friend, so she'd never second-guessed her decision to hire him.

By the time Liz reached Emily Watts's name, she was getting blurry eyed and worried about what was taking Alex so long at the hospital. She gave Emily's forms a quick glance, stopping only when it came to the background check that she'd never seen before. When Emily had moved to town and applied for a concession, Liz had been in the very pit of despair, her uncle newly dead, her husband refusing to see her, her own body rebelling at her pregnancy. She just hadn't had much to do with mall business for a while and Jane Ridgeway and Ron had covered for her until she felt better.

Now she saw that Emily was only eighteen months

older than her brother and had had a different last name as a child. Apparently, Ron and Emily were half sister and brother. They'd never mentioned this fact, but why should they?

Another notation was more worrisome. Emily had a police record.

Emily?

There was no explanation of what the record was for. It might be those parking tickets she and Alex had joked about, but it might be something worse, as well. It was odd that there wasn't additional information, but perhaps Ron had shielded his sister from scrutiny by being honest but not thorough. Liz had a hard time thinking it was for anything serious.

And then she thought of the way Emily had reacted to the knowledge that the sheriff was nearby. Liz realized she'd have to dig further.

She was reading all about Meg Miller, the woman who ran Miller's Landscaping and was still caring for the Hiller estate, when she heard a key in the lock. She made it to the living room just as Alex came through the front door.

"How's Harry?" she asked.

He took off his jacket and faced her with his hands in his jeans pockets. "The same," he said, his voice as crisp as the outside temperature. "They wouldn't let me see him. I did meet his daughter, Patty, though. She's fresh out of rehab and seems straight, at least for the time being. She seemed very appreciative that you and I found him in time and passes along her thanks. Apparently, the sheriff hasn't been around since she got there."

Liz couldn't help but say, "Good."

"Not good," he said, walking into the kitchen. She

followed him. "I need to ask him about Harry. I need to know for sure if he tried to commit suicide. I stopped by the station, but he wasn't there, either."

"I guess the man has a private life. It is the weekend, you know."

"I guess it is," he said, opening cupboard after cupboard. He apparently didn't find what he was looking for. As he peered into the refrigerator, he said, "Listen, when you picked up that prescription bottle, did you happen to notice the date on which it was filled? If it was recent, that would give us an indication of how many pills he took."

"I didn't think to look," she said.

"I know some of the paramedics," he said. "Even though they might not talk to me, they might talk to Dave. Meanwhile, what did you find out about our erstwhile sheriff? Can you access your uncle's files from your computer? We need to know what Roger Kapp had on your uncle."

"I haven't gotten around to that yet. I did the mall first and am just now starting in on private individuals. I'll get into Uncle Devon's files next."

"Great." He closed the refrigerator and, hitching his hands on his waist, looked around the small room as though expecting a new cupboard full of yummy tidbits to appear. With a sigh, he added, "Well, what did you find out about everyone else? Anything interesting?"

Much as she hated to, given his continuing negative relationship with Emily, she admitted she'd discovered evidence of some kind of criminal record in Emily's background check.

"Fantastic!" he said. "Cross your fingers they got her for animal cruelty or tampering with beach stairs."

Liz picked up her coat from the back of the chair

where she'd left it the night before. Unable to stand the thought of facing the computer again, she said, "I'll treat you to lunch at the fish and chips place, then how about we go see Emily and ask her?"

He straightened slowly. "You mean actually go to Emily's house?"

"Yes. I know she doesn't go into the store on Sundays."

"But her house? I don't know—"

"Chicken."

He produced a half smile. "She doesn't like me."

"I know. Aren't you curious why? Let's ask her that, too."

"Let's not. I have several theories about it and frankly, I don't think I want to know the truth."

"Cluck, cluck, cluck," Liz said.

He grabbed her hand and pulled her close, steadying her when she almost stumbled, both of them laughing. For a second, it was like old times as she smiled in anticipation of a kiss.

He did kiss her, but it was on the cheek and not the mouth. A new wave of anxiety attacked her, or perhaps more accurately, another wave of the same old thing. Since she'd given him the impression she was ready to resume a sexual relationship and he'd pulled away, he'd been kind of distant. He looked deep into her eyes now and she couldn't tell what he was thinking, didn't have a clue if he found her desirable or not.

It was one thing, she thought, to be cautious yourself. It was another thing entirely to have someone you care about treat you with the same wariness.

"Emily wants you as a sister-in-law," he said softly.

"That isn't true—"

"Yes, it is. Last night Ron told me he found out that

Emily was the one who encouraged you to file for divorce.''

"I'm a grown-up," Liz said, though she hadn't realized Ron hadn't known about Emily's endorsement all along. She added, "Emily supported my decision, but Alex, it was *my* decision, not Emily's."

"I know—"

"Do you?" she interrupted, leaving the warmth of his embrace, backing up against the barrier that kept Sinbad from roaming on his pinned leg. The cat yowled in anticipation of additional attention or something to eat, but she didn't even look at him. Instead, she stared hard into Alex's blue eyes. "You still think I don't have a speck of self-determination."

"That's not true."

"*I* wanted to go forward with my life. *I* wanted to build a new future. Not Emily, not Ron, *me*. Why is that so hard for you to believe?"

Returning her intense stare, he responded immediately. "Because it hurts," he said before looking away.

She reached out for his hand and held it in hers, rubbing her thumb over his knuckles. He had big, competent hands, hands that cradled her, hands that saved lives. "I know it hurts," she said softly.

He turned back to her, and this time he kissed her lips.

LIZ HADN'T BEEN to Emily's for a couple of weeks, since before Alex came home, a real departure from the months before where visits between their homes had been relatively common. Once again, Liz felt a pang of guilt for ignoring Emily, whose rude behavior toward Alex last night had driven even more of a wedge between the two women. She also felt guilty for the phone call she'd made from the fish and chips place, asking Emily if she could stop by but not mentioning the fact that Alex was with her.

Emily lived in a duplex butted tightly against Ron's. The two residences were mirror images of each other, two stories high with kitchen, half bath and living area on the bottom, two bedrooms and a full bath upstairs. Ron used his spare room as a painting studio and Emily used hers for needlework projects. In the past, Liz had envied them their close relationship.

Now? Now she wondered if she really knew them at all.

Both buildings were strung with Christmas lights in such a way it appeared as though the same person had decorated both. An illuminated Santa Claus and his sleigh straddled the property line.

Emily opened the door with a smile that quickly faded when Alex offered a pleasant, "Hi."

She looked at Liz, her face flooded with disappointment. "I thought we were going to have an intimate talk, like old times," she said, turning into the predominantly green room. The carpet, the walls, the furniture, even Emily's hand-knit sweater were all different shades of the same hue. The decor had always been this way and Liz wasn't sure why she hadn't really noticed it before. Perhaps she'd been too numb to notice much of anything.

She recalled Emily's remark that Ron had suggested new furniture and wondered if he found all this green a little suffocating. In a place as perpetually damp as Ocean Bluff, green upon green was an odd choice.

There was a tray set up on a low table in front of the sofa. Liz noticed an old-fashioned teapot and china covered with roses, a plate of lemon cookies, delicate cups resting on fragile saucers.

"Just you and Liz?" Alex said.

Emily nodded.

He pointed at the tray, at the three cups, and raised his eyebrows.

There was a sudden knock on the door and Ron let himself in. He smiled when he saw Liz and held out a hand to Alex. "Great to see you two again so soon," he said. His glance went to the tray. "Em, looks like you'd better fetch another cup."

"I'll...I'll get it," Emily said, and rushed into the kitchen.

"I didn't tell her Alex was with me," Liz said. "I should have told her. I'm sorry."

Ron gestured at the sofa. "No, no. Don't worry about it. Emily has a few ideas it's about time she got over. Seeing you guys together will be good for her. When she called me a few minutes ago and asked me to come, I didn't know what she had in mind. I'll just go and see if she needs help." He excused himself and joined his sister as Liz and Alex both sat down.

Alex leaned close to her and whispered in her ear. "Told you."

She half laughed as his warm breath fanned her cheek and seemed to travel with lightning speed right into the core of her body. She turned her face and for a second, they were nose to nose, mouth to mouth....

"There now," Ron said, reentering the room. "Emily found another cup."

Liz and Alex jerked apart.

Emily, cheeks pink, eyes downcast, stopped near Liz. "Ron says I shouldn't have tried to plan a little impromptu party for the three of us," she said. "I just thought it would be nice to catch up on the news. Just us. You know.''

"And it will be," Liz said, "but there's no reason we can't include Alex, is there?''

"I don't know him," Emily said.

"I know you don't.''

"Maybe it's time we get acquainted," Alex said. "How about a cup of tea? Those cookies look delicious.''

Emily finally sat down and poured tea.

Liz had to admire Alex. He hated tea and looked somewhat ridiculous holding a tiny little cup between two fingers, but he made the right noises to imply he liked it. He complimented Emily on her cookies and on all the knickknacks that cluttered every horizontal surface. Oddly enough, Emily seemed to appreciate praise for her cooking, but looked uneasy as Alex asked her about the doodads.

Ron changed the subject. "There's something I want to clear up," he said, setting his cup on the butler's table. "Emily told me that last night you asked her about attending your uncle's party. She told you she didn't, but that's not the truth. She was there as my guest.''

Alex had already set aside his empty cup. He leaned forward now, pinning Emily with his blue stare. He looked incredible to Liz, who suddenly realized she was having the most sexual responses to him at the most inopportune times! Sitting there, gaze intent, he looked heart-stoppingly strong. She put her cup down when it rattled against her saucer, and tried to concentrate.

She said, "Why did you lie, Em?''

"She lied to protect me," Ron said. "She'd come to town to see how she liked it this far away from San Francisco. I had an invitation to your uncle's big party and I convinced her to come with me. The next day, after we learned what happened, Emily begged me not to tell the police she'd been at the party. She was afraid it would get me in trouble. I went along with it. After all, we weren't killers so what did it matter?''

"I was thinking of Ron and his job," Emily said.

Ron cast her a swift glance.

The excuse seemed flimsy to Liz. Why lie about something so inconsequential to the police during a murder investigation? So what if you brought a guest to a party? The gala was so big, did Ron and Emily really think anyone would notice or care? It didn't ring true to her and she could tell from the look on Alex's face he felt the same way. Giving them both the benefit of a doubt, she mumbled, "I'm just glad to know the truth."

"Good," Ron said.

"As long as we're talking like this, there's one more thing I'd like to ask you, Emily," Liz continued. "You know that Alex and I are trying to find out who the real killer is, so we have to understand as much as we can about everything."

"As much to rule things out as to count them as important," Alex added.

Liz nodded. "That's right. Earlier today, I was looking through some files. There's something on your lease application I don't understand."

Emily's hand flew to her neck where she clasped her pendant, the same prancing horse she'd worn the night before.

Liz went on. "I noticed you've had trouble with the law. The information I have is incomplete. I can instigate another background check to find out the particulars if I need to. It's all a matter of public record. I don't want to do that, though. I was hoping you might just tell me what happened. I'm sorry to pry.''

Looking right at Emily, Alex said, "I'll leave the room if you'd be more comfortable discussing this with Liz and your brother in private."

Emily's eyes flooded with tears. She shook her head. Liz didn't know if it meant that Alex should stay or that she wouldn't talk.

Ron jumped in again. "That's my doing," he said with a sigh. "I, of course, knew about Emily's... troubles. I didn't want them following her to this new town where she was determined to make a new start. You were homesick and Jane Ridgeway was only too happy to accept my help, so I managed a little cover-up. Yes, my sister was in trouble, but she did complete the required sessions with a therapist and she did make retribution. I don't see why her...problem...should follow her around forever. It's not fair."

"What problem?" Liz asked.

Emily looked up, wiped tears from her eyes, and stilled Ron's answer by raising her hand. "No, Ron."

"Em, we have to tell the truth."

"I'll...I'll tell them," she stuttered.

"But—"

As more tears tumbled heedlessly down her round cheeks, Emily blurted out, "I am...I was...a kleptomaniac. I stole things. I got caught."

Liz's gaze went immediately to Emily's hand which slowly dropped to her lap, revealing the jeweled horse hanging from her neck.

"You finally recognize it, don't you?" Emily said.

"It was Uncle Devon's, wasn't it?"

Emily nodded. "I took it from his curio cabinet," she said, lips trembling, "the night of the party."

"Oh, Em—"

"It's yours now," Emily said, her hands suddenly in frantic motion, clawing at the clasp as though the chain burned her skin, so anxious to rid herself of the offending piece of jewelry that she all but tore it from her neck.

Liz swallowed hard. "Emily—"

"Take it," Emily insisted, pressing it on Liz. "That's the real reason I lied about being at the party. He had so much stuff, how could he possibly miss one little ornament? How did I know he was going to get himself killed? Take it."

Liz felt as though the ground was shifting under her feet. Lovely as it was, she wanted nothing to do with the pendant. Her gaze met Alex's. He nodded and she reluctantly folded her fingers around the tiny horse.

Meanwhile, Ron had stood and was staring at his sister as though he'd never seen her before. "Emily," he finally cried. "I thought you were cured!"

She laughed. It was not a pleasant sound. "You wanted me to be cured," she said. "It was easier for you to think I was cured."

Ron couldn't seem to get past his feeling of personal betrayal. "You stole from Devon Hiller," he said, his voice incredulous. "*That's* the real reason you wanted me to keep quiet about your presence at his party, isn't it? Not because you were afraid of how *I* would look, but because you were afraid of a background search without a kindly, gullible brother to distort the facts. You were afraid you'd be revealed to the cops for what you were…what you are! I'm shattered, Emily. You lied to me."

Emily, by this time, had become a heap of shuddering tears, gasping for breath.

"I trusted you!" Ron added, his hands rolled into fists. "I can't believe this."

"You better help her, honey," Alex whispered to Liz as he put himself in front of Ron. Addressing him, he said, "Now it's your turn to calm down, Ron. What your sister has is a disease, so lay off. Until you can find her the appropriate help, call her doctor and see about getting her a tranquilizer."

Liz dropped the pendant in her pocket and helped Emily to her feet. As they climbed the stairs, Liz glanced back. Alex had found an address book and was thumbing through it. Ron stood in the same spot, his hands now uncurled and hanging limply by his side, his gaze traveling the room, absorbing the dozens of knickknacks scattered throughout his sister's house.

He had to be wondering the same thing Liz was—how many of them came home secreted away in a purse or a pocket or under the flap of a coat?

"I SHOULD HAVE stayed with her," Liz said.

It was raining and the steady thump of the windshield wipers was like a metronome, beating out the rhythm of their conversation. "Ron said he'd stay until she fell asleep. The doctor was there and I gave Ron my cell phone number in case he needs help," Alex said.

"That was so kind of you," Liz said, her hand landing on his arm. She was quiet for a second before adding, "I don't know how I could have been so blind to her troubles. I didn't even recognize that necklace. How could I not recognize that necklace?"

Alex had no trouble answering that question. The curio cabinet Emily had swiped it from was tall and poorly lit and crammed full of all sorts of things. He could remember the first time he'd seen that case; he'd thought at the time that it was a perfect representation of Devon Hiller's life—a closed-up space crowded with stuff, all of it valuable but none of it valued.

He didn't tell Liz this.

She said, "Why did she purposely wear it in front of me? She obviously thought I'd recognize it a lot sooner than I did, so why did she bait me like that? Does she hate me that much?"

He gripped the wheel tighter, miserable that he couldn't find the right words to ease her pain. He said, "I think she wanted you to know because she trusted you to help her," he said. "And now you have."

"You have," Liz said softly, laying her hand on his thigh. He covered her hand with his own and she grasped his fingers, holding onto him again for support. He would always be there for her in this way—it was his destiny to protect her. But he wanted so much more from her and she seemed unable or unwilling to give it.

"You were the one who called the doctor, you were the one who got Ron to calm down," she added. "It's what you're good at, Alex."

He didn't know quite what to say so he said nothing.

With a sigh, she added, "At least we can rule Emily out of some insane plot to kill my uncle and hurt me."

Alex wasn't so sure. Could Emily really be a calculating hard-hearted killer? Was the theft a diversion from a greater crime? Had she stolen the pendant during the party or after she killed Devon Hiller? Who was to say she didn't know the old man from years before? Who knew if she truly was sick? She hadn't come forward with the truth of her illness until pressed by Liz; they had no way of knowing if she was truly ill, only her word. And Ron's.

He didn't mention all this to Liz, either.

"Stop by the hospital," she said as they drove past the emergency entrance. "I want to make sure Harry is okay."

"It's been such a long day for you—"

"I want to make sure Harry is okay," she repeated, "and maybe help his daughter. She must be about my age."

"She looks ten years older."

"She's had a hard life," Liz whispered.

Alex swung into the hospital parking lot. He helped Liz out of the car and they made as quick a dash as possible, given her pregnancy, to get under the awning and out of the cold rain. They rode the elevator up to the third floor and ducked inside the ICU waiting room.

Patty Idle sat in the same chair she'd been sitting in that morning when Alex first met her. She was a faded, emaciated looking blonde, dressed in jeans and a turtleneck, the same clothes she'd worn that morning, only now she'd added an additional layer, a bulky orange sweater.

Sheriff Kapp sat across from her.

Patty popped to her feet the minute she saw Alex and almost jumped into his arms. "Daddy still can't talk to me!"

He patted her back. She'd confessed earlier that day that she'd been away from Ocean Bluff for most of her adult life and had few remaining friends in town. Alex had experience with people in crisis and he knew that a sympathetic ear and nonjudgmental attitude was like a warm blanket to someone like Patty. However, he couldn't help but notice the way the sheriff stared at Patty's clinging figure. It didn't take much of an imagination to figure out that he was seeing something that wasn't there.

Alex's gaze met Liz's. She smiled warmly, and the chill the officer had introduced to the scene disappeared.

Liz held out a hand. "My name is Liz, I'm Alex's wife. Let's you and I take a walk," she said. "We'll find some coffee."

Patty seemed delighted to escape the small room. She grabbed her handbag and the two women were suddenly gone.

Kapp got to his feet. "Have to admit that I can't quite figure out what you're doing here," he said. "Patty told me she'd never met you before this morning, but you two seem mighty friendly."

The sheriff still wore his padded jacket and Alex could see a veneer of sweat glistening on his forehead, beneath the brim of his hat, despite the cool temperature. "What exactly are you hinting around at?"

"Let's play us a game of 'What if.' *What if* Patty decided her daddy was worth more to her dead than alive. She's his only kid, he dies, she stands to get his house and property. A woman like Patty could do a lot with that kind of money. *What if* she and you knew each other before today and she convinced you to help her get her daddy out of the way, maybe split the money with you."

Alex kept his rising temper in check. He said, "And why would I murder for money when my wife stands to inherit a small fortune anytime now?"

"*What if* you and Patty are more than friends and Elizabeth found out about it. She kicks you out, Patty's money starts to look better."

"Did Liz look angry or upset to you? Come on, Sheriff, you don't honestly believe I've had the time or inclination during the few days I've been out of jail to hook up with a woman who until Saturday was down in

Los Angeles, and agree to help her kill her father? All this while I'm trying to keep myself out of your wily clutches? Just how stupid do you think I am?''

"I don't think you're stupid at all," Sheriff Kapp said. "I think you're an arrogant killer."

"You're wrong. Did Harry's toxicology report come back?''

The sheriff chewed on the inside of his cheek as though trying to decide if he wanted to share information. It was obvious he didn't, but just as obvious that he had a point to make. He finally said, "Old Harry ingested more than enough of that stuff to kill him. My deputies went back to the house and studied things. They got a funny feeling that maybe Harry wasn't alone when he took the stuff, which leads to the next speculation. If Harry wasn't alone, did someone help him take it? Where were you on Friday evening?''

"Harry was at our house at five-thirty. He left. Liz and I ate dinner and went to check on Harry about seven-fifteen. During that time, I never left Liz's sight nor she mine.''

"And I'm sure she'll happily swear to all that," Kapp said, sarcasm dripping from his words. "Well, it won't be a problem much longer. Doctor says Harry ought to be able to talk for himself pretty soon. Think I'll post a deputy outside his door, just to be safe.''

Alex refused to rise to the bait. Instead, he said, "Say, Sheriff, how about you answer a question for me? How about telling me what you had on Devon Hiller?''

The sheriff's eyes narrowed.

"I've heard it's the blackmailer who usually ends up dead, not the one being blackmailed, so I figure something went wrong. Did Hiller get tired of being fleeced,

did he fight back? Did you kill him and try to blame it
on someone else?''

The sheriff shook his head. ''You're either grasping
at straws or trying to deflect your guilt, Chase. Say good-
night to Elizabeth for me. Tell Patty I'll see her once
her daddy is conscious again.''

Alex watched Sheriff Kapp leave.

Kapp was never going to admit to blackmailing
Devon Hiller; he'd be an idiot if he did. But Kapp had
apparently tried this same thing on Battalion Chief
Montgomery.

It was time to come clean with Montgomery. Alex
would have to convince the chief he was innocent. He
did some quick math in his head. Dave was working a
regular shift, twenty-four hours on, forty-eight hours off.
That meant he would be back at the station tomorrow.
There would be a change of shift meeting at 7:00 a.m.
After that, barring a fire, there would be training exer-
cises or tours of old buildings they might someday have
to save, or even physical training. If he was lucky, Chief
Montgomery would be at the station. *If he was lucky…*

His mouth slid into a grimace. Luck and he hadn't
been on speaking terms for quite some time now.

Chapter Eleven

As tired as she was, Liz insisted they go back to Emily's duplex and make sure she was okay. She knew Alex would protest and he did. He'd been acting jumpy since talking to the sheriff, and as they drove along the dark, wet streets, he finally told her the gist of their conversation.

"He's going to try to pin Harry's incident on you," Liz said. "I knew it!"

"He won't get very far."

"Why would anyone want to kill Harry?"

"Unless he really did see someone in our yard and the perp heard him, I can't imagine. His daughter seems genuinely upset about her dad's condition."

"Patty is a nice woman, just a little scared. She told me she's going to stay with her dad when he comes home, she wants to get to know him again and help him. I'm hoping Harry might actually help her."

"Yeah. She'll get him hooked on cocaine and he'll have her guzzling beer."

"Alex."

"Sorry." They pulled up in front of Emily's place. A few lights were on downstairs, glowing through the rain. Ron's duplex looked dark and empty.

"I bet Ron is still there with her," Alex said. "I have to admire the way that guy is sticking by her."

"He's a good brother. Half brother, that is."

"Half brother?"

"Emily and Ron had different fathers," Liz said as Alex helped her out of the car. Ron had apparently heard them arrive. He opened the door while they were still on the stairs and led them into the living room. The rain outside combined with the mossy green color inside gave the place the look and feeling of a cluttered cave.

"How is she?" Liz asked.

Ron shook his head. "Out like a light. I can't believe her doctor actually made a house call. I wonder what that will cost her. He referred her to a shrink. To tell you the truth, I'm relieved this is all out in the open. Emily has always been squirrely, but since her divorce, she's been obsessing like mad, doing crazy things, acting weird."

"And I didn't even notice," Liz said.

"You didn't know her before. I've tried to help her, that's why I bought her this duplex next to mine."

"I thought she bought it."

"No, I did. She put all her money into her store."

"But I didn't think your mother left you much, Ron, just some antiques that Emily said weren't very valuable."

"There were a couple of gems in among the more ordinary things. Listen, can I get you guys something warm to drink or maybe something to eat? I'm afraid to leave her and I don't know what she has on hand—"

"We're fine," Alex said.

Liz could tell Alex was anxious to leave, and truth of the matter was that she was too, but Ron seemed desperate for them to stay a bit. She said, "How about coffee? I know Emily always has that on hand."

Ron bustled off to make coffee and Liz smiled at Alex, asking him with her eyes to understand that they had to stay. He squeezed her hand and called softly, "Hey, Ron, does Emily have any bread?"

In the end, the three of them sat down at Emily's small table and chairs for a hastily prepared meal of coffee, toast and scrambled eggs. Oddly enough, it hit the spot.

"Take my mind off my sister," Ron said. "Tell me what's going on with you guys."

Alex and Liz took turns bringing Ron up to date on their frustrating search for the identity of the real killer and their plans for the next day. "We're going to search Hiller's den tomorrow afternoon," Alex said.

"What if the sheriff finds you there? Won't that strike him as mighty suspicious?"

Liz said, "Remember the other night when you asked what was going on and we hemmed and hawed a lot? That's because there's incriminating evidence hidden in my uncle's den."

Ron's startled gaze flicked over to Alex. "I thought you were innocent," he said, almost rising from his seat.

"The evidence he hid incriminates *me,* not *him,*" Liz said before Alex could contradict her. She'd felt his body tense the minute she started down this path, but as they'd explained their so-called investigation to Ron, she'd come to the realization that they had gotten exactly nowhere on their own. If she told Ron about the scarf then the information would be out there, so to say, and perhaps Alex would finally feel comfortable with the idea of her telling the sheriff the truth and asking for help.

"He found my scarf at Uncle Devon's," she continued, "and he hid it. He thought I killed my uncle and he took the blame."

Beside her, she could feel Alex's anxiety radiating outward from him like rays from the sun. She dared not look at him. She added, "I'm trying to convince Alex to let me turn the scarf over to the sheriff and come clean about the fact I visited Uncle Devon later that night for a fruitless try at reconciliation."

Ron shook his head vehemently. "Absolutely not," he said, looking from Liz to Alex and back again. "Liz, are you crazy? If you give Sheriff Kapp that kind of information, you'll wind up in jail."

"But if I don't, Alex might. Again. I can't sacrifice him to save myself."

"Did you kill your uncle?"

"Of course she didn't," Alex said. Liz could tell from his voice that he was seething and kept her gaze averted. He'd thank her for this in the end. Wouldn't he?

"Then keep your mouth shut and follow Alex's advice," Ron said. "Listen, you told me that Alex is going to talk to the chief tomorrow and then you're going to look over your uncle's house. Every day you stay free gives you a chance to find the murderer. You go talking to Kapp, it's over, you'll be neck deep in lawyers and courtrooms."

Alex said, "Ron is making sense, Liz."

"Of course he is, he's agreeing with you," she said. "On the other hand, aren't we already neck deep in lawyers and courtrooms? Have you forgotten you still have a new trial to face?"

"I haven't forgotten," Alex said softly.

"Think of it this way. If the original investigation was a little slipshod, perhaps Sheriff Kapp will go all out this time and that might include DNA testing on things like the carpet. Maybe they'll find blood from the real killer. Why not? I mean how do we know the killer wasn't scratched or cut during the fracas? We can't do that kind of thing on our own.''

''Too risky,'' Alex insisted.

''Alex is right,'' Ron said. ''Find that scarf and destroy it before you tell the sheriff a thing.''

''What scarf?'' Emily said from the doorway. She was dressed in blue pajamas and seemed to sag against the frame as she repeated, ''What scarf?''

''Liz lost her scarf,'' Ron said softly, rising and going to his sister. He put his hands on her arms and steadied her.

''I smelled the coffee,'' Emily said.

''Liz will get you a cup while I take you back upstairs. Do you want something to eat, too? Come on, Em, you shouldn't be up and about in your condition.''

''What scarf?'' Emily said as Ron led her away.

Brother and sister left the room, leaving Alex and Liz alone. She darted a look to his face, and felt stricken. She'd expected him to be angry, but his expression was one of intense disappointment. ''I'll...I'll get her the coffee,'' Liz said.

Alex nodded curtly. ''I'll wait for you in the car.'' Then he was gone.

THE NEXT MORNING, after convincing Alex she could manage being alone for a couple of hours, Liz watched Alex drive away with a heavy heart. They'd quarreled about her disclosure to Ron, she trying to explain her reasoning, him acting as though she'd betrayed him. She'd told him to get over it. What harm had been done? Ron had reacted exactly like Alex had, adamant she be protected. Honestly.

Her thoughts momentarily turned to Emily. Liz imagined Ron would take the day off to be with his sister, and the parallels of his selflessness with his mother and now his sister were too big to ignore. When would Ron be free to lead his own life?

Somewhere out there, people were happy, she thought suddenly, vowing to join them as soon as possible. She cleaned up the kitchen, then settled down to comb Sinbad who, as his bone mended, was growing increasingly restless with each passing day.

"You deserve a little happiness, too," she told the cat as he tried to find a lap in which to curl. She smiled as she kissed the tip of his beautiful brown ear and ran the comb down his sable back. "When this is over and you're all better, you can go outside again," she said. "No bluff though, okay?"

He purred in agreement, or so it seemed to her. "You're welcome," she crooned.

ONE OF THE bay doors stood open which made getting into the fire station that much easier. No ringing the public bell and waiting for an old workmate to let him inside—or not let him inside, as the case may be. There was a new guy checking out the equipment piled into the search and rescue rubber raft, and Jimmy Thurmond was busy tinkering with the paramedic truck. The new guy accepted Alex's wave and obvious familiarity with the place. Alex breezed behind Jimmy's back and quickly climbed the stairs.

He walked into the day room that served many duties. This was where they gathered to eat the meals they prepared for themselves, and indeed, each shift had its own refrigerator lined up against the wall along with an extra fridge full of soft drinks. However, the room also served as the heart of the station. A place to socialize and conduct meetings, it also housed the equipment to run videotapes used in training. There was a table nearby painted with city streets, topped with moveable wooden structures and vehicles to mimic Ocean Bluff. Visiting kids loved this table, but it also came in handy when used to plot courses through town or refine fire fighting strategies.

This morning, the room held three men Alex had once counted as brothers. Actually, given the fact he hadn't seen his own brothers in several years, closer than that. Dave was there as well as Mike Sinclair and Drew Soffit. Dave's smile froze on his affable face. The other two men crossed their arms and gave Alex a chilling look that said he wasn't welcome. Considering the circumstances and the cloud of guilt under which he'd left, he didn't blame them. With identical scowls, they both left the room.

"I need to talk to Montgomery," Alex told Dave with a wistful look at his former friends' backs. Hopefully, soon enough they'd learn the truth and this awful feeling of having lost a second family would leave. He faced Dave and said, "Please, Dave, I need your help again. I'm sorry to do this to you. Is Montgomery here?"

Dave nodded, then shook his head. "I don't think you should have come."

"I know you don't. Is he here?"

"He doesn't want to see you, Alex."

"I guess that should matter more than all the other problems I have right now including a bum murder charge, a pregnant wife with misguided loyalties who seems to attract danger like some kind of magnet, a neighbor in jeopardy, friends going haywire, but you know what? It just doesn't."

"If you want your job back here someday—"

"I want my life back," Alex interrupted. "I want my wife safe. I want to see my kid be born. Now, is Montgomery here or not and will you help me see him or not?"

Dave took a couple of steps toward Alex. "On one condition. If I help you see him, then you have to tell him what you told me, about Liz and the scarf and what you did, the whole nine yards."

Alex nodded. Thinking of Liz's disclosures to Ron the night before, he grumbled, "It's not like he'll be the first to know."

CHIEF MONTGOMERY was a fit-as-a-fiddle, flat-stomached forty-three-year-old man who wore his dark-blue uniform with unmistakable pride. In the past, he'd all but taken Alex under his wing, letting him know that he expected great things and Alex had been willing to work hard to prove Montgomery right. He had looked forward to working his way up the ladder. All that seemed impossible now.

Because he and the battalion chief had been relatively close, Alex could only imagine the depth of Montgomery's disappointment when Alex confessed to the murder of his wife's wealthy uncle. It would be an uphill climb to win him over.

He entered the chief's office behind Dave, but as he was a head taller, the chief's eyes went from Dave to him immediately. Montgomery had been at his usual position in front of the computer, keeping an eye on all the 9-1-1 calls that came in over the line, both police and emergency.

"Sullivan," Montgomery said, his small blue eyes

piercing. "What's the meaning of bringing *him* in here?"

"He needs to talk to you," Dave said. "It's important."

"I don't need to talk to him," the chief said calmly.

"Just listen to him, Chief."

Alex decided to be blunt and direct. He said, "I didn't kill Devon Hiller."

Montgomery got to his feet. "You confessed."

Dave patted Alex on the back and left, closing the door firmly behind him.

"I confessed to save my wife," Alex began. "When I found Hiller's body, I jumped to the wrong conclusion. Believe me, I'm paying for it. The trouble is that now Liz is in danger. There has been at least one attempt on her life in the last few days, perhaps two. Can I sit down and talk to you? Will you listen?"

Montgomery drilled Alex with his stare. Finally he said, "Liz is in danger? You're not making this up?"

"I'm not making this up."

Montgomery motioned at a chair close to his desk. "Tell me what's going on," he said.

With a curt nod of thanks, Alex sat down.

LIZ LEANED close to the computer screen. Unless she was mistaken, there was something a little untoward about the way her uncle had acquired the land for his latest strip mall. The property had been zoned residential when it first came on the market but it was difficult to develop—too close to poor neighborhoods and highways, no view, little sunlight. As such it had languished for years until her uncle bought it for a song. The zoning magically changed within weeks of her uncle's acquisition. He'd built the mall immediately.

Could that be what Kapp had on her uncle? Had Uncle Devon paid off the planning commission and had Kapp found out about it?

Hmm…

As she'd been doing at odd moments, she turned her attention to the bundles of her uncle's letters that had been mixed in with her childhood keepsakes. She'd scanned the biggest group over the past few days, hoping to find an old grudge having to do with some nefarious business scheme, but had come up dry. Now, a little excited, she started in on the personal letters, the first few from her own father. They were all very short and she was soon disabused of the notion that she would uncover new and fascinating details about the father she'd adored. He'd put very little of himself into his letters. One notified Uncle Devon that Liz had broken her arm, a fact she'd all but forgotten, another discussed selling a house, a third canceled a meeting with their lawyer, the fourth dealt with the funeral arrangements for Liz's grandmother. It was easy to see her father and uncle had not been particularly close.

With a sigh, she set those aside, thumbed through a half dozen from distant relatives including an irate cousin who berated Uncle Devon for not lending him the cash to hospitalize his late wife, and at last picked up the final letter, this one in a plain envelope with no return address and a San Francisco postmark of April 10th, 1969.

It was short, too, and she read it fast, then reread it.

Devon, it began without salutation or endearment. *The baby is a girl and she is healthy. I received the money order you sent. As you say, no looking back. Irene.*

Who was Irene? And where had Liz recently heard that name? She drew a blank and moved on. A baby?

Was it possible her uncle had a baby? She almost laughed at the thought. Irene could be anyone. The baby could have been anyone's.

Interesting, though. Mighty interesting.

Alex would be home pretty soon and she'd run it by him if he was talking to her. A flash of irritation was replaced by the realization that they didn't have time to bicker. Perhaps this letter would give them a new place to start looking. After lunch they were going to her uncle's house to retrieve her scarf and check the place out, and after that, perhaps they could figure out a way to research birth announcements in San Francisco for April of 1969.

The thought of lunch reminded her that there still wasn't a thing in the house to eat. She grabbed her purse and car keys with the intent of rectifying that.

It was the first time since Alex had returned that she'd been shopping alone, and she celebrated by choosing all his favorites. It wasn't until she found herself bagging Satsuma oranges that a question popped into her head. Was this her way of apologizing to him? With food? Was she ready to admit that her trust in Ron somehow compromised her loyalty to Alex?

No. Yes. She wasn't sure.

She was surprised to find Emily's car in the driveway when she returned home. The front door of the house stood ajar, and Liz thought of the cold drizzly air circulating through her house. For a second she was annoyed that Emily had failed to shut the door, and then she remembered what kind of shape Emily had been in when she'd seen her last.

Should she have been behind the wheel of a car? Maybe Ron had driven her over…

Juggling the bags, Liz managed to carry everything

into the house in one load, pushing open the door with her hip, calling out Emily's name.

The call died in her throat. Emily sat in the middle of the sofa, gazing at nothing, her hands lost in the folds of her heavy wool skirt.

"I used the key you gave me to get in," she said, her voice an odd monotone. "I waited and waited for you."

Shutting the door with her knee, Liz said, "I'm sorry, Em. I didn't know you were coming. Give me a second to put the ice cream in the freezer."

Emily nodded.

Liz deposited the groceries in the kitchen. Sinbad sat up in his enclosure, square in the middle of his sandbox, eyes huge but oddly silent as though he, too, was aware of the tension emanating from the distraught woman in the living room. She dug out the ice cream and slipped it into the freezer, but the kitchen was so cold she knew the meat and milk would be fine for a few minutes. Emily, on the other hand, didn't look as though she had a few more minutes in her.

ALEX FOUND himself thinking Montgomery could do quiet like no other man on earth. A rock had nothing on this guy.

He'd listened, he'd asked two or three questions, and now he was thinking. At last, he took a deep breath. "So let me get this straight. Sheriff Kapp is convinced you're guilty, you can't get him to look anywhere else unless you compromise Liz, Liz is in danger from some unknown person, you suspect Hiller was blackmailed by Kapp."

"You got it."

"And now you want me to tell you why I used the word blackmail with Kapp."

"Yes."

Montgomery thought some more. "I assume Mike told you about this."

Alex shook his head once.

"You're trying to keep Mike out of it."

Alex didn't reply.

With a heavy sigh, Montgomery said, "Kapp is a pompous, arrogant jerk."

Hearing Montgomery label Kapp as arrogant less than twelve hours after Kapp had used that word on him, made Alex feel vindicated in a way. The fact that the chief was talking to him spurred a flame of hope. Alex said, "I'm up against a wall. Kapp is determined to hang me out to dry. I can't prove he's a blackmailer. If you can't tell me what he said to you, will you just confirm that the man approached you? Maybe that would be enough."

Montgomery got up from his desk. "And maybe it wouldn't. Let me tell you what I know." The chief perched himself on the broad windowsill and looked thoughtful. "You're not a dad yet, but you're pretty darn close. Someday that baby of yours will be all but grown-up. You won't still think of him or her as a baby, say, when you take them to college, but you will still feel protective. It comes with the territory.

"Well, my last baby is seventeen years old and we took him off to school down in L.A. a few months ago. The boy is smart as a whip, graduating a year early from high school but maybe that wasn't a good idea. He's immature. He started drinking to fit in and then he drove a friend's car into an old lady's front window. The friend ended up with a broken leg. The old lady had a stroke. Now my kid's got a DUI and trouble with the law."

"I didn't know."

"No one up here did, but Kapp found out. He even got hold of a picture of my kid taken at the scene, obviously three sheets to the wind and obviously belligerant. Now pay attention, because this is the way Kapp's mind works. Kapp knows I'm looking to become fire chief when Purvis retires. He offered to keep my son's trouble off the front pages of the paper if I agreed to enlighten him about a rumored affair Purvis had with an underage girl. He wants the power to threaten Purvis's marriage so Purvis will endorse him come re-election time. Purvis is an out and out critic of the sheriff's, so there's no way that endorsement will come without coercion. Kapp figures I want to protect my son. He even hinted that I won't stand much of a chance for promotion if Kevin's debacle is front page news and maybe he's right."

"So Kapp tried to blackmail you to blackmail Purvis."

"Yep."

"And you then accused him of trying to blackmail you."

"I did indeed. He balked at that, told me it was 'business,' not blackmail. He said I should just scratch his back the way old man Hiller had."

Alex sat up straight. "He mentioned Hiller and blackmail in the same sentence?"

"He mentioned Hiller and business in the same sentence, but with him, it's all the same."

"I can't figure out what he had on Hiller."

"I gather he had a lot on Hiller. I have no proof. I have a feeling this is business as usual for Kapp and that he'll pretty much do anything he wants in this county for as long as he wants. It galls me, and frankly I have to admit that I don't see how any of this will get you closer to Hiller's murderer.''

Alex shook his head. "I don't either. But the whole thing is like a puzzle. Who knows which piece will be the one that makes all the others fit?'' He stood up and held out his hand. "Thank you for being so frank,'' he said.

Montgomery stared at Alex's hand, stood and shook it. "Best you stay away from here until this is all resolved,'' he said firmly. "When it is, come see me if I'm still around.''

Alex nodded. "Yes, sir. If you don't mind me asking, what's Kapp going to do about your kid?''

"Ruin him. Ruin me.''

Alex left the station preoccupied.

Kapp was a class one scoundrel—was he also a murderer? He heard his name called as he walked to his truck and turned to find Dave under the protection of the station overhang. "Tell me what happened,'' his friend said, handing him a steaming mug of coffee and taking a sip from his own mug.

As much as Alex longed to return home to Liz and make up for the tensions of the morning, he knew he owed Dave an explanation. Leaning a shoulder against the building, Alex started talking.

LIZ SAT in the rocking chair and looked anxiously at Emily. "Are you okay?''

Emily nodded her head, then shook it. Tears rolled silently down her cheeks, plopping unceremoniously onto her blouse. Not a blouse, Liz realized suddenly. A pajama top, the same blue one from the night before.

"Let me call Ron for you,'' Liz begged.

"No.''

"Then how about I drive you home?"

Emily finally stopped staring into space and turned her attention to Liz, who shrank back against the chair under the intensity of her friend's gaze. She said, "Why couldn't you just leave it alone?"

Furrowing her brow, Liz said, "Leave what alone?"

Emily closed her eyes for a moment and her head swayed. "Me. Us. You," she said. "Why couldn't you just leave everything the way it was? Why did you have to meddle, why did you have to bring Alex around again, why couldn't you love Ron?"

Liz blinked several times. She wasn't sure what to say.

"I knew I had to have it," Emily said, her voice now dreamy sounding. "The minute I saw it, I knew. It's like that sometimes. Oh, most of the time it's just an urge, like being a little hungry, like wanting a snack. But sometimes, the feeling is overpowering, like being ravenous, like killing the first beast you come across and devouring it whole. Your uncle was a beast, Liz. Ron told me how much you hated him."

Yikes, Liz thought as the first prickling of fear tingled her spine. Rising, she said, "Em, you aren't well. I'll drive you home."

"Sit down," Emily demanded. "I'm not done. The least you can do is listen to me."

Liz sat.

"I knew I had to have it," she continued. "I could see myself wearing it before I even touched it, I could feel it around my neck…I wanted it and I took it and I saved you. But did you appreciate what I'd done? You only had eyes for Alex, you couldn't even see Ron. You couldn't see that I saved you, that I offered you a second chance. You didn't care—"

"I don't understand," Liz said, fear escalating from a prickle to a drumbeat. Searching for the right thing to say, she added, "You can have the necklace, Emily. Like you said, it's mine now to do with as I choose and I want you to have it. Let me get it for you. It's in the bedroom."

As she said all this, she stood.

"Not the little gold horse. The green scarf."

Liz felt like shaking her head to clear her ears. "*You?*" she whispered. "*You* took my scarf?"

Emily nodded.

Liz looked at her friend beseechingly. "Emily, listen to me. You must have left the scarf where someone else could find it. Think, Em. Who was nearby when you set it down—"

"And those beach stairs," Emily said.

The stairs! Liz was trying not to react, trying to keep her cool, but the words just shot out of her mouth. "You broke Sinbad's leg and tied him down there? *You* sabotaged the stairs and tried to kill me?"

"It had to be done," Emily said.

Liz stared at Emily and tried to make sense of this information. It was no use, she couldn't. She needed help. She said, "I'm calling Ron. It'll be like old times, just the three of us."

"Sit down."

"No, Emily, you can trust Ron, you know he'll help you."

Emily's hands shifted as she withdrew a black handgun from the folds of her skirt and rested it on her lap.

Liz swallowed a lump the size of a basketball. "Where did you get that?"

Emily lifted the gun until Liz was all but staring down the barrel. "I don't remember where I got it," she said.

"Maybe I borrowed it from somebody. I must have borrowed it...."

"I'm calling Ron."

"Sit down. You aren't calling anyone."

"But—"

"Don't make me kill you, too."

Chapter Twelve

"Who else did you kill?" Liz mumbled.

Emily shook her head.

Uncle Devon? But Emily had never known him, she'd never met him until the night of the party. Even Uncle Devon couldn't provoke a killing frenzy that quickly. Who then? Had Emily drugged Harry? Did she think he'd died? Or had she shot Ron or Alex—

Liz battled panic as she said, "Who, Emily? Who else did you kill?"

Emily kept shaking her head. Liz glanced at the phone. If only she could call Alex and tell him to come home! When could she expect him? Ordinarily, he'd come directly from the fire station, but he'd been perturbed with her when he left so who knew what he might do to blow off steam. Run on the beach, go to the gym, drive up to the national park and hike along a wintry trail—anything was a possibility.

Come home, she cried in her heart. *Please, come home to argue with me, come home to be angry, just come home!*

Liz's mind was so focused on trying to figure out a way to get the gun, cursing her present ungainly state, calculating trajectories without having the slightest idea

what it all meant, that it took her a while to figure out
that Emily had asked a question. But what question?

Emily waved the gun at Liz and said, "Tell me why."
Why what?

"Tell me!"

Liz jerked. "I...please, ask me again."

"I said, why can't you love Ron?"

Liz inched closer to the edge of the rocker. "Um,
well, I didn't meet Ron until I was already married,"
she said, a sudden plan popping into her head. She
grabbed her leg and groaned, struggling into an upright
position. "I have a horrible cramp, Em! I need to walk.
Don't make me sit."

"Over there," Emily said, gesturing with the gun to
the area by the Christmas tree. "You can walk around
over there. Just don't get too close to me."

"I won't."

"If you'd met him first—"

Ron. She was still talking about Ron. Liz said, "Your
brother is a fine man. You and he are valuable friends."

"He loves you," Emily said.

She wanted to argue this point but the gun made hon-
esty a difficult policy, at best. She said, "I love him,
too. Like you love him. Like a brother."

"My mother was so happy when he was born. She
and Daddy used to sing to him. They loved him. But
me..." Her voice trailed off.

Liz heard a noise outside and held her breath. Tires
crunched, the sound muted by the rain that had started
up again as Emily's talk drifted from one thing to another and back again. Liz prayed that Emily, unaccus-
tomed to the particular sounds that heralded visitors at
this house, might not recognize the fact that someone
was coming.

Please, please, be Alex...

Emily said, "Your uncle had to die."

"Why, Em?" *Keep her talking...*

"Ron said you hated him."

"I—"

"So I killed him."

Liz stopped pacing. "But Emily, you didn't even know him. Did he catch you stealing the necklace, is that what happened?"

"Ron said you hated him."

"We had our troubles—"

"He fell on his letter opener, but if he hadn't, it wouldn't have mattered because there was your pretty green scarf. He had to die. He wouldn't cooperate. So old, so feeble, so stubborn." She paused for a second, looking confused. "It's like a dream, like a story," she said, her voice almost sing-song. "But now he's dead. Did you hate him, Liz?"

"I don't know."

"You try to like everyone. It doesn't matter, Ron still wants you so Alex has to go."

Liz's heart had been beating like a marathon racer, but as Emily's intent finally sank in, it stopped cold. Emily was going to shoot Alex the second he opened that door.

With a lurch, her heart leaped back into the race. *No. It's not going to happen. I won't let it.*

Liz made a decision, born of fear, strengthened by the knowledge that she had to do something right now. Coddling hadn't worked, perhaps authority would. She held out a hand and moved with all the bluster she could manage. "Enough is enough, Em. Stop this right now and give me that gun."

Emily sprang to her feet, grim determination filling

her eyes, her mouth a slash of rage. Liz suddenly understood that Emily's fury had been building for years
and had now been fueled and honed by a psychosis no
one had even known she had. Her fury was demanding
an outlet, consequences be damned. If she couldn't kill
Alex, she'd kill Liz. She'd already admitted she killed
Uncle Devon; somewhere in her mind she had to know
she'd burned a bridge that could not be reconstructed
and that Liz was now an enemy.

All these realizations passed through Liz's mind in
less time than it takes to blink, but they formed the foun-
dation for her next move. Still staring at Emily, she
dodged into the kitchen. Sinbad howled as she tore past
him, upturned a chair in her path, yanked open the back
door, stumbled down the cement steps, fled into the yard,
toward the bluff, Emily in hot pursuit. She cradled her
belly and kept moving, hoping that Alex would come in
time, knowing the only way to give him a chance—him
and the baby she so ponderously carried—was to draw
Emily away from him.

She heard a shot and a bullet whizzed by, striking a
tree to her left. Gasping, she struggled on through the
deep, wet grass, rain beating on her head, sliding into
her eyes. Another shot. Her arm burned, she tried to
crouch. She heard Alex's voice and ducked behind a
tree, driven to look back, afraid Emily would turn the
gun on him, unable to bear the thought.

Emily stood thirty feet away, her attention focused
toward the house. Alex stood at the back door, completely vulnerable, the gun now pointed at him. He'd
started talking to Emily much the same way Liz had,
coaxing her to put the gun down, to give it to him. Emily
let him approach, down the stairs, across the wet grass,

rain flattening his hair, staining the shoulders of his leather jacket.

Liz opened her mouth to warn Alex. She knew this was a trick, a trap, that Emily would only let him get close enough to be sure he couldn't escape, then she'd shoot him. At close range.

Behind Alex, another man appeared in the open doorway. "Emily!"

Emily's attention shifted from Alex, up to the house, to her brother.

Ron stared at his sister with frantic eyes. "What are you doing?" he yelled. "For God's sake, Emily."

Emily yelled, "I'm taking care of things…for you. Like I did old man Hiller. Like I—"

"Stop it," Ron said in a softer tone. He held out his hand in the same beseeching way Liz and Alex had done and added, "No more, Em, you know what you have to do."

Liz's view of Emily was restricted to her back. Long, wet hair, clinging pajama top, skirt drooping, boots dark from moisture. She saw Emily nod as though she understood.

Someone had finally gotten through to her!

Emily lowered the gun from Alex's head and then, in a flash, she raised it to her own temple and pulled the trigger.

ALEX HAD KNOWN Emily was going to shoot herself the minute she'd changed the aim of her Glock 9mm. He'd seen it in her eyes. He'd tried to move forward to stop her, but it all happened too fast. Even as Emily's body crumpled to the ground, even as the noise of the shot seemed to ricochet off every tree in the yard, he ran past her, toward Liz whom he'd seen hiding behind a trunk, reaching her as she screamed and sank to her knees, deep sobs consuming her.

He held her trembling wet body in his arms and soothed her with soft words that sprang from the very depths of his soul, words that originated in his devoted love of her, words fine-tuned by the last few minutes when he thought for sure that Emily would shoot him in the heart and then turn the gun and her madness on Liz and their baby.

In the distance, he heard sirens, he heard Ron, he heard the ocean, he even heard Sinbad cry, but it was all lost in the part of the world that didn't include him and Liz, the far away part, the unimportant part. He kissed her wet head and held her until she grew still and silent and then he held her even longer, trying to absorb her fright and pain.

Eventually, paramedics arrived and he realized that Liz was bleeding, that the bullet had grazed her upper arm. Ron was pale and silent, sitting on the steps in the rain, his eyes vacant as he stared at the covered body of his sister, protected by a canopy, waiting for the medical examiner.

Eventually, Sheriff Kapp asked questions. Liz refused to leave with the paramedics until she'd recited what Emily told her, how Emily confessed to murdering her uncle.

Eventually, he heard Ron tell the sheriff about finding his gun and his sister missing, how he'd raced here to elicit help, how he'd almost been too late.

And Alex had thought to himself that he'd almost been too late, too.

Eventually, he rode with Liz to the hospital and stayed by her side as they treated her, stayed by her side as her doctor examined her, stayed by her side as they wept with relief that the baby was okay, that they were okay, wept with great sorrow for what had happened to Emily…and Ron.

Eventually, he arranged to have Sinbad taken to the vet's for boarding, and checked them into the nearest hotel, a plush place overlooking the rain swept sea where, still dressed in their damp clothes, they fell into each other's arms and slept.

IT WAS ALMOST midnight when Liz woke from a sleep as dark and quiet as death. The rain had stopped and a sliver of moon now hovered over the ocean. For some time she lay there looking out the undraped window at the remarkable vista, Alex's regular breathing a peaceful sonata beside her.

Emily would never see the moon again.

Liz felt her eyes fill with tears. She felt the bed shift and then Alex's finger gently wiped a tear from her cheek. "No more crying, my love," he whispered.

"But—"

"Not now," he said. "You're cold, I can feel you shivering. I know just what you need."

He kissed her cheek and got off the bed, walking around to her side and helping her stand. "The only room they had left was the honeymoon suite," he said softly, leading her toward another door. He flicked on a switch and the bathroom came to life. The star of the show, a pink heart-shaped bathtub sat smack-dab in the center.

"I don't believe it," she said.

He laughed as he turned on the faucets. "I figure what you need is warm water and plenty of it." From the array of supplies provided by the hotel, he picked up a trio of pink spheres and plunked them into the roaring water. "And bubbles," he added.

"My arm—"

"We'll be careful," he said. Looking deep into her eyes, he added, "You'll need help."

It was time to let go of her fears. She nodded. With a slow smile, Alex disappeared back into the bedroom. As he spoke on the phone, she looked into the mirror; for the first time she got a good look at her face, her hair, the big white bandage on her upper arm, the blood-stains…

What a mess.

Oh, Emily.

New tears blurred her eyes and she flicked them away as Alex came back into the room. Smiling at her, he dimmed the lights, casting a soft glow over the small room. He touched her chin, kissed her lips, his own warm and soft.

"Let me undress you," he said as his hands ran across her body. She managed a nod, but by then he was unbuttoning her top which was actually one of his shirts. She spent one moment wondering what he would think of her new underwear. No wispy brassiere; a woman as pregnant as she had to think about support, and oddly enough, at least in Ocean Bluff, maternity underwear did not come in lace, black or otherwise.

He unhooked the bra and her full breasts suddenly filled his hands.

"I look different," she whispered shyly.

"You look beautiful," he said, kissing each nipple.

Forgetting about her appearance, she gave herself over to her husband's tender care. He untied her shoes as she sat on the edge of the tub, pulled off her socks, then helped her take off her slacks. He smiled at her bright white undies printed with frolicking lambs and daisies and she laughed. The laughter felt wonderful, it felt like a spring bubbling out of the ground after months of lying under a thick layer of permafrost.

He pulled her panties down and ran his hands over her swollen belly, trailing moist kisses that rivaled the steam rising from the bath. There was a knock on the outside door and he stood up, kissing her lips again, excusing himself as he closed the door behind him. She turned off the tap.

In a moment he was back with a tray. An icy pitcher of orange juice and two crystal goblets, beautiful scones with currants and orange zest, a white tulip in a vase. He set the tray on the vanity and pulled his shirt off over his head. She felt her heart accelerate at the sight of his muscular chest and shoulders, at his tapered body and the fine mist of dark hair that disappeared under the waistband of his jeans. As he pulled off his pants, the sight of his excitement, miraculously—she had to assume—evoked by her, left her breathless.

"Oh, my," she said.

He smiled again, but this time his smile was confident, a smile that wrapped her in its warmth while at the same time exciting her with its promise. He stepped into the tub first, then extended a hand to steady her, helping her climb in beside him. As their bodies pressed together, she felt the last doubts and fears melt away.

Together they sat in one curve of the heart, his back against the porcelain, her cradled in his arms against his chest, her feet floating, toes poking through the bubbles, his hands on top of her belly, her head tucked under his chin.

"I love you," he whispered.

Speaking was hard for her. There was so much that

needed to be said and she wasn't sure where to start, or if she did find a place, if she'd ever be able to stop. At last, she mumbled, "When I thought she might shoot you, I panicked. I'm sorry I told Ron about the scarf—"

"It's okay," he whispered, his breath ruffling her hair. "It doesn't matter anymore."

"But Emily took the damn thing," she said, because she couldn't pretend all this hadn't affected her profoundly. "I think hearing me tell Ron was what set her off. I don't understand why she killed Uncle Devon, I don't think Ron's in love with me, I think that was all in her head. How did she rig those stairs, how could she have hurt Sinbad, how—"

"Tomorrow," he said against her neck. His fingertips grazed her nipples and suddenly she realized that he was right, that there had been enough death and pain for one day, that it was time to shut off her mind and give herself to her husband. Instead of mourning, she would celebrate the fact that Alex was free and their life could resume….

"YOU'RE STILL thinking too much," he said, moving his hand between her legs and touching her in such a way that she was no longer capable of any thought at all. He caressed and stroked her until her excitement matched his, until all her thoughts were a maelstrom of sensation, until she climaxed with a shudder that shook her to the center of her body, then he lifted her in the water and she turned to face him, straddling him, at first awkward because of her shape, but eventually finding a way to fit together. His eyes were midnight-blue and gleaming the way they did when he was fully aroused and ready to possess her. His mouth was hungry and demanding and she gave herself willingly, lovingly, sharing in his release, ultimately shedding more tears and not caring which originated from happiness and which were the holdovers of grief, all of them twining together and becoming the same thing.

They spent the rest of the night dozing, nibbling on the scones and talking.

Liz told Alex about the letter sent to her uncle by a woman named Irene. He couldn't think of anyone they knew with that name and eventually Liz attempted to put it out of her mind. She'd gone to school with an Irene, so maybe she'd made a subliminal connection that only seemed recent. Irene's baby, well, she was harder to dismiss....

Alex brought Liz up to speed on what Battalion Chief Montgomery had disclosed about the sheriff's use of blackmail to get what he wanted. It took a long time for them to both realize that none of it mattered anymore, at least not on a personal level, because Emily had been behind all their troubles, she'd confessed, and it was over.

AT ELEVEN O'CLOCK the next morning a deputy approached them in the hotel restaurant. "Sheriff said I was to bring you two into the office to give a formal statement in the suicide death of Emily Watts," he said.

Alex shook a few drops of tobasco sauce on his French fries and said, "After we finish our early lunch. Pull up a chair, have something to eat."

The deputy declined and said he'd wait in his car. They took their time with their sandwiches, then Alex held Liz's hand as they walked out into a crisp winter day and climbed into the back of the deputy's car.

Alex was pleased that Liz kept the existence of her green scarf out of her statement, and decided they were going to go get the damn thing and burn it at the first opportunity. Meanwhile, he was a free man. He could barely believe it.

Sheriff Kapp came in as they were about to leave. He stopped them with one of his glares and Alex, knowing what Kapp had in store for Chief Montgomery, felt his blood boil.

"Not so fast," the sheriff said.

Beside him, he heard Liz groan. "Sheriff, honestly, haven't we been through enough? We gave the deputy our statement. Ron and Alex both heard Emily say she killed Uncle Devon—"

"Now, I won't say Emily Watts wasn't nuttier than a fruitcake," he said deliberately, staring at Alex. "But I also don't know that she killed Hiller. And even if she did, Harry Idle is suddenly talking though he isn't making a whole lot of sense yet. He swears someone came to his house that night and he's talking about a feud with Alex. It's clear someone tried to kill the old guy. My money is on you, Chase."

"Are you charging me with something?" Alex said gruffly.

"Not yet. But I don't buy this story about Emily Watts so don't go too far away, you hear?"

Liz opened her mouth. Alex could see she was about to blurt out something about the blackmail attempt with Montgomery so he gently pulled her away. There was no point in riling the man at that particular moment.

His feeling of freedom had lasted about eighteen hours.

They met Ron Boxer coming into the station as they left. Liz immediately embraced Ron who closed his eyes as they filled with tears. Alex shook his hand and expressed his condolences.

"What I feel worst about is how sick she was and

even I didn't know it," Ron said. "Maybe if I hadn't always tried to shelter her—"

"You can't blame yourself," Liz said quickly. Alex wasn't so sure. Liz added, "She had delusions, I think, about you and me—"

"And that's my fault, too," he said. "I had a little crush on you, Liz. Unfortunately, before Emily ever moved to Ocean Bluff, I told her about it. It's humiliating to admit this. Anyway, Emily apparently blew it all out of proportion, made up some fantasy in her head. She stole your scarf at the party. I saw it, you know, and at first she told me you gave it to her and then later she claimed she lost it and swore me to secrecy. The other night, when she heard you talking, she must have realized I'd know she was lying again, and that eventually I'd wonder how it ended up with Hiller. She sent me out to fill a prescription, took my gun and drove to your house. She could have killed one or both of you. I can't help feeling it's my fault."

Alex watched Liz comfort Ron. He felt bad for the guy, but there was something about Ron that bothered him. Perhaps it was the fact that he'd been coveting Liz for a year and a half, telling his sister about his feelings for a married woman, unwittingly feeding her neurosis.

Ron looked at the glass doors ahead of him and said, "All I have to do is read and sign the statement I gave them yesterday. I know you guys don't have a car here. Wait for me to finish here and I'll give you a lift home."

Before Alex could say no thanks, Liz told him they would. Alex bit down his irritation even as he admired his wife's sense of loyalty.

"I feel so bad for him," she whispered, then she turned to face Alex and added, "Sheriff Kapp thinks you tried to kill Harry."

"Forget Harry. He'll eventually explain what really happened. The bigger problem is that Kapp still wants to pin your uncle's murder on me. He doesn't buy Emily's confession."

"But how could he not? Three of us heard her—"

"If Kapp killed your uncle himself, then he knows Emily was lying. If Emily didn't murder your uncle, then it means she left the scarf at the house and Kapp picked it up to throw suspicion on you or me and away from himself. He may be wondering how he could have missed it and that it might suddenly be more important. All along he's said that he's going to re-examine the crime scene. We need to go over there right now and take care of that little detail, Liz. After Ron gives us a ride home, we'll get it over with."

"Sounds good to me," she said.

Chapter Thirteen

The Hiller Estate sat on half an acre of manicured land. Consisting of three stories of white paint and gray gingerbread, the one hundred year old Victorian house had been built by a lumber baron for his third wife. As it domineered a prominent place in the high rent district of Ocean Bluff, Alex hadn't been aware the place existed until he met Liz.

Back then he'd thought it impressive if intimidating. Now he thought it presented something of a firetrap. Too many trees growing too close, too little access and an old wood shingle roof that needed replacing. Liz had called ahead and given the housekeeper the rest of the day off, so they knew they'd have a few hours to themselves.

It had been over six months since Alex had rushed into the house, determined to tell Devon Hiller what he could do with his money. Today he entered it slowly, deliberately, trying to think like a killer. As Liz closed the door, he flipped on the overhead chandelier.

The house was predictable in its layout. Kitchen and dining room occupied the back of the house, while double doors on one side of the foyer led to Hiller's den, identical doors on the other to a formal living room.

When they were all open, as they were now, the front of the house was huge. Sweeping stairs led to the second-story bedrooms and baths, a more modest stairway accessed the attic and nursery on the third floor. The current housekeeper had separate living quarters above the detached garage.

"This is the first time I've been back," Liz said.

Alex squeezed her hand as he looked around, amazed at all the nooks and crannies in which to hide if that was what a person had in mind. Closets, huge potted palms casting mysterious shadows, a grandfather clock at least eight feet high…and that was just in the foyer.

Liz ran her hand along the polished banister. "I always wanted to slide down this thing but I never dared."

"Why not?"

"It was forbidden," she said. She wrinkled her nose and added, "What a great house this would have been if a child had been allowed to be a child." She cleared her throat and added, "Alex, I love our place on the ocean, but lately, with so much happening there and that bluff, well, I was just thinking that it may be a difficult place to raise a child. Maybe we could move back into this house."

He stared at her. She couldn't be serious.

She must have seen the skepticism on his face. "This was my home for most of my life. Why shouldn't I want to reclaim it and fill it with happy memories?"

"I can't believe it," he said, interrupting. "Your uncle was murdered here."

"And Emily killed herself in our backyard."

"Okay, that's true, but so is this. Assuming I don't wind up in jail again, this house is way too expensive for me to even pay the taxes on, let alone renovate."

She narrowed her eyes. "I have money left to me by

both my parents and Uncle Devon,'' she said. ''*I* can afford it.'' Her eyes grew wide as she apparently heard her own words. ''What I mean is that my money is your money—''

''Most of your money is your uncle's money. I won't live off your uncle.''

''That's ridiculous.''

''Take it or leave it.''

Narrowing her eyes, thrusting out her chin, she said, ''Are you issuing me some kind of ultimatum?''

''I'm relating a simple fact. I won't live off your uncle's money. Period.''

''Even if it means living apart from me?'' she said, eyes wide.

''I'm hoping you won't force me to make that kind of choice,'' he said, and took her hand and rubbed the bare fingers of her left hand. ''You still aren't wearing your wedding band,'' he added. ''Why not?''

She shook her head, her eyes filling with tears.

Another moment or two of tense silence followed, then he sighed. ''Listen, honey, we don't have time for this now. Can we agree to disagree and get this over with?''

She took a deep breath and turned to the den. Both their gazes went to the desk and the empty carpet in front of it. ''I don't know what I expected,'' Liz said.

''Your housekeeper did a good job of cleaning up after the police. No fingerprint dust, no tracks on the carpet.''

Behind the desk loomed a wall of books, hundreds of them, all dark and forbidding looking, not the kind to curl up with in bed. The aroma of ill-gotten cigars lingered in the room.

Alex moved quickly across the room, coming to a stop

behind the desk. He moved three thick volumes, stacking them on the desk, just as Liz had done, as a teenager, the one and only time she'd sneaked him into her uncle's den and revealed the secret cubbyhole.

"I can't believe you didn't leave any evidence of having fooled around over here when you hid my scarf," Liz said, coming to stand beside him.

"My prints were all over the room which was expected as I'd been here before so that wasn't a giveaway, and your uncle didn't...well, he didn't bleed much from his wound." Glancing at his shoes, he added, "No bloody footprints," before pressing on the hidden hinge which was so cleverly built into the back of the book case that it was almost impossible to see. A small door sprang open.

It was a relatively shallow spot, and the scarf fell out on its own. Alex picked it up reluctantly, the memories associated with it almost unbearable.

"What's that?" Liz said, peering over his shoulder. "Behind my scarf, what's that dark paper?"

He stuffed the green silk scarf in his pocket and withdrew a brown envelope from the hidey-hole. He handed it to Liz who shook the contents onto her uncle's desk. Two tiny cassette tapes, one piece of paper, a folded document of some kind.

"Did you see the envelope when you hid the scarf?" she asked as she picked up the single sheet of paper.

He replaced the books. "No. But I didn't look, of course. I was in a hurry. It must have already been there."

Liz scanned the paper while Alex unfolded the document. As the realization of what he held sank in, he heard Liz gasp.

"According to this paper, these tapes are recorded

conversations with Roger Kapp,'' she said, talking so fast it was hard to understand her even without the distraction of the document. ''This paper lists the times and contents of the calls, and makes a note of the money Uncle Devon handed over in return for Kapp's silence. Geez, it wasn't just the rezoning thing. Alex! This is proof of what Roger was up to. I can sue him on behalf of my uncle's estate. I think. I'll have to talk to his lawyers. At the very least, this information will ruin his public life! I can prove he was a blackmailer!''

As she said all this, she stuffed the tapes into her purse. ''Alex?''

So focused was he on the riveting words in front of him that he barely heard her. The document was the result of a private investigator's research into the Chase family. Alex's head reeled as he read the summary.

His father: deceased.

His mother: retired teacher, San Diego.

John, his older brother: former cop in New York City, present whereabouts unknown.

Theo, his middle brother: Seattle, current occupation unknown.

Juliet, his younger sister: a student, San Diego.

His sister? He had a sister?

''Alex?''

Dazed, he refolded the papers. Devon Hiller had investigated his family, looking, no doubt, for something so scandalous that Liz would immediately consent to a divorce.

Alex hadn't thought of his brothers in a long time. He'd been so wrapped up in making a life for himself that he'd put his family's fate and whereabouts out of his mind, out of his heart. They came stampeding back with a vengeance that pierced his soul in a million dif-

ferent ways. And with them, they brought a sister named
Juliet.

"Alex? What's wrong?"

"Nothing," he finally said, tucking the folded papers
into his jacket pocket. When she raised her eyebrows,
he shook his head. "Later," he said.

"But—"

He kissed her quickly, shutting her up for the moment,
then kissed her again because it was impossible not to.
They spent the next few minutes looking around the
room, opening closets, peering behind draperies, turning
up corners of area rugs until Liz finally threw up her
hands and sighed.

"It's hopeless," she said. "I mean, what are we looking for?"

"I don't have the slightest idea." He moved close to
her, took her hands in his, and smiled when she looked
into his eyes. He leaned down and kissed her, hoping
against hope that she wouldn't ask him to choose between a life with her and profiting from her uncle's fortune sometime in the future. He loved her with all his
heart; all he wanted was for her to love him in the same
way, to trust him again.

Perhaps he needed to go first. "We have the scarf,"
he said softly. "More importantly, those tapes will prove
the sheriff is a blackmailer."

"If Kapp knew my uncle had recorded him doesn't it
make sense he might have tried to find the tapes or even
that Uncle Devon may have turned the tables and started
blackmailing the sheriff?"

"Exactly. Maybe it's time to do what you've wanted
to do from day one. Maybe it's time to hire a really good
attorney and fight this the legitimate way. You're right

about DNA and forensics—a good investigation might turn up clues we can't begin to uncover for ourselves.''

She threw her arms around his neck. ''I'm so relieved! And, Alex, the killer may have left some of himself on my scarf. We'll turn it in, too.''

''Maybe,'' he said, still not ready to put Liz's fate quite so openly on the line. As he spoke, he felt a vibration in his pocket and withdrew his cell phone. Flipping it open, wondering who could possibly be calling him, he heard a voice broken by static, but the message was clear and set his adrenaline pumping.

''What is it?'' Liz demanded as he folded the phone and fought with himself over what to do. ''Alex!''

He put his arms around her. ''It's the dispatcher. There's a fire in Old Town. Half the buildings…Liz, they want every available trained fireman and that means me. This is my chance to be part of the team again, but…''

''Go,'' she said.

''I can't leave you here by yourself—''

Gesturing at the phone on the desk, she said, ''I'll call for a taxi. I'll be fine.''

''Come with me. I'll drop you off—''

''Our house is in the other direction and you know it. People are in danger, Alex. A fire. They'll burn. Go!''

''But—''

''Alex, for goodness' sake, go!''

He kissed her soft lips and did as she asked, half worried about her, half thrilled at being back in the loop no matter how unconventional the approach. He heard her call to him as he tore open the front door.

''Be careful, come back to me,'' she cried.

They were the words she always called, and for a second, he paused, then he thought of her parents, dying

in orange and red flames, and realized that she wanted
him to go—she needed him to go—to do his job, or at
least what had once been his job, to save another child
from what she'd suffered.

As he ran to his truck, he listened for the sound of
sirens.

LIZ TURNED to pick up the desk phone and paused. Out
of the corner of her eye, as it had since the minute she
walked into the room, the huge curio cabinet seemed to
beckon to her. Made of polished walnut and glass, the
cabinet stood about six feet tall and held on its shelves
a plethora of items both large and small.

She pulled a chair close and opened the glass door.
Where had Emily found that necklace? Here with the
delicate jade dragon or on the top shelf with the oriental
lacquers? Everything was spotless, as usual, and she realized the housekeeper had no doubt been dusting the
cabinet each week as usual. If she'd found an empty
spot, she'd probably just moved something over to fill
in the space.

Liz stared at the valuable, beautiful things, and heard
herself say, "What does any of this *mean* to me?"

She'd lived in this house from the ages of eight until
twenty-one. Fourteen years. She could count on one
hand the times she'd dared to sneak downstairs and open
this cabinet, touch these things. She'd never slid down
the banister, her room upstairs held few happy memories. She'd lived in a gilded cage just as Alex had lived
in one with too many bent and twisted bars.

As she touched her bare ring finger, she realized that
from the moment she'd walked into this house today,
she'd been overcome with conflicting emotions. Nostal-
gia for the past, greed for the opulence, desire to replace

bad memories with good ones, and maybe even fear, an unconscious desire to push Alex away because she was so afraid of losing him.

The solution came to her as she stared at the lead glass bowl which occupied a place of honor on the middle shelf. Alex was right. These things and this house represented her uncle's accomplishments, as nefarious as they now seemed. They were the sum of *his* dealings and passions, not hers.

Her passion was Alex. Her future was snuggled deep in her body, almost ready to embrace life. Her desire was to make the safest, most wonderful home possible, where she and Alex and their children could find genuine happiness.

When the estate was finally settled, she would sell it all and give the money back to the community, to build, rejuvenate and preserve. Generosity would be her uncle's ironic epitaph.

As she replaced an exquisite string of ivory beads, she heard a noise in the foyer. By the time she rose and turned the corner, she found Ron closing the front door.

"Ron? What are you doing here?"

"The door was unlocked. Where's Alex? Did you find the scarf? Is everything okay?"

"Everything is fine. Alex had to go fight a fire."

"I thought I heard sirens. I knew you'd be here and I wondered if I could get a tour of the place."

She glanced through a front window. "Where's your car?"

"I parked a few blocks away and walked awhile for the exercise. It…it helps take my mind off…I just can't seem to force myself to…well, to go…home."

She immediately understood. Look how long it had

taken her to come back into this house. "I'm glad you came. I was going to call a cab—"

"Now you won't have to," he said. He whistled as he ran a hand over the high back of a carved wooden chair. "Is this a Caquetoire chair? What a beauty."

Liz was more excited about her new plan than the old chair. "Listen, Ron, you know how I've been struggling with what to do with my uncle's belongings? Well, I've reached a decision. I'm going to sell everything and set up a philanthropic organization to administer the money to help the community! I'm so relieved to have figured this out. And I'd be happy if you'd consent to choose something for yourself. I know how you admire antiques."

He stared at her for a moment, finally saying, "You're amazing, Liz. I mean, who else would even consider giving away a fortune?"

Alex would, she thought with pride. She said, "Where do you want to start your tour?"

"I'd like to see your uncle's den." With that, he strode across the foyer and into the den, coming to a stop in front of the open curio cabinet.

As she watched with ever increasing amazement, he reached in, scooped up a handful of small items and dumped them into his overcoat pocket. "I'll save the Fabergé egg and the Breguet carriage clock for my satchel," he mused.

Liz stared at him, too shocked by his behavior to speak.

Another handful, another bulging pocket. In his haste, he knocked the glass bowl to the floor.

The noise made her jump. "Ron? What's going on?"

He looked at the shattered glass. "Damn! That was

18th century. Ravenscroft, I think. Well, don't worry, Liz, really, in the long run it won't matter.''

Was he this upset about her plan? Is this how he interpreted taking something? Unsure what to do, but suddenly uneasy being alone with him, she walked quickly toward the desk, her attention focused on the phone.

Ron's words stopped her. ''You know, your uncle tried that same thing.''

It was odd how a few words could turn everything upside down. Turning, she mumbled, ''My uncle?''

''This time, I used Alex's wire cutters on the phone line. You guys should have figured out that the house key you gave Emily also opens your garage. I made a copy for myself. It's come in handy a couple of times lately.'' As he spoke, he pulled the wire cutters out of his breast pocket and dropped them to the floor. Looking back at her, he said, ''Liz, you look stunned! You didn't honestly believe Emily killed your uncle, did you?''

Liz's hand flew to her mouth. Mind churning, baby ominously still, she finally managed to mumble, ''Why?''

''Why what? Why did I kill your uncle? Money, of course, why else? Why did I do my best to kill Harry Idle? The man messed up all my careful planning. See, I drove my car out your way and parked it off the road, took the bike from the back, rode it the rest of the way and got here in time to see Alex going down the stairs. I quickly followed him, untied his rope, climbed back up and was on my way for you. Only a matter of time before Harry figured out I was the one he saw lurking in your yard.''

He reached into the other coat pocket and produced a small silver pistol which he aimed at Liz. ''Don't worry, I'm not going to shoot you. Come with me.''

He pulled her arm and stuck the muzzle against the back of her neck, directing her to move through the silent house. "Open the door," he demanded when they got to the kitchen, and she did as he asked, her fears lifting for a second as she thought he might be taking her outside. Perhaps he'd tie her to a tree or something while he robbed the place. She didn't care, she just wanted to be away from him and the icy circle pressing against her neck.

Two small gasoline cans and a satchel rested on the porch. *Gasoline cans!*

Ron said, "Do you know that the wooded area back there goes straight through to a nice, private little country road? Of course you do, you grew up here. I keep forgetting."

Despite the gun, Liz tried to turn, to look into his eyes, to demand an explanation even though the logical one seemed all too clear.

"Ron—"

"Ssh," he said as if to comfort a child.

She stumbled down a couple of stairs, but he caught her arm and pulled her back. "Not so fast," he said in that same warm tone. "You aren't going anywhere. Fact is, Liz, you're a hard woman to kill, but all's well that ends well."

The gun trained right at her belly, he scooted one can inside and then the other, directing her to lift the satchel and come back into the house. Though she knew she couldn't outrun a bullet, the thought of flight entered her mind. In the next instant, she knew she couldn't try. Ron wasn't as scattered as Emily, and in this instance, she didn't have a head start. As long as there was a possibility of survival, she had to keep her head.

Prodded with the gun, hoping against hope that an

opportunity to save herself would arise, she shuffled back through the house. Could she swing the satchel and knock Ron off his feet before he shot her? He stayed far enough back that she knew she couldn't. Besides, the bag was too light to do any damage.

"Drop the satchel and sit in that exquisite Louis XVI chair," Ron said once they re-entered the den. As the realization of what he had in mind burned in her head, he pulled several lengths of rope from the satchel.

"No!" she said. "I won't. Ron, we're friends—"

He laughed as he lowered the weapon to her swollen belly. "Sit down, friend," he said.

He tied her hands to the arms of the chair and her feet together at the ankles. It looked to Liz like Alex's rope, stained with the dirt from their bluff.

Ron tightened the knots until they bit into her flesh. He patted her stomach and she reeled with disgust. "Too bad about the baby," he said, "but we don't need a little heir hanging around now, do we?"

Gasping with fright, she babbled, "Ron, if it's money—"

"Too little, too late," he said.

He took off his long coat and draped it over a chair, then splashed gasoline out of the first can. Tears rolled down Liz's cheeks and her heart pounded with the futile instinct to run. She twisted her neck and craned to see as Ron picked up the second can and moved across the foyer, his footsteps echoing on the floor. He quickly doused that room as well, tossed the can aside and threw in a lit match. Flames blossomed at once.

"Nice tall ceilings, plenty of air to get a good fire going before a window blows and the fire is reported," he mused as he came back into the den. "Shame to destroy all these expensive things. Your uncle's collection is so delightfully eclectic. Just about breaks my heart.''

''Ron—''

''By the way,'' he added, ''I bought these cans in Meyer's Junction. My shirt with the Ocean Bluff Fire Dept. insignia on the front and the cap with the same logo pulled down low over my face was all the clerk ever really noticed about me. Well, that and the fact that I talked about my darling wife, Liz. When Alex is convicted of murdering you for your money, he won't be able to inherit a penny.''

''Ron,'' Liz said, nauseous now from the fumes, the smoke and the abject terror she could feel crawling inside her skin like fire ants. ''Ron, think. You can't inherit anything from me. You're not in my will. This is pointless—''

He held up a finger. ''I can't inherit, but the estate of my dear departed sister can and I happen to be *her* sole beneficiary. Now, I admit, her dying before you is tricky, but since you'll die before your baby is born, Alex will be your only heir and he'll be ineligible. I believe I can make a good case and at this point, what have I got to lose?''

Liz had a moment of insight. ''Emily's middle name is Irene. It was on her lease application.''

''My dear mother gave her first-born child her own name as a middle name. Couldn't use the last name of Hiller because your uncle wouldn't have a thing to do with either of them. After Mother died, I found the letters she'd kept and a copy of the birth certificate. That's when I moved here.''

Liz was close to choking on her own fear. ''Emily could have told me—''

A derisive laugh was followed by a snort. ''Emily

never knew. The knowledge and proof of the identity of her real father was like money in the bank and you don't trust money in the bank to a loose screw like Emily.''

"So you approached my uncle?"

"A most disagreeable man. Told me to get lost. Told me he would amend his will to specifically *exclude* Emily. I thought, well, I'll wait until the old guy dies and then approach Liz. But you got pregnant and your uncle threatened to give the whole ball of wax to a few birds and some fish. Obviously, he had to go. Right away. I couldn't believe my luck when you showed up later that night, right as I was getting ready to strangle the old goat.''

"You framed me."

"Alex almost screwed it up when he took the blame. Still, with Emily's prodding, you were close to a divorce and I was making headway in the marry Liz campaign, so I wasn't too worried. My plan was to wait until your divorce was final, but then Alex got out. I had Emily pretend to be from the sheriff's department and call you. She was such a romantic, that girl, and so pitifully easy to manipulate. By the end, she thought she killed your uncle and that the best way to make sure you loved me was for her to kill Alex. Frankly, I didn't care which one of you died on those stairs. If it had been Alex, I'd have let it slip little Emily was really your uncle's daughter. I knew you well enough by then to know you'd fall all over yourself making sure she got her fair share. If it was you, Alex would look guilty as hell and be convicted of killing you as well as your uncle. Either way, Emily would inherit, and I'd be set.''

"But you left your gloves and took Alex's."

Ron laughed. "No one is perfect. Unfortunately, neither of you died. Emily knew I didn't go home with her the night of your uncle's party and I think she always suspected I'd swiped the green scarf from her after she swiped it from you. She knew about me taking my bike out at late hours and about my absences. As they say, she might have been crazy, but she wasn't stupid.''

"You used her."

"You bet I did. She was so doped up on medication, she didn't know who did what to who. Now, I admit giving her that gun wasn't my best idea—I mean, she was supposed to eliminate Alex, but instead came close to gunning you down. That would have wreaked havoc with the inheritance angle. Thankfully, she killed herself. Now, let's see, are we through here because that fire is getting serious.''

Liz struggled against the ropes, seeing in her mind's eye the drawings from her childhood, seeing the tiny figures caught in crayon flames. He wrapped the carriage clock and Fabergé egg carefully in separate cloths, then working quickly, scooped up a few of the enamels and the ivory. Zipping the satchel closed, he looked around the room.

"Listen to me, Ron," she begged. "No one will ever believe Alex killed me. He's fighting a fire, everyone knows exactly where he is.''

"You mean that big fire in Old Town, the one he just now is figuring out doesn't exist? The call he'll puzzle over as his former colleagues tell him to get lost? The false call it will appear he tried to use as an alibi?'' He put on his overcoat and took a book of matches out of his pocket.

"They'll trace the call—"

"Made from a pay phone," he said as he came back into the den, "just like the call Kapp received the night your uncle died. Who's to say Alex didn't call himself to cement his alibi? After all, he's an opportunist. Everyone knows you can't expect much from a Chase.''

"Then someone saw you come through the front door—"

"Who says I came through the front door? Did you see me? Actually, I came in the back way. Give it up, Liz.''

The actual flames were beginning to catch up with those of her imagination. "Don't leave me and my baby here to burn to death," she cried. "Please, Ron—"

He took out his gun and smiled at her. "Would you rather be shot?"

She stared at the gun.

"See, that's the thing about people. Any chance is better than no chance, right? Besides, I know about your history with fire. Don't they say the best way to conquer your fear is to face it?"

He turned then, so anxious to flee that he didn't take into account the location of the now heavy satchel and it tripped him. Down he went, bracing himself with his hands. As he hit, the gun spiraled toward Liz. Ron screamed curses. He'd fallen right into the shattered glass from the broken bowl. Jagged shards pierced his palms, sending bright red blood streaming under the cuffs of his overcoat.

The gun skittered to a stop by Liz's bound feet. She quickly nudged it out of sight with her toes and then rested her feet on it.

She watched Ron stand, search the floor for the gun, tug at the glass in his hands, swear as the deep cuts bled profusely. Liz's gaze followed his to the living room where the blaze he'd started precious minutes earlier now raged, sending smoke and waves of heat across the foyer.

Ron seemed to weigh the problem of his gun turning up in the fire investigation against the possibility of ending up caught in his own trap. Finally, bloody hands trembling, he managed to light a new match and throw it at the gasoline soaked drapes. As they burst into flames, Liz turned her face away.

And in that moment, her body decided it was time for her baby to abandon ship. A sharp, painful cramp rolled across her abdomen. The heat and pain joined forces, one threatening to destroy her from the outside, the other threatening to tear her apart from the inside, her mind darting between the two, trying to regain control.

As Ron gingerly picked up the satchel again, Liz took shallow breaths, trying to hide her baby's struggle to live from the man determined to make sure it died. She thought about Alex being blamed for their murder, spending the rest of his life in prison, blaming himself even if the courts somehow let him go. She thought about all she had and all she stood to lose. And she thought of dying without her wedding band, without telling Alex how much she loved him, how much she needed him, how sorry she was that it had taken her so long to realize that she'd always been able to trust him when it came to the truly important things, when it came to his love and devotion.

With strength born of anger and desperation, she kicked the gun toward the fire.

Ron dived to intercept it.

Another pain shot through Liz's body as the gun powder exploded.

Chapter Fourteen

"Whose idea of a joke is this?" Alex demanded of the nine men who sat staring at him in the day room of the fire station.

Dave tried to pull Alex away, but Alex stood his ground. "I want to know which one of you thought it funny to call me to a fake fire!"

Dave said, "You know none of us would do something like that. Think, Alex."

And just like that, Alex understood that this was still another ruse to get Liz alone and he'd fallen for it. Kapp!

He turned on his heels just as Battalion Chief Montgomery came hurrying into the room. "Fire at the old Hiller place," he shouted, running down the stairs as the alarm sounded. All nine men jumped to their feet and using the pole or the stairs, descended to the engines below.

Liz was still at that house. He had no proof, but deep in his gut, deep in his heart, Alex knew it was so. He caught up with the chief as he started his truck. Jumping in the passenger seat, he yelled, "I'm going with you."

The chief paused for half a second, then tore out of the station. Before long, the sounds of sirens ripped through the air.

BATTALION CHIEF Montgomery talked on the radio as they raced through the city, communicating with both the arriving units and dispatch. All Alex could think of was Liz caught in flames, her worst childhood fear come to life. Would she have the strength to hold on until he found her? Was she already dead? His heart screamed.

He heard the chief say, "Well, at least it's empty."

"Listen to me," Alex demanded. "Liz and I were both in this house less than an hour ago. She's still there, I can feel it in my bones. When we get there—"

"You listen to me," Montgomery said, eyes blazing. "This is my fire. You don't know for sure where Liz is. Stay in this truck and out of the way. If Liz is there, we'll find her."

Alex clamped his jaw shut, but even before the truck came to a halt, he jumped out. The living room side of the house was ablaze and flames showed through the windows on the den side. Around him he heard the fire engines rolling to a stop, he saw pedestrians standing, pointing, insisting they'd heard an explosion, he heard the chief shouting orders, firemen unwinding hoses, but he paid little attention.

The fire was going to be fought as though the building was abandoned. He tried yet again to catch the chief's attention, but Montgomery shrugged him off. Alex knew the chief wouldn't risk his men when there was no evidence of occupation. Well, he wasn't one of Montgomery's men, was he?

Montgomery had assigned designations to the house, and now moved around to the back, preoccupied in his attempt to save property. The reflective lettering on his incident commander's vest made tracking him easy. Alex knew where on the truck to find equipment and he knew the house layout. He would bet his life Liz was in the den, right at the place where this whole nightmare had started.

He heard a new siren, and turned in time to see the sheriff's car squeal to a stop. Kapp! What was he doing here? In one instant, Alex answered his own question. The sheriff had started the fire and come back to watch it.

Alex longed to tear through the crowd and force Kapp to reveal what he'd done to Liz but he realized the sheriff still held the power to restrain him, and if Alex planned on getting in that house and saving his wife, he'd better do it before Kapp made a move to stop him.

He grabbed an ax and a spare set of turnouts, pulling on the gear and boots as fast as he could, rushing the front door while yells and shouts followed him.

The door was hot and locked and Alex started in with the ax. He sensed someone approaching and tensed, ready to fight if need be, but it was Dave who stood there, ax in hand, Dave who joined him in destroying the door.

"I'm going in," Alex shouted. "Liz—"

Mike Sinclair pressed a gas mask attached to a rescue bottle into Alex's hands and a helmet down on his head. As Alex dashed inside, he knew Dave and Mike were behind him.

They crouched low, moving quickly. The living room was engulfed in flames. The foyer with its slate floor was smoky, the den was also ablaze, flames licking the heavy drapes. Through the fire and smoke, he saw Liz, tied to a chair, eyes squeezed shut. As if sensing his presence, her eyes flew open and their gazes met.

"Alex!" she screamed, and then she kind of folded over on herself and cried out. "The baby," she sobbed, tears making tracks down her sooty face. He rushed toward her, tearing off the oxygen mask as he ran, pressing it over her face as he struggled with the ropes.

Dave arrived and produced a knife which Alex used to slice through Liz's restraints. Dave forced his mask on Alex's face for a moment, and Alex took a few deep breaths. Mike had moved closer to the flames and Dave joined him. There was a prone body over there, but Alex had his arms filled with Liz.

Darting through fire made more intense by the influx of air from the broken door, Alex jumped the last hurdle. Coughing, gasping, he finally made it outside and across the grass. Dave followed a few moments later with a man draped over his shoulder, Mike right behind him. They set the man on the ground as paramedic crews swarmed.

Alex caught sight of the man's bloodstained, blistered face. *Ron?* Liz's gaze followed his and she tensed. "It's okay," he said, cradling her.

She pushed the mask from her face. "It was Ron," she cried, "all along, Ron. Not Emily, Ron. Ron started the fire, Ron killed my uncle, Ron tried to blame you."

He stared at her with wide eyes.

"I love you," she sobbed. "I don't want to ever be without you, not for a moment, not ever."

He kissed her brow. "I know, honey—"

"I don't want my uncle's things, I don't want anything but you and our—"

Another contraction stilled her and she cried, grabbing her stomach, gripping his hand, groaning as a labor pain she had neither the opportunity to anticipate or the time to prepare for wracked her body. She was in labor, close to giving birth. Glancing once more at Ron, he made the effort to compartmentalize the cold knot of fury that burned like black ice in his gut. *Later...*

Paramedics with a stretcher showed up, and he lifted Liz to the clean white sheets and followed her to the van, refusing to be pushed aside, refusing to relinquish her hand even as he heard Kapp's raised voice demanding he stop, issuing threats, promising all sorts of mayhem. He heard Chief Montgomery tell Kapp to stay back and shut up.

There wasn't time to get to a hospital, barely time to wash, and then Liz was pushing and he was encouraging, and at the last moment, it was Alex who caught his baby girl in his big hands, Alex who cut the cord and held the delicate pink infant as the paramedic checked her over, Alex who swathed her in a soft blanket.

He handed her to Liz and gazed into eyes that seemed as deep as the sea and yet as internally illuminated as the inside curl of a wave. "Your daughter," he said, crying and laughing at the same time.

"Our daughter," she whispered.

He smiled at her. He didn't know what lay ahead, he really didn't care. At that moment, none of it mattered. His daughter was here, Liz was safe and he felt his own heart swell as he held them both in his arms.

Epilogue

Two Months Later

Alex was almost positive the warehouse fire was arson. First of all, the burn patterns were all wrong, then there was the fact the building had been abandoned for years and yet rumors flew that it was heavily insured. He was certain lab tests would uncover traces of an accelerant.

Fraud. He knew it. And it intrigued him.

Eventually, that's what he wanted to do. Not right now, but someday soon, someday when he could stand being cooped up in school, someday when he didn't relish every single second of being outside and free, of having time to spend with Liz and with little Grace, he wanted to switch from fighting fires to finding the people who intentionally started them.

People like Ron Boxer who lived through the explosion Liz had instigated when she had the presence of mind to kick that gun into the flames and bring Ron down. Though badly burned, Alex had heard that Ron was talking up a blue streak, looking for a deal.

Alex felt no compassion for the man. Ron had killed once, tried to kill several times, willfully driven his own sister to suicide. He'd come close to destroying so many lives; he was beyond compassion.

As was Roger Kapp. Kapp had made his choices, and now thanks to those cassette tapes that made it through the fire safe in the depths of Liz's purse, he would face the consequences and decent men like Chief Montgomery wouldn't suffer.

Alex pulled up to the house on the bluff, the house neither of them could bare the thought of leaving, not just yet, anyway, and smiled at the sight of Liz's little SUV with the baby seat in the back. He felt a jolt of anticipation knowing he would soon see his girls.

As he grabbed the tiny jewelry box, giant stuffed panda and can of hideously expensive cat food he planned on distributing on this joyful Valentine's Day, he thought of his other family, his mother, brothers, his sister, and wondered what they were up to.

Maybe soon he would follow Liz's advice and attempt to contact them. Until then, he crossed his fingers that they were as happy and filled with hope as he. Then he opened his front door and called, "I'm home."

* * * * *

Look for Alice Sharpe's next book, a Silhouette Romance, in June 2004!

HARLEQUIN®
INTRIGUE®

has a new lineup of books to keep you on the edge of your seat throughout the winter. So be on the alert for…

BACHELORS AT LARGE

Bold and brash—these men have sworn to serve and protect as officers of the law…and only the most special women can "catch" these good guys!

UNDER HIS PROTECTION
BY AMY J. FETZER
(October 2003)

UNMARKED MAN
BY DARLENE SCALERA
(November 2003)

BOYS IN BLUE
A special 3-in-1 volume with
REBECCA YORK (Ruth Glick writing as Rebecca York),
ANN VOSS PETERSON AND PATRICIA ROSEMOOR
(December 2003)

CONCEALED WEAPON
BY SUSAN PETERSON
(January 2004)

GUARDIAN OF HER HEART
BY LINDA O. JOHNSTON
(February 2004)

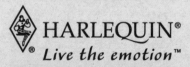

HARLEQUIN®
Live the emotion™

**Visit us at www.eHarlequin.com
and www.tryintrigue.com**

HIBBONTS

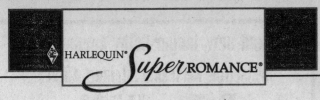

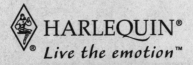

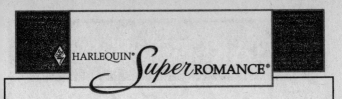

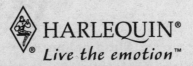

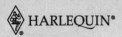

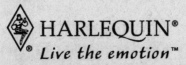

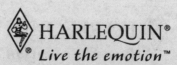